BROKEN ROAD

TO A GHOST

CHERYLE THOMPSON

Edited by: Crystal Mann

Cover Design: Dreamstime.com
dreamstime_xxl_72742283

Special thanks to: Destin Writers Group

COPYRIGHT REGISTRATION: TXu 2-316-895
ISBN#: 9798844198151

PROLOGUE

Director Brennen paced the floor. "Let me stand on my soapbox for a moment. Who do the asylum seekers believe lied to them? What led them to think the trip across the river into Texas would be easy? How many ISIS members penetrated the caravan's leadership? Our process to citizenship is long and tedious for a reason. Millions have taken the right road and succeeded. If that path is shut down, we face the imminent possibility of a hostile takeover by those wanting to destroy this country. I haven't said anything you two don't already know. My concern is terrorist members are already here and it's a matter of time before they show their true colors."

A no-win political nightmare over immigrants detained at Mexico's and the U.S. southern borders. Innocent led by the guilty. Internet sites, social, and news media reporting fake news. Hearsay overshadowed the truth. Isolated cases of violence and death were being dramatized on every media source possible, while the many positive and successful cases were brushed aside as unnewsworthy.

The difficult process of determining the difference between those having the desire to honestly become U.S. citizens, and those seeking to abuse the system, were being processed by unqualified staff members due to the lack of personnel to handle the overwhelming numbers. Those encamped south of the border, faced additional issues by remaining in Mexico. Mexican authorities turned a blind eye to the responsibility of taking care of the South American's critical needs. Struggles on both sides as to how to cope with the problems were as tangled as a Slinky after a two-year old played with it. Lack of food, shelter, and medical help battled for top slot on the list, but an underlying problem gained ground.

FBI Director for more than three years, Lance Brennen leaned against the edge of his desk. Occupying the two chairs in front of him were Agents Brad Sebastian and Sheila Garrett. Agent Garrett, a DEA agent in the San Antonio office, had been temporarily assigned near the border of Laredo, Texas. Brad Sebastian, a senior FBI agent, specialized in kidnapping and sex trafficking.

Dressed in a black suit, starched white shirt, and a light blue tie matching the color of his eyes, Brennen adjusted his black rimmed glasses and continued. "We have an issue that needs to be addressed before the media gets wind of it. News reporters will have a field day making it a major humane disaster. You each have a special attribute leading me to request you specifically for this case."

"Mexican cartels?" Sebastian asked.

"No. We have reason to suspect a Somalian with a distinct ability to disappear. He's currently known as Greygo…short for Grey Ghost. When he started out as a teen, contacts called him The Somalian Ghost. His real name is Abid Hasan."

"Is this about the two transport buses that disappeared on their way to Nuevo Laredo?" Garrett asked.

"Yes."

Sebastian picked up his briefcase and stood. "Tijuana to Nuevo Laredo? Hmm. Why is it our problem?"

"As soon as the immigrants started arriving at our borders, the media has dramatized every bad thing that has happened. The accidental deaths from swimming across the river, our fault.

Starvation, lack of medical attention, our fault. So, funds were allocated to the Border Patrol division aimed at breaking down the highly concentrated camps south of the U.S. border. A joint effort to help alleviate crime and overcrowding. My understanding is the California Border Patrol office received a written request from Chief Lorenzo. His jurisdiction includes the Tijuana caravans. Supposedly, his office requested the use of two of our vans to move asylum seekers with one escort to oversee the transport."

"I don't see how the loan of two vehicles made it our problem," Sebastian said.

"The two Tijuana officers assigned to drive the refugees are dead. Lorenzo denies signing the request. Said his name was forged on copied stationary."

Sebastian glanced over at Sheila. "You haven't said anything. What are your thoughts?"

Sheila smiled as she stood next to Sebastian. "Why am I involved? I'm due to return to the San Antonio office next week."

Before she became a DEA agent, Sheila was a detective for the San Marcos Police department. While still a detective, she joined forces with two DEA agents out of the Dallas office to solve several murder cases involving Carlos Reyes, Robert Reyes's father and leader of the Reyes Cartel south of Nuevo Laredo. Knowing Carlos either instigated or committed the murders added up to zero without physical evidence.

"Because of your history with the Reyes family. I've already contacted Robert and Rita Livingston," Brennan replied.

"Funds to Mexico don't mean shit. Politicians probably gave themselves bonuses with it. Sebastian's right. Loaning two vans doesn't make the disappearance our problem."

Brennen glared directly at Sebastian. "You sent Billy Wright to train with border patrol in California fresh out of Quantico. We haven't found out who told Wright you approved the assignment as the escort to make sure vans were returned."

Sebastian's brow furrowed. His face reddened as he stepped closer to Brennen. "He has no experience in this type of situation. When you find out which asshole decided he could make decisions for me, I better be the first call you make. If anything happens to him, this fuckup is on you." He turned to leave.

"That ship sailed the second the immigrants left Tijuana. That's why I need you two."

Chapter One -- South Walton, FL

Nicholas Jacobson gazed out over the white, sandy beach. Beyond the clear, blue water, shades of orange and yellow brightened the horizon. His peaceful serenity had come to an end. Spring breakers were descending on South Walton beaches earlier than usual. When his phone vibrated on the table next to the lounge chair, he checked caller ID but didn't answer. *Sebastian again.* Weeks had passed since anyone had tried to call him. Other than his cousin, Mitch Reeves, Nicholas hadn't spoken to anyone except his furry and feathered friends in almost five months. Not even his business partner, Robert Reyes, or close friend Father Simon.

The day he left Father Simon and Robert standing on the sidewalk in front of Saint Vincent's church, north of McAllen, Texas, he rented a car and disappeared. Before he left town, Nicholas waited until dark then returned to the animal refuge across the street from Saint Vincent's. Jillian's ashes were delivered to the administrative building before he and Robert drove the priest home from New Orleans. After he spread her remains among the grape and muscadine vines, Nicholas found Shadow and Coal, his two cats, and headed east a few weeks before Thanksgiving. Christmas, New Years, and his birthday came and went with no one to celebrate them with.

He grabbed his coffee cup, stood, then moved toward the rail where pieces of fish filled a bowl on the rail. Bucky, the pelican, arrived for his daily breakfast. After several vocal quacks, Nicholas tossed the contents of the bowl onto the sand. He pushed strands of hair behind his ear then turned to watch his two furballs desperately trying to scratch their way through the sliding glass door.

His daily routine had become taking care of the animals, then checking the live feed from of his antique shop in Grapevine from his laptop. He missed the regulars who showed up for daily wine tasting. After his morning run, he spent time reading the Bible Father Simon had given him. He found himself highlighting verses of his own and pondering the reasons for the ones Father Simon highlighted long before passing it on to him. Nicholas smiled as he ran his hand across his scraggly beard. His favorite entertainment of the day turned out to be watching Bucky chase the seagulls trying to steal his free meal.

He let his mind drift back to the case he finished before leaving the real world behind. On the way to Florida, he stopped in New Orleans. Rita requested his help to tie up loose ends on the sex trafficking case which involved his uncle. Rita Livingston, an FBI agent, worked under the direction of Brad Sebastian. She let Nicholas stay with her at the house on St. Charles, a property seized by the FBI during the investigation.

Rita didn't listen as patiently as Jillian had and expressed her opinions on every subject. The matter of whether he wanted to hear her view fell to the wayside, but he trusted Rita. Nicholas knew he was being tracked through the satellite phone Sebastian gave him. Being a part-time contractor for the FBI did not equal an anytime status to Nicholas. He wanted time and distance away from the life he thought he knew every detail about. All his efforts to make sense of the chain of events in New Orleans that led to the death of his uncle never altered the outcome.

Nicholas waited for Bucky to quack his appreciation and waddle away before he went back in the house. After several days of the pelican showing up, Bucky seemed to fit. Nicholas was surprised when the big bird responded to the name. He once considered selling his beach house, but for some reason never found the desire. Shadow and Coal were taking their morning nap on the couch. He refilled his cup and recalled the last conversation he had with Rita before leaving New Orleans.

"You know, I have a million questions with no answers. Like, why didn't my mother tell me Sebastian was my birth father after my dad was murdered? I was barely fourteen then. All the time I spent in McAllen, why didn't Father Simon tell me sooner?"

"Well, I talked to Robert. Father Simon told him what he told you. In the old man's defense, you took off on foot without an explanation. Father Simon had a burden to tell you. Did you ever think God had a time and a place for you to find out? As far as your mom not telling you before she died, maybe she wanted to spare you from suffering through the pain of her mistakes knowing she would not be there to carry you through them."

"Logical conclusions."

"You know, they watched you run toward McAllen until you disappeared. Robert ended up spending the night in hopes you would return. He sat on the front steps of the church and watched you scatter Jillian's ashes."

"I knew he was there, but I need to figure this out for myself. Jillian requested her remains be spread among the vines she planted long ago."

Jillian Lewis's vet clinic was a few blocks away from Nicholas's antique and wine shop in Grapevine. They met the day he took Shadow, a stray kitten he found in bad shape behind his warehouse that needed medical care. Several months later she volunteered to help with medical care and brought homeless animals to the sanctuary in McAllen.

"Robert and Father Simon said they will not tell Sebastian. They're leaving that decision to you. Your mom loved your father, but she was the love of Sebastian's life. He's never married."

"But Micha was more of a father to me than the ones most of my friends had. He was and always will be, my biggest hero. When he returned from long missions, he made sure to stop in my room first before going to bed."

"I'm sure Father Simon told you this in some form or fashion, but love has nothing to do with the blood that runs through our veins. We can start with Jesus but look at how many people give their children away without a second thought. What about the rate of child abuse cases, and the number of children in foster homes? Like parents who adopt, don't you think they love them just as much?"

Nicholas had let Rita climb on her soapbox that day and ramble her opinion of love and children. But in his mind, it hadn't resolved the reasons why his mother never told him the truth. Maybe she was trying to protect him from the pain. *Was she ashamed?* Debating the issue once again would not change history. He needed to return to the real world, his antique shop in Grapevine, and his friends. He put his empty cup in the dishwasher and headed to the shower.

Chapter Two -- South Walton, FL

Rita and Robert were crouched between a row of evergreen shrubs and an eight-foot wood fence. "We've been out here for almost an hour. Sand has made its way up the crack of my ass. Let's go knock on the front door."

"You actually think he'll let us in?" Robert laughed.

"He's your business partner. So, trespassing in his neighbor's yard and spying on him through the small gaps in the privacy fence is okay?"

"Rental property and currently vacant." Robert dug a rubber band out of his pocket. He pulled his long, black hair into a ponytail.

The sound of a sliding glass door opening then closing drifted with the breeze. Nicholas ran his fingers through his blonde hair as it brushed across his shoulders. With a clean-shaven face, he headed down the steps toward the ocean. *Why didn't they knock? Were they afraid I wouldn't let them in?*

Rita whispered, "What's he doing?" Their backs were against the fence.

"I'm squatting right beside you. If you can't see, then how do you expect me to know?"

Nicholas paused and listened. As he peeked around the corner, he said, "Did you think I couldn't see you?"

Robert glanced up. As he stood, he brushed sand off his jeans. "Well, yes, but we didn't think you'd even speak to us, much less open the door."

"I saw you approach on my way to the shower."

"Then why in hell did you make us wait?" Rita asked.

"Curious as to what you'd do. I really expected to see you on my back porch by the time I got out of the shower. Have you eaten breakfast?"

"No. Remember, we've been hiding out here. I feel like I've been buried in sand." Rita stepped out of her flip flops, shook the sand off, and trudged passed Nicholas. "You two coming? I'm assuming you already fixed something. I'm starving."

Nicholas turned toward Robert. "Well, I guess she didn't miss me."

"If it's any consolation, I did. Really could've used your help at the shop the last few weeks. We've been busier than ever. Appears people are beginning to panic over this COVID pandemic thing. Online orders have tripled while in store shopping is slow."

"Who's covering today?"

"Oh? Now your concerned? Don't worry. I got it covered."

Nicholas poured coffee and sat plates of scrambled eggs, bacon, and French toast on the bar. Robert and Rita pulled up bar stools while Nicholas leaned against the counter. "So, why are you both here?"

"Sebastian sent us. He didn't want to bother you after the clusterfuck in New Orleans. He needs your expertise."

"The two buses headed to Nuevo Laredo for what was said to be better work opportunities for the South American immigrants?" Nicholas asked.

Rita's jaw dropped as the eggs fell off her fork. "How do you know?"

"My turn to remind you of the fact that I have a cousin who works for Director Brennan."

"Okay. Okay. I get it. You have friends in high places," Rita replied.

"So, what does he expect me to do?"

"Intelligence believes Greygo is behind the attack." Robert said.

"Hmm. Abid Hasan. Among his alias's, he has used Greygo and Somalian Ghost, but rarely goes by his real name. Who's he working for now?" Nicholas asked.

Robert pushed his plate away. "Do you remember Old Man Greyson? He ran the property next to ours for the Garcia Cartel until we bought it."

"Yes."

"Well, his three sons took off to Monterrey after the old man's assassination. Supposedly, they were eliminated by an assassin working for the Garcia family. Rico Jr.'s remains were never found. Sebastian tracked Rico Jr. to Tijuana. For some reason, he believes Rico and his sister are mixed up with Hasan."

"I heard Brennan requested the assistance of a DEA agent from San Antonio. With you two and Agent Garrett, what do you need me for?" Nicholas asked.

Rita picked up their plates. She walked around to the sink, rinsed the dishes, and put them in the dishwasher. "You hunted Hasan once before for Marcus Garcia. You know his habits, and weaknesses."

"I took a picture, sent an encrypted email to Marcus with Hasan's location, then caught the next plane out of Cancun. Hasan never saw me. That was close to fifteen years ago. Habits and weaknesses change with age."

"Did your cousin tell you Billy Wright was sent as the escort? Young girls and healthy men are disappearing faster than Homeland Security can keep up with. Anything that goes wrong at the border is blamed on the U.S. Anything right…well, you know the answer for that." Rita said.

"Yes. He told me the border officers in Southern California told Wright it was supposed to be an initiation assignment ordered by Sebastian, but Sebastian knew nothing about it until Brennen told him. Three agents were suspended without pay pending further investigation. How many people were being transported?" Nicholas asked.

"The extended vans were designed to carry eleven people. Ten female teens, nine males, and Billy. Both vans were set on fire with the Tijuana officers zip tied to the steering wheels. Large truck tires covered the entire area making it impossible to know how many vehicles or suspects were involved. Destination suspected to be Nuevo Laredo." Rita started the dishwasher then returned to her barstool.

"If Hasan sees Wright, he might recognize him." Nicholas said.

"Really? How?" Robert asked.

Nicholas hesitated. Telling them the truth would mean admitting he had been hired by the Garcia Cartel to get rid of Billy's father. For more than a decade, Nicholas completed contracts as a paid assassin to fund the construction of the antique shop in Grapevine. Billy Bowlegs Osceola Lewis, Wright's father, had stolen a shipment of cocaine from the South American cartel. Nicholas knew Lewis had a son, but never believed he'd end up working with the man years later.

After several moments, Rita spoke. "If you can't say it, then I will. Sebastian knew about the contracts you completed for Marcus years ago. Specifically, the contract on Billy's father. You may not be aware of the fact that Sebastian had a team watching Lewis. Distributing cocaine through the Everglades is still an ongoing battle. You solved Sebastian's problem."

Rita tucked strands of her auburn hair behind her ear then continued. "He believes if the FBI had captured Lewis, the thief would've never made it out of Florida alive. Marcus needed a new connection to transport cocaine between South America and the Everglades. Part of your contract to eliminate Lewis included Hasan as a replacement. Am I right?"

"Pretty much, but if he is planning to steal a drug shipment, the Garcia Cartel will be looking for Hasan too unless they were led to believe he's dead. If Rico Jr. is with him, are they still headed to Nuevo Laredo?"

"Sebastian has intel stating Hasan picked up a drug shipment south of Tijuana. Destination is somewhere along the Texas border," Rita replied.

"So, Robert, since Diego married your sister, do you think Hasan is headed to your property?" Nicholas asked.

After Marcus Garcia's assassination, Marlon assumed his position as head of the Cartel's businesses. Under him were two additional brothers and one sister with the youngest sibling being Diego. The history between the Reyes family and the Garcia Cartel went back further than Robert could remember. When Robert's family purchased the Greyson property next door and combined the two properties together was when he found out that the Greyson family was related to the Garcia family by marriage and the Garcia Cartel owned the property.

"Shit! Hell no." Robert removed his cell phone from his shirt pocket and headed out the sliding glass doors to the back deck.

Rita stood. "Hasan may not recognize Billy. He shaved his head and grew a beard to cover the scar along his jawline for this assignment. Sebastian's letting him work off his past crimes. Billy still has a long list of connections in the illegal drugs and sex trafficking markets. Only thing we don't know is, does Hasan know about Billy's partial prosthetic leg?"

"Hasan may use Diego for a pit stop, but I think he's looking for an easier way to cross the Texas border. If Rico is travelling with Hasan, then Diego may be in for a fight." Nicholas said.

"Why do you think that?"

"Robert had two main routes when his family transported illegal marijuana across the Texas border. Rico grew up next door.

He may know those routes. Because Diego's last name is Garcia, Hasan may expect access to those routes."

"Robert shut both routes down last year," Rita replied.

"No barriers to overcome at the river tunnel. May be still be shallow enough to drive across. Besides, what makes you think a closed door or barrier means anything to Hasan?"

Chapter Three -- Santa Ana, Mexico

Billy Wright thought he had seen it all in his lifetime until the vans were run off the road about fifty miles from Santa Ana. His first so-called assignment turned out to be escorting teen refugees to another part of Mexico where they had better opportunities for work. A trial run to see if relocation helped alleviate crime, health issues, and overcrowding. He wondered who leaked the information about this special expedition when very few knew about the project. *Was it someone on the coordination team, a Tijuana officer on the take, or maybe a desperate parent of one of the teens?*

When the two Tijuana officers were shot in the head then tied to the steering wheels, Billy assumed the snitch had to be a corrupt cop with a seriously twisted vendetta. The necessity of zip ties and then setting the vehicles on fire was beyond his comprehension. Forcing the young migrants to watch could only be the act of a psycho. To his surprise, no one questioned his age difference. From his perspective, the ten-year gap should have raised immediate questions.

The guard who confiscated their cell phones along with his Glock resembled a baboon; a brainless soldier without the ability to know when he needed a bath. All their suitcases were searched

15

before the bags were hurled onto the bed of an aging military transport truck. Faded camouflage paint with dark green canvas covered the bed. Billy intentionally lined up behind the teenagers being forced to climb onto the bed of the last cargo truck.

Billy wondered what army this small band of soldiers belonged to. Before each teen was pushed in the direction of where they were expected to sit, a soldier zip tied their hands together. This process went on until all twenty prisoners were shoulder to shoulder on wood benches. Instead of seatbelts, the soldiers used a crude, braided rope to tie them in place.

The images reminded him of the old black and white TV show, '*Hogan's Heroes*', he watched as a kid except these guys were South American and Mexican, not German. Their reality was more of a horror show than a sitcom, but prisoners all the same. The guard next to him and the one directly across from him held loaded AK-47s. Understanding the soldier's conversation with hot air funneling its way through the slit in the door flaps turned out to be impossible. His basic Spanish course may help order dinner at a restaurant, but not here.

Billy leaned his head back, closed his eyes, and pretended not to pay attention. Knowing they were somewhere near Santa Ana did not help. He had no way to tell anyone. He tried to recall the maps of Mexico he studied before leaving Tijuana. Determining why these men chose to travel east across barren land raised more questions than answers. *Why not cut a path southeast back to the Pacific Ocean? That makes sense, this doesn't.*

He tried to relate his current situation to his prior line of work but found it impossible. He wasn't going to be shipped overseas to some foreign country. He wasn't going to be forced into slavery as an unpaid prostitute. Memories of him snatching young, innocent teen girls from their happy life in different towns along the Gulf Coast then delivering them to New Orleans seemed so much worse once he knew the complete picture of what truly happened to the girls. *Why did Sebastian think I would be good at this?* Being the one taken turned out to be a nightmare beyond his imagination. *Is this what karma looks like?*

Jostled and jerked by the bumpy ride led him to believe they were not on any paved road. Minutes dragged into hours before the sun dipped below the horizon. The caravan made camp for the night. Soft sniffles from the teens were muffled by the soldier's laughter. With no trees to block the humid breeze, sticky grains of sand drifted across the rows of sleeping bags clinging to every inch of his bare skin.

Surrounded by six transport vehicles and one gas tanker, reminded him of the vehicles he saw while stationed in Iraq; left over inventory from the Desert Storm War era. He struggled to lay still. All twelve soldiers appeared to be Mexican or South American descent, except for the one pacing back and forth in a large tent. A generator kept a fan blowing and a light burning on a desk for Abid Hasan.

Hasan appeared to be talking to a fat, bald Mexican. Billy wondered if they were partners working on some human trafficking scheme, but that opened the question as to what was in the back of the other five trucks. Provisions, MREs, and what was left of their suitcases would not take up that much room. Even if he could hear their conversation, his basic Spanish fell short of understanding.

Sniffles graduated to faint sobs from the ten young girls on the other side of the fire. Their cries echoed on a feeble breeze. While embers flickered with the dying flames, so did the stench of burnt human flesh. The canned beans they were given for lunch wasn't enough to satisfy a small child's hunger, yet his desire to eat turned to nausea. The soldiers were drinking either vodka, or maybe a clear tequila.

Billy closed his eyes in hopes of awakening to find the live horror scene he witnessed turned out to be another nightmare. His mind struggled to move beyond the screams and images of the boy's body as it was tossed onto the hot coals. A helpless situation, no backup, or posse on the horizon. The young migrants were told not to speak unless spoken to. Hasan ordered his faithful men to demonstrate punishment for disobedience. Shot in the gut, but still alive, the soldiers drenched the boy with kerosene. Billy didn't even know the kid's name. Torture and death were the penalties for a brother's effort to save his sister from the hands of Hasan.

After Hasan completed his show of dominance in front of everyone, he made his soldiers add the boy's body to what appeared to be burning limbs with all the trash that had accumulated. Hasan walked right in front of Billy several times. A thick, coarse beard covered the scar that ran down Billy's left jaw line. Once known for his long, black hair, Billy struggled to recognize himself which helped to ease his anxiety, but an escape from an area that appeared to be a lifeless desert, in a country he knew nothing about would be suicide.

The soldiers cut their zip tied hands when they were served MREs for dinner, but Billy couldn't fight all the big baboons by himself. *What does Sebastian expect me to do? If saving myself is out of the question, how am I supposed to help these kids? Why didn't they tie us up again?* The females slept on the other side of the fire. An empty sleeping bag where the dead boy once laid separated him from the other boys. The soldiers eventually climbed on the bed of the truck, but the feeling of being watched remained. With his back to the trucks, Billy drifted off sometime after the light dimmed in the tent.

Chapter Four -- Santa Ana, Mexico

Wham! A single blow from a steel toed boot landed dead center in the middle of Billy's back hard enough to knock the breath out of him. Out of instinct, he was off the sleeping bag standing in a boxer's stance within seconds. Unfortunately, he came face to face with the fat Mexican from Hasan's tent. Billy found himself staring down the barrel of his own Glock. Clouds blanketed most of the night sky, but a dim light still flickered inside the tent. As if cutting a path through the darkness a thin line of light outlined the fat bastard, but this was no angel.

"Greygo will see you now."

"Who the fuck are you?"

"None of your fucking business. Move!" The man said with a low, gruff tone while he continued to keep the pistol aimed toward Billy's head.

Billy lowered his fists, turned, then headed toward the man standing outside the tent. *Why wait until after everyone settled down? Why now? Why not when we were first captured, or the many times Hasan walked within inches of me?* Billy stopped six feet short.

19

Hasan stared at him a few moments, then proceeded to circle Billy with the appearance of completing a military formation inspection in search of a tiny infraction. Hasan stopped inches from his face. "Habla español?" Hasan asked.

"Pequeño," Billy said.

"Your name?"

"You took my wallet. You have the damn passenger manifest. You know who the fuck I am."

The bald man with Hasan rammed Billy's shoulder as if it were a bolted door and the man's fist had transformed into a demolition ball dangling from a crane. Hasan stepped aside allowing Billy to land face down in the sand.

Hasan kicked sand on top of him. "Get up, Will Carter. Look me in the eye and explain to me why I should believe the information on your California license."

Billy moved slow and methodical. He pushed himself up and brushed the grit off his face onto his shirt sleeve. Anger filled his expression. "I am a U.S. citizen. I crossed the border into Tijuana long before the caravans from South America arrived. My wife died, Asshole. I stayed drunk longer than I should have. My money, credit cards, and fucking passport were stolen. Even with a California driver's license, border officers refused to let me return without a passport."

"What about a replacement?"

Billy's eyes narrowed. "What part of money and credit cards stolen did you miss?"

20

Hasan smiled but seemed to ignore his response. "How did you end up traveling with the teens? Other than the drivers, you were the only one with a weapon."

"Been in Tijuana more than a year. No family. Friends quit taking my calls a long time ago. When choices were being made as to who would be transported, I lied. Told the man taking volunteers I had a connection in Nuevo Laredo that would find manual labor jobs for strong young teens. By the way, I grabbed the Glock off a strangers table in a bar one night about a year ago. Don't know who it belongs to."

Hasan stopped pacing. "Don't give a shit about the weapon, who do you know in Nuevo Laredo?"

Billy didn't respond until he felt the barrel of a weapon against the back of his head. "Met a man while in Tijuana. Said he lives near Nuevo Laredo. Told me if I ever made it that way to look him up."

"What's this so-called friend's name?"

Hasan crossed his arms over his chest. A few inches shorter than Billy, but Hasan made up for it in width. Wearing American military, black BDUs, a black t-shirt and jump boots, Billy wondered why the Somalian dressed more like a member of some special forces unit if he never served one second protecting any country, much less his own.

Billy clinched his fists. "What the fuck does it matter?"

In less than a second, Billy hit the sand face down. This time the power of the bald man's fist landed hard against his cheek. The force rendered him unconscious. He awakened with the sun's rays warming his face. With a sleepy haze over his eyes, he realized he had been returned to the sleeping bag and all the young boys were gone. He heard voices behind him. The vibration of footsteps growing closer shook the ground beneath him.

"Get up, Asshole. You missed breakfast. Grab your shit. We're leaving," The bald Mexican yelled, then kicked Billy again.

Billy was shoved in the back of the last truck when the engines roared to life. All the teens watched in silence while he crawled to the front and sat on the floor. His brow furrowed as he glared at the two guards laughing at him.

"You do anything stupid we kill wimpy kid in glasses, not you," one of the soldiers said.

Billy's head felt like a hard rock band used his brain as the base drum for an all-night concert. He touched the knot on the right side of his head. A small indention below the bump felt like it was coated with dried blood mixed with sand. His focus moved to the boy tied to the bench next to him. The teen's eyes were closed, but his legs trembled against Billy's shoulder. He wondered if the boy believed in the power of prayer. *Maybe I should do the same.* The air reeked of urine. *Must be afraid to ask.* On the other hand, Billy hadn't felt the urge since they were lined up in front of a five gallon bucket the night before. How long could they go without water? Their supplies were taken by guards.

Wearing jeans and lace-up leather boots concealed his partial prosthetic leg, but the distinct clicking sound should have raised curiosity. *Am I being self-conscious?* He pulled his knee to his chest, leaned his head against it then closed his eyes. They had at least eighteen more hours in the back of that cargo truck if

Hasan's intended destination was Nuevo Laredo. *If he asks again, can I use Robert's name? Is there a way to get a message to Robert through his sister? Have I missed a weakness in Hasan's small brigade? What's the plan?*

Chapter Five -- Nuevo Laredo, Mexico

Robert Reyes told his sister, Anita, many times over the past few months that he would come see his new nephew. He hadn't been home since the day he left Mexico and moved to Grapevine. With a new career, a new house, combined with the time he spent doing contract assignments for Sebastian, Robert hadn't had a single day off to travel.

With one brother in Dallas and one in San Marcos, he wanted to sell the compound in Mexico and take his sister, Anita with him to Texas. She refused to leave the home they grew up in. Diego Garcia agreed to partner with the Reyes family to manage and take care of the crops but ended up falling in love with Anita.

Eight-foot block walls surrounded the compound with watch towers at each corner. Before he left Nuevo Laredo, Robert worked long days to make sure their marijuana fields were converted to avocado trees, vanilla, and cocoa plants. Not much to do maintaining the fields as it would be at least three more years before the plants would produce. Avocado trees could take as long as thirteen years to bear fruit, but the plan was set for long term goals. Fulfilling the promise, he made to his mom to legalize all the illegal pot trade and integrate the business with their eight legal pot shops and planted fields in Colorado and Washington had finally been completed.

Robert's body had its own internal clock. It seemed to know when five o'clock rolled around no matter what time he went to bed. He considered waking Rita, but the drive from the Florida panhandle to his family's compound located about thirty miles south of Nuevo Laredo had taken almost seventeen hours. He poured a cup of coffee then walked out on the porch to watch the sun rise. He found himself feeling like a stranger in a place he spent nearly forty years of his life.

He sat on the wood railing as he recalled his conversation with Diego before their departure from Florida. Diego told him he sent Anita and little Rafael to Dallas the second he found out Hasan planned to pay him a visit. Diego separated himself from his family in South America when he married Anita. But when his older brother asked for one last favor, Diego said he couldn't say no.

"I was told Hasan needed a place to stay one night. Something was mentioned about waiting on a boat to arrive near Abasolo. I can only assume Marlon is still running cocaine and weapons across Mexico. There was no mention of refugees," Diego explained.

Robert's thoughts were interrupted when the front door opened and closed.

Nicholas handed Robert a fresh cup of coffee. "I feel out of place here."

"I can relate. I returned once to Moscow a few years after my mom died. The only time I returned to visit my cousin. It seemed like I had never lived there."

"I remember you saying something about that. Wasn't it when you planned your fake death?" Robert asked.

"Yes. Have you spoken to Diego this morning?"

After Nicholas's mom's death, he did special assignments for the SVR. The Russian SVR was tasked with intelligence and espionage activities outside the Russian Federation and successor to the KGB. Nicholas's cousin worked for SVR intelligence at the time and helped Nicholas cut ties with the organization. Since then, his cousin defected to the U.S. and currently worked for the CIA.

"Not yet. Saw lights on upstairs when I walked out, but now they're off. Rosa, our housekeeper must've left the front door open. I smell bacon. Won't be long until he comes outside," Robert said.

Three houses were lined up next to each other near the northeast corner of the compound. The middle one belonged to Diego and Anita. Robert, Rita, and Nicholas spent the night in the main house where Robert's parents lived before their deaths. Two warehouses were close to the northwest corner. An office building, cafeteria, and four bunkhouses were boarded up near the gated entrance.

After purchasing the old Greyson property from the Garcia family, Robert had the south wall torn down and enclosed both properties as one. Rosa shared the old house on the Greyson addition with two field hands. After all the illegal drugs were disbursed between the family's stores in the U.S., all security personnel were let go.

Robert added a pad lock to the tunnel crossing that ran under the Rio Grande. The strip of rocky, overgrown beach front property near Abasolo remained pretty much uninhabited except for the crabs, mice, and sea life that considered it home. One small gravel parking area and one dock were the only things added to nature's sand, rocks, and weed landscape.

"How many men is Hasan bringing with him?" Nicholas asked.

"I don't have a clue. Diego made it sound like it would be Hasan and Rico, Jr."

"Hmm. So, we still have no idea of how many trucks, what they're carrying, or their final destination."

"You think Wright's still alive?" Robert asked.

"Your guess is as good as mine. What concerns me are Hasan's drunken guerillas around young females. Doesn't paint a pretty picture. How much do you remember about Rico, Jr.?"

"I went to high school with him. After that I spent sixteen hours a day working. Not much time for socializing. My family always assumed that Old Man Greyson owned the property. We didn't find out until after he died the Garcia Cartel owned it and allowed the Greysons to live there. Something about Old Man Greyson being a cousin to their mother. According to Diego, Rico called his brother, Marlon a few months ago. Apologized for running out and disappearing. Asked Marlon for a job. That's how he ended up with Hasan. My brothers don't trust Hasan anymore."

"And he trusts Rico, Jr.? Last rumor I heard was that the Garcia family had a price tag on his head. Stealing and abandoning the property, family or not, the penalty is death. You think he wants revenge for the murder of his two brothers?"

Robert stood and turned toward the front door. "If that's his intention, then we may need to prepare for a war. I'm going to wake Rita, then we can ask Diego. Breakfast is ten yards away."

"So, no carpooling?"

"If you want to get in the truck and drive, go ahead. I'll beat you on foot," Robert laughed and walked away.

Chapter Six -- Nuevo Laredo, Mexico

Nicholas sat in a recliner next to the window that overlooked the fields. He opened the Bible to Samuel, chapter seventeen. Father Simon had given the old, leather-bound book to him almost a year ago. During the time he spent in Florida, he searched for answers and direction. He made time every day to read at least one chapter. After a visit from the Archangel Michael, Nicholas knew his purpose wasn't the life he created for himself. He skipped down to a section highlighted in yellow.

49 And David put his hand in his bag, and took thence a stone, and slang it, and smote the Philistine in his forehead, that the stone sunk into his forehead; and he fell upon his face to the earth. 50 So David prevailed over the Philistine with a sling and with a stone, and smote the Philistine, and slew him; but there was no sword in the hand of David. 51 Therefore David ran, and stood upon the Philistine, and took his sword, and drew it out of the sheath thereof, and slew him, and cut off his head therewith. And when the Philistines saw their champion was dead, they fled. 52 And the men of Israel and of Judah arose, and shouted, and pursued the Philistines, until thou come to the valley, and to the gates of Ekron. And the wounded of the Philistines fell down by the way to Shaaraim, even unto Gath, and unto Ekron. 53 And the

children of Israel returned from chasing after the Philistines, and
they spoiled their tents. ⁵⁴ And David took the head of the Philistine
and brought it to Jerusalem; but he put his armour in his tent.
⁵⁵ And when Saul saw David go forth against the Philistine, he said
unto Abner, the captain of the host, Abner, whose son is this
youth? And Abner said, As thy soul liveth, O king, I cannot tell.
⁵⁶ And the king said, Enquire thou whose son the stripling is. ⁵⁷ And
as David returned from the slaughter of the Philistine, Abner took
him, and brought him before Saul with the head of the Philistine in
his hand. ⁵⁸ And Saul said to him, Whose son art thou, thou young
man? And David answered, I am the son of thy servant Jesse the
Bethlehemite."

Nicholas closed the book and returned it to his overnight
bag. He wondered how hard David's battle to kill Goliath really
was back then. David saved an army. He needed to save nineteen
refugees and Billy Wright, but a slingshot wouldn't be enough.
Nicholas knew everything history told him about King David's
journey, but none of it explained the direction he was headed.

His focus returned to what needed to be done before Hasan
arrived. The two field hands and the housekeeper would have to
leave. The biggest question was, how many guerillas would Hasan
have with him? He knew little of the Somalian according to the
facts listed in the file he received from Marcus Garcia more than a
decade ago. Time had changed him, so how much had Hasan
changed?

According to the information Sebastian sent with Rita and
Robert, Abid Hasan built a small network of transport routes for
the Garcia's drugs through Tijuana into the U.S. but lost it with the
heavy influx of immigrants seeking asylum. Hasan fell off the

CIA's radar for almost a year until he hijacked the two vans. *So, what has he been doing?*

Nicholas walked over to the window and gazed out over the flourishing greenery. *So, that's what avocado trees, vanilla, and cocoa plants look like. Could I become a farmer or a shepherd like David? What are the possibilities of disappearing into another life?* His dreams of the future had been turned upside down. *Is this my true calling?* He checked the time on his phone and headed downstairs.

Chapter Seven -- Nuevo Laredo, Mexico

Diego pushed his plate aside. "I spoke to Hasan this morning. He estimated their arrival to be late tomorrow. He plans to camp somewhere around Chihuahua."

"If he's on the run, why would he camp anywhere?" Nicholas asked. When no one responded, he continued. "Can't be much more than sixteen hours from here. Why the detailed update on travel plans?"

"Didn't ask."

"What about sleeping arrangements and meals? Does he expect you to feed his small army and the refugees?"

"No. He said his men would stay with the trucks. Didn't specify where. He wants overnight accommodations for him and Rico."

When Rosa came out to clear their dishes, Nicholas picked up his coffee cup and walked to the end of the screened-in porch at the back of Diego's house. He stared beyond the office, cafeteria, and the orchards hoping to magically come up with an idea to solve all their problems. No one spoke. They all seemed to be waiting on his direction as if he were commander in chief of their team.

As a contract assassin, he only had one life to worry about. His teammates were his friends, yet they all turned to him expecting the perfect solution to any problem.

"Did Hasan say anything about where they were headed from here?"

Diego pulled his hair back with a rubber band. "Something about Abasolo, so I can only assume Rico told Hasan about the two routes the Reyes family used to transport their marijuana. I explained that Robert shut them down before leaving Mexico. Hasan said if the tunnel was locked, make sure it was opened then hung up on me."

Nicholas leaned against the support beam and wiped sweat off his forehead. "Robert, from what Diego found out, I'm assuming Hasan's been using the dock and property near Abasolo for a while without permission. Is it possible to remove the tunnel lock without alerting the police chief in town?"

"I have keys. The police chief doesn't know the location. The tunnel is about fifty miles from town in the middle of nowhere. I should've put the waterfront property near Abasolo up for sale a long time ago. I hoped with time it would increase in value. I never considered anyone else would trespass and use it. The shrimp boats we once kept there are currently in drydock at our property east of Biloxi. You interested in ten acres of rocky oceanfront? Your view in South Walton's about a million times better."

Nicholas didn't respond, so Robert smiled and continued. "Never mind. It's too overgrown to build any structures without extensive land development. We cleared a small gravel parking area. It had a decent dock last time I made a trip that way. I could send the two field hands to check on it today. It's about a nine-hour drive round trip."

"Who's police chief now?"

"Chief Vito replaced Rojas. We would be in prison by now if we hadn't replanted our fields. Vito promised to clean up the city. Something about building the tourism market," Robert explained.

"He's right." Diego Interjected. "Last year, Vito showed up to check our warehouses. I already moved the weapons in the back warehouse to the underground storage long before then. Rumor has it, Vito doesn't take hush money like Rojas did."

Nicholas turned to face Rita, Robert, and Diego who were still sitting at the table. "Diego, have the field hands finish early. See if Rosa can fix something for dinner and leave it on the stove. Have them stay at a hotel in town tonight and tomorrow."

"Okay, but why?"

"Hasan and Rico are coming here for a reason. I doubt it's a social call or a one-night visit. Rico lived here most of his life and may believe he has a right to take it back. Marlon agreed to let him work with Hasan. They'll have no problem killing you then forging a bill of sale for this property with your signature on it."

Robert stood so fast that the oak chair fell behind him. "They can't do that. This property is part of the Reyes family trust."

"So, Hasan forges your name. Just because Vito is clean, doesn't mean shit. Rico must have connections in town and enough money to buy a judge. I don't know if that's their intent, but the scenario makes sense. This compound would give them a secure and permanent location."

"If your scenario is correct, how do we stop them?" Robert asked.

"You and Rita ride out to Abasolo. I assume Hasan's been using it since you moved to Texas. I'd be willing to bet that if Rico knows the location, then they have a team waiting somewhere close by to transport Marlon's cocaine to the distributors. Possibly a fishing boat anchored off the coast."

"Rico knows the exact location. Remember, we're cousins," Diego said with a tone of anger in his voice.

Nicholas smiled. "I didn't mean to make you angry, but I don't think family matters to Rico anymore. Old Man Greyson didn't own the property, but he may have never communicated that fact to his children. Now that he's backed by Hasan's little army, I'm thinking Rico wants vengeance. He knows that it was Marcus who ordered the execution of his two older brothers. He would've died too if he hadn't found a way to escape."

Diego's shoulders sagged as he took a deep breath, exhaled, and stood. "Then what do you need me to do?"

"You make sure that your staff plans to be out of here by three. I'll meet you in the warehouse office in about an hour to go over the property layout. We'll figure out a strategy then."

Robert checked the time. "If we leave now, we'll be back about four this afternoon."

"Good. I doubt Hasan told Diego the truth about their ETA. Probably more like a sixteen to eighteen-hour drive, not a day and a half," Nicholas said.

Chapter Eight -- Nuevo Laredo, Mexico

After Robert and Rita left for Abasolo, Nicholas returned to his room to take care of his two kittens. Shadow and Coal were used to traveling. Checking out their new surroundings seemed to be a game between the two furballs. This time he found them cuddled together in the center of the bed. He sat in the chair then picked up his laptop.

Nicholas closed his eyes a moment. Images of a dark-skinned man wearing military camouflage BDUs with a black baseball cap pulled down to his brows drifted through his thoughts. He wondered if Hasan wore the same thing every day no matter what degree registered on the thermometer. He took a deep breath and exhaled, then opened his laptop. Among all his contract folders from years ago was a file on Hasan.

Nothing more than he remembered. An old picture, full name, and a history of intermittent work completed for the Garcia family. *He disappeared from the cartel then, but why? Lack of assignments? Must've been a mutual agreement or Hasan would've been dead long ago. So Abid, what have you been up to lately? Working for two masters is an impossibility. Who else is jerking your chain?*

Nicholas shut down his computer and stared at his phone. His next conversation with Father Simon needed to be done in person. He ran his hand through his hair. Sebastian would call again. *I'll eventually have to answer, but what will I say? How long have you known? No. That would be a question further down the line of many. Another conversation that has to wait.*

All his questions could only be answered by Sebastian. Nicholas had asked himself the same questions every day since Father Simon told him. *Maybe Sebastian only suspects the truth. Did Pops know?* His thoughts drifted back to the last time he had seen the only father he ever knew. Micha had taken him and his mom to the airport.

After kissing his mom, Micha knelt to his level. Tears puddled in his father's eyes as he smiled and said, "*Son, it may be a while before you see me again. Please take care of your mom for me and remember, no matter what happens, I love you.*"

Pops knew he wouldn't make it out. Mom never told him the truth either. Nicholas's thoughts were interrupted by his phone vibrating in his hand. He wiped the tear making its way down his cheek with the back of his hand, took a deep breath, and answered.

"Good morning, Sebastian."

"Good to hear your voice. I assume you had a quiet vacation in Florida?"

"Yes, but I didn't expect to return to the real world and find out Billy Wright and nineteen immigrants were captured by Abid Hasan."

"When you didn't answer my calls, I hoped if Rita and Robert explained the situation in person, you'd be willing to help. I assume you're at the Reyes property?"

"Yes."

"Do you have a feel as to what to expect from Hasan?"

"It's not Hasan I'm worried about at this point. It's Rico, Jr. Hasan is in this for the money. If I put myself in Rico's shoes, I'd be looking for vengeance. He knows half of this property better than we do. He lost everything with the wave of Marcus Garcia's hand."

"I agree. I texted you Agent Garrett's cell number. She's prepared to cross the border as a civilian and lend a hand. Got another call. Talk to you later."

Sebastian clicked off without waiting for a response. Nicholas put his cell phone on the nightstand and sat on the edge of the bed. As he petted the two furballs, he realized what needed to be done. Memorizing the complete lay out of the Reyes property would be a priority. Next issue, the backup plan.

Chapter Nine -- Nuevo Laredo, Mexico

Billy found it impossible to nap. Hours passed before the convoy stopped. They were left untied when the two guards on the end jumped out. Minutes dragged by before the teens were directed one by one to get off. Billy was last to use the pee bucket. An out-

35

house covered in spider webs would have been better than this. Killing the little eight-legged creatures would be easier than the three hundred plus pound goons watching him. With a guard at both ends of the line, they had no privacy. Images of using both men as punching bags intensified with each lude comment every time one of the females took their turn.

His heart ached while he watched the young girl who had been raped by Hasan the night before. The swollen bruises visible on her cheeks were very prominent, but the ones on her body were concealed by the faded jeans and t-shirt she wore. Trying to fathom the severity of her long-term mental scars would be difficult even for a psychologist specializing in the field. All the turmoil had turned her black braids into frizzy bird's nests. When she stumbled and fell to her knees, the two guards laughed. He wondered if the broken angel would ever recover from the horrific abuse. A damaged asset could become a potential liability. *Will Hasan kill her too? Does the bastard have a buyer for all of them?*

For almost five years, Billy collected young girls from the panhandle of Florida for a sex trafficking ring near New Orleans. His last assignment changed his life dramatically when he learned he had a son. The three weeks Sebastian allowed Billy to return to Tampa to see his mom and find his four-year old son turned out to be the happiest time of his entire life. He married his high school sweetheart, Kaylee, before he left for Quantico. Instead of jail time, Sebastian worked out a deal to where he would train with California border patrol for six months. Away from anyone he knew and might possibly run into, however a trip from Tijuana to Nuevo Laredo wasn't part of that deal.

When Billy stepped up to the bucket, the guard announced this would be the last stop until they camped for the night. He intentionally kept his gaze toward the ground to keep from meeting the guard's stare. He zipped his pants then accepted the MRE without looking up. The teens were almost finished with their meals when he sat down. Billy didn't know any of the young refugee's life history, but nothing could be as bad as this. All of them volunteered to leave their family behind. Each accepted the risk in lieu of a chance for a better life.

How could anyone prepare for this? Questions as to why Sebastian would send him on this trip without calling first swirled through his thoughts. *Shit! He wouldn't. Why didn't I call him? Bastards set me up. But why?* If Sebastian didn't know about this, then he was on his own. While his mind debated the situation, he studied the teens as each one finished their meal. The young girl used as an example by Hasan was the first to stand and toss the remains of her MRE in the trash then return to her spot in the back of the truck. One by one, each refugee followed like a programmed robot receiving commands from a remote-control device.

His focus shifted when one of the trucks drove off. Billy realized the tanker and two of the trucks were missing. *Where did they go? Why separate the caravan now?* Hasan and his Mexican buddy appeared to be laying out instructions to four of his men. He wished he could be a fly on the one tall enough to be a small tree. Images of the old *Jolly Green Giant* commercials came to mind, except this man was nowhere close to jolly or green. His thoughts had drifted so far away, he failed to realize everyone returned to the truck except him until he felt metal pressed against the back of his head.

"You will die or tell me the name of your contact in Nuevo Laredo."

Billy placed his palm against the hot sand and cocked his head to the side. "So, if I tell you I get to live? Hmm? Doubt it. Go ahead, you son-of-a-bitch. Kill me."

He closed his eyes and prayed. Seconds ticked away. Nothing. The pressure from the barrel of the gun disappeared.

"You're not afraid of me?" Hasan asked.

Billy stood, rubbed his hands across the back of his jeans in an effort to knock away some of the gritty sand. "Why should I be? I spent the last year in a Tijuana hellhole. Nothing left worth fighting for."

Hasan holstered the Glock and stared at Billy. "Do I know you?"

"Don't recall ever seeing you before. Spending most of the last year with a bottle in my hand makes remembering anything a little fuzzy." Billy's brow furrowed as he crossed his arms then met Hasan's gaze.

Hasan's eyes were as black as his hair. Buzz cut to military style, but not quite as short as his. Hasan had changed clothes but had on the exact outfit as the day before. He started to wonder why the Somalian wore lace-up boots with BDU pants and a t-shirt until his peripheral vision picked up on something shiny on the outside rim of each boot. Thanks to his Quantico training or he may have never noticed. Then he recalled Hasan had perfect accuracy with knives.

"Hmm. I see threats will not work. We arrive at our destination later tonight. You introduce me to your local connection…" Hasan hesitated then continued. "I'll let you go."

"You're not very convincing. What about the innocent kids?" Billy asked.

"Not your concern."

"I'll think about it." Billy didn't blink an eye as he turned and headed toward the truck.

Hasan followed close behind until he climbed on the back of the last truck. Billy never turned around to watch Hasan walk away. Billy's lack of fear had earned a level of respect. *Maybe this will be my ticket out alive.*

Chapter Ten -- Abasolo, Mexico

"When you said the property was located near Abasolo, I expected civilization somewhere." Rita stated.

"You saw the sign. Matamoros is fifty-six miles ahead." The terrain around here is uninhabitable except for wildlife. Too desolate. If you built a house, within a week, you would be robbed, murdered, and your house burned to the ground. Chances are you'd be raped too. Speaking from experience, this area is run by the big cartels."

Almost an hour had ticked away since another vehicle had passed them. Not even one gas station. Robert slowed as he approached the gravel parking lot. The last tropical storm flooded the property all the way to the road. Damage to the dock appeared to be more than he recalled. Emailed pictures from his sister didn't show this much devastation. His concern now were the two deep sea fishing boats tied to the dock. *Are they waiting on Hasan?* Men wearing black t-shirts, camouflage pants, and toting automatic weapons strapped across their shoulders were meandering on the

dock and boat decks. Robert's dark blue F150 did not go unnoticed.

On her knees and facing the back window, Rita focused the binoculars "Four on each and two fishing off the dock. You think anyone's below deck? Weapons look to be AK-47s. I feel like we brought BB guns to a war zone."

Robert pulled over to the emergency lane then shifted to park. "I'm going to call Nicholas. It appears that we're the mouse and that's the trap."

"No time. Drive, NOW! There's a Jeep rumbling across the rocks with two hanging on to the roll bar and they're not empty handed." Rita slid back into her seat and fastened the seatbelt.

Robert dropped his phone in front of the gear shift, switched to four-wheel drive, and pressed the pedal to the floor. Rocks and dirt blew with the wind until the tires gained traction. He glanced in the rearview mirror. Beyond the haze, he saw the men lining their sites on his location.

Ding noises from the truck bed were getting louder. "Hold on." Weaving back and forth, he created a thick cloud of dust. When the air behind them cleared, the Jeep was nowhere to be seen. Robert turned the truck around and stopped on the side of the road. They were almost five miles away with no one behind them.

Rita took a deep breath and exhaled. "Damn. And I thought mud racing was a bumpy ride. What now?"

"That's my fucking property." Robert banged his palm against the steering wheel. "Hasan's become too comfortable taking advantage of the fact we don't have security here. He expected Diego to send someone. Look under the seat. This used to be my dad's truck. Hopefully, you'll find his Uzi."

"If we go back, they'll shoot and never ask questions," Rita said.

"This truck has bullet proof panels and glass. The problem is, I don't have a fucking clue as to what type of ammunition that includes. If we take a chance and go back, we could become prisoners. It may be the leverage Rico wanted. Also, it could be the reason Hasan asked Diego to have them checked. They were expecting company. Now, I'm concerned about how many soldiers are waiting to ambush us at the river crossing."

"You really think Rico wants his property back?"

"Yep. Dad may've been in bed with Chief Rojas to eliminate Old Man Greyson, but Rico blames the Garcia family. It won't take long for him to round up enough good ole boys around his old stomping grounds. Drug wars are all the Greyson family has ever known. Bet your bottom dollar, if he finds out I'm in Mexico, he'll try to put an end to my days on earth."

"Well, Mr. Sunshine, do we return to Nuevo Laredo to prepare for a fight or your funeral?"

"Ha. Good one. Maybe looking at his intentions from this perspective will be our saving grace. Sad thing is, what about the innocent immigrants just looking for a better life?"

Chapter Eleven -- Nuevo Laredo, Mexico

No architectural drawings had ever been done of the Reyes property. All tunnels and structures were constructed by the family, skilled carpenters, or field hands when they were not tending the crops. Maps of the underground tunnels and building floor plans were sketched by hand. While Diego checked on his three employees, Nicholas climbed the ladder leading to the southeast security tower. Eight-inch square, pressure treated posts supported a six-foot-by-six-foot hut.

After killing a few spiders, then shooing off the lizards for not eating the little creatures, Nicholas scanned the area using binoculars. Specifications for the lenses listed the field of view to be one-thousand yards. He didn't believe the ratings any more than the breakdown of ingredients listed on the boxes of most prepackaged foods. Diego had explained the big boulders marked the actual property line which were located at the intersection of the dirt road used to travel east and west around the city. Heading west would lead to the Rio Grande crossing into Texas. Robert and Rita took the eastbound route to the Gulf.

Not a cloud in the sky or a breeze to cut the humidity. Sweat drizzled down the back of his neck. *This is why Robert pulls his hair back with a rubber band all the time.* The few leafless trees across the road marked the approximate location for the east tunnel exit. He recalled the sketched drawing of the underground pathways. All the tunnels originated in the main warehouse except one. The one Old Man Greyson partially completed before his demise. Robert's father used the laborers who stayed in the bunkhouses on their property to complete the digging at night. The only unfinished item when Carlos Reyes disappeared for good was a door.

Nicholas contemplated removing the golf cart used to travel from tunnel to tunnel especially since the Greyson house was close to three-hundred yards away. Since Rico was aware of the tunnel, any chance of him accessing the rest of the Reyes property had to be prevented. The opening from the warehouse to the master bedroom of the Greyson home would need to be sealed. *If Rico wants revenge bad enough, how far will he go? What means and to what end?*

Nicholas's thoughts were interrupted when his phone vibrated in his shirt pocket. He leaned against a post and answered.

"Hello."

"Nicholas, this is Sheila Garrett. Sebastian asked me to call and find out how I can help. Do you need me in Mexico, or would you prefer I set up a team on this side of the border?"

"I sent Robert to check their property on the Gulf. He should be on his way back. Let me talk to him and we'll call you back. Are you in the Laredo office?"

"Yes. Call me on this number. It's a secure line. I don't think I trust the locals yet. It appears they don't trust me either."

"Got it. Talk to you soon." Nicholas clicked off finding himself comparing Sheila to Casey. He knew Agent Sheila Garrett's history from the time she started as a street cop for the San Marcos P.D. up to her current position with the San Antonio DEA's office. From her long, blonde hair and blue eyes to her smile that seemed to light up a room full of people reminded him of Casey. All his efforts to protect Casey from becoming another sex trafficking statistic failed when his uncle had her murdered. She had been the only woman he had ever loved.

The purpose for Sheila's temporary assignment with the border patrol had two underlying purposes. First, find out if any border office locations had agents who received payoffs to aid kidnapper's transport unaccompanied minors across the Texas border. The second issue of illegals crossing the border without following proper protocol had grown from minor to critical. Corruption caused by the wrong kind of migrants had risen dramatically.

Sheila's knowledge of the Reyes family and drug trafficking across the border could be a big help. But if Nicholas asked her to come to Mexico, he would be placing her in harm's way. Could the four of them capture Hasan and Rico without Sheila's help? That depended on how many guerillas Hasan had with him. He didn't need a Trojan horse showing up.

Hasan would have to believe Diego was alone on the property. How to achieve that and protect Diego at the same time created a difficult quandary. Would he, Robert, and Rita hide in the tunnel system within close proximity of Diego? Maybe the best solution would be for Diego to stay in the master bedroom of the old Greyson house and make Rico and Hasan stay in the rooms upstairs. *Is this a Catch-22? Dammed if I do and dammed if I don't. Need to tell Diego not to board up the tunnel.*

Nicholas climbed down the ladder. When he reached the ground, his cell buzzed again. This time it was Robert.

Chapter Twelve -- Nuevo Laredo, Mexico

"Hey Nicholas. We're near La Palma. Stopped to get a bite to eat," Robert said.

"Any issues at the property?"

"Yep. I would've called you sooner, but phone service has been lousy. We arrived to find two fishing boats. Rita counted ten oversized dudes toting AK-47s. Could be Mexican or South American. They had a Jeep parked near the dock. Chased us a few miles, but we managed to outrun it."

"Hmm. More likely a mixture of both. If he already has a team waiting, then he may skip your property all together. What time do you think you'll be back?"

"About four."

"Did they get close enough to get your plate number?" Nicholas asked.

"I doubt it, but they could describe it to Hasan. This truck belonged to my dad. He had it when the Greyson's lived here."

"Diego was told to make sure both gates were open. Question is, were they there early to get rid of or capture anyone who showed up?"

"Good possibility since they opened fire on us. One drove and two were balancing their weapons on the roll bar. I created a dust storm and eliminated their ability to see us."

"I'll send Sebastian a text alerting him on what you found. When you get back, I need you to find holes in the idea I have. Be careful. Hasan's guerillas may have sent the Jeep to hunt you down."

Nicholas put his phone in his pocket as he walked into the warehouse office. He glanced out the window to see Diego on a four-wheeler near the southwest corner of the property, surveying the field. Nicholas had laid the groundwork that turned Diego's life around. He had showed Diego in a roundabout way the truth of how his older brothers were turning profits at the expense of the innocent.

Diego's older brothers shielded him from what truly happened to all the young girls who were being captured and transported to other countries. Once the youngest son of a large cocaine cartel, Diego transformed into an honest farmer, father, and husband with the help of his wife, Anita. Now, happily married and raising a son. It was of no concern to Diego that little Rafael was technically his stepson and didn't have Garcia blood running through his veins.

Transforming the vast pot fields into avocado, chocolate and vanilla plants reminded Nicholas of the months he spent at Saint Vincent's church while constructing the animal refuge across the street. Every day the schedule changed, or another obstacle arose from turning a barren, lifeless sand pit into an animal sanctuary. What he missed more than anything was Father Simon's daily inspirational speeches. As he sifted through their conversations, one caused him to pause.

"Remember when one door shuts behind you, you're worth more than what was left behind it. God brought Diego to you at a time He knew you could change a drug dealer's path just as He brought you to me. If someone had told you a year ago that you would be standing on the roof of a church overseeing the creation of an animal sanctuary, would you have believed them?"

"No," Nicholas said aloud as if Father Simon were in the room with him. *Are You guiding my direction again? God, if you're listening, all I ask is that the young, innocent kids do not suffer due to an error in the calculations or mistakes I might make. I've come to realize that without you, I'd be lost. Thank you for Father Simon and my team of misfits.* He smiled, found a rubber band in the top desk drawer, then used it to twist around his hair. *Time to review the drawings one more time.*

Chapter Thirteen -- Torreon, Mexico

Billy dozed on and off until the trucks stopped again. The guards at the end climbed off. All eyes were on the flapping tarp. No one spoke. More questions piled up. He wondered if this was what it felt like to be a prisoner of war. *Has this been a way of life for these young people? Has the art of standing up for what's right been forgotten by these goons who sought an easy payday stealing from the weak?*

For a moment, guilt overwhelmed Billy. He had been the goon that trapped young girls across the panhandle of Florida and transported them to a shipping contact outside of New Orleans. For almost five years, he closed his eyes to what happened to the young girls after he dropped them off until Nicholas, Robert, and Rita showed him the ugly truth. The young girls were drugged, shipped to Russia, Africa, or South America to become slaves in countries that turned a blind eye to the market.

Several minutes passed. His thoughts were interrupted by banging and clanging sounds as if the trucks were being refueled by the tanker. He heard Hasan yell for someone named Rico and assumed it had to be the fat, bald man. Most of the conversation was muffled. Billy pictured Hasan dictating new orders. He counted three engines restart and drive away. *If that is accurate then there are three trucks with at least six of Hasan's team left. Can I fight Hasan, the fat Mexican, and the other guerillas?*

Billy's questions went unanswered as the flaps opened and they were instructed to get out.

Again, the same plastic bucket had been placed out in the open. It appeared to have been emptied but not washed. Without being told, the teens lined up in single file as if they were back in elementary school. Each of them received an eight-ounce bottle of water. None of the teens opened the water, but Billy guzzled his down in two swallows. He ran his hand over the stubble on his head as he pretended to stare at the ground. His calculations were accurate. Hasan and his buddy were speaking to the two men climbing into the gas tanker.

By the time Billy finished at the bucket and turned to throw his empty bottle away, Hasan and Rico were headed toward him. He pretended not to see them as he walked toward the truck bed.

"Stop walking Mr. Carter, I need to speak to you," Hasan said.

Billy ignored the command until a bullet hit the sand less than a foot in front of him.

"The next step you take will be your last."

He stopped and cocked his head to the side enough to see the two men.

"Shoot him. I told you if it's who we think it is, I'll introduce you if he's in town," Rico said as he stopped walking.

Hasan's swung his arm around and aimed the .45 at Rico's head. "Fuck! This is the last time I will say this. If he knows you're with me, he'll never agree to meet. I know your history."

Rico's eyes widened. "Okay, okay. You're the fucking boss. You handle it," he grumbled and walked away.

Hasan waited for Rico to climb behind the wheel of one of the trucks then asked, "You know how to drive one of these trucks?"

"Stick shift or automatic?" Billy asked.

"Automatic. You're driving."

"What makes you think I won't intentionally wreck the vehicle and kill you?"

"If you make any mistake or refuse to answer my questions, Rico's men are to shoot a migrant in the head and shove them out the back. Wild coyotes and dogs will have time to remove all evidence that would lead back to me. You are a man with a conscience. You'll be the last, so you know the deaths of all the others will be your fault. Move." Hasan nudged Billy's shoulder with the barrel of the gun.

He had nothing left to threaten the Somalian with. Hasan was right. He did have a conscience, but even more he wanted to make it back to Kaylee and his son. As Billy climbed behind the wheel and started the engine, he noticed the radio mounted to the dash.

"Where are we going?"

"Doesn't matter. Follow the truck in front of you." Hasan waited until the other trucks began moving to continue. "What was your line of work in California?"

"Construction. Paint and drywall."

"You have the build of someone who spent time in the military."

"Two years. IED ended that career." Billy paused to consider how much of a partial truth he needed to confess to make the rest of his lies believable. "Why the sudden interest in my life? I have nothing worth stealing and not a dime to my name. I doubt my phone has minutes left."

"What did you plan to do in Nuevo Laredo?"

Billy's brow furrowed as he cocked his head. "I answered that question. Did you forget?"

Before he blinked twice, the barrel of Hasan's weapon was pressed against his temple. "Looking up an acquaintance is not sufficient. I need to know who you were going to see."

Before Billy responded, the radio came to life. "Why are you falling behind?" Rico asked.

Hasan's focus switched to the road ahead. "Speed up. Keep the truck ahead in sight."

Billy pressed the gas pedal until the speedometer reached seventy. This was his first view of the road they were traveling on. Sweat beads slid down his back like rain on a tin roof. The twenty miles per hour increase in speed caused the front end to vibrate. No air conditioning, but the windows were down. It was a dirt road with no signs of civilization in site. He wondered if someone created separate road maps specifically for illegal drug runners.

Had Hasan used this route before? The pressure of metal against his head brought Billy back to reality.

"Answer the fucking question."

"Like I told you before, I haven't spoken to the man since last year. I was going to wait until I got there to call."

"I don't give a shit. What's his name?"

Billy hesitated. Thoughts raced through his mind calculating the odds of snatching the gun out of Hasan's hand, shooting him, then turning the truck around. *No phone, no money, and no wallet, so quit thinking you have options.* He took a deep breath and exhaled. "Robert Reyes. Said his family owned a large spread south of Nuevo Laredo. His brother-in-law and sister run it. He had a restaurant in town until it burned down. He is in the process of rebuilding. Told me with my construction background, I had a job if I wanted it."

Hasan holstered the Glock. "How well do you know Mr. Reyes?"

"I don't. We drank beers a few times at the same bar. Discussed life and politics. Had a few laughs. He loaned me money to get by. That's it, dammit. Fuck! I don't know him any better than I know you." He clutched the wheel so tight his knuckles were almost white. His frustration rose to breaking point, but if he screwed this up, more than his life lay on the line.

The ride from behind the wheel turned out to be no better than sitting on the hot, metal floor of the truck bed. Potholes were more like small ditches. Billy watched Hasan from his peripheral view. The man appeared to be deep in thought. Billy recalled all

51

the times he had seen Hasan's ship take the same path transporting the Garcia's family's cocaine his father once made. *Did the Coast Guard shut down that route? If he knew who I was back then, I would've been cut up and fed to the gators. Did Hasan still work for the cartel? This Rico dude is a loose cannon. What's the purpose of knowing an acquaintance's name? Has he connected the dots?*

Answers only led to more questions with nothing resolved. Almost a half hour passed before Hasan spoke. "I need to know if Mr. Reyes is at his property in Nuevo Laredo. Call him now."

Billy turned his head to see his own cell phone in Hasan's hand. "Why?"

"None of your fucking business. Make the call."

Chapter Fourteen -- Nuevo Laredo, Mexico

"I need a beer. Is there a convenience store somewhere in our near future?" Rita asked as she finished her bottle of water.

"Nope. Nothing. Remember, I mentioned when we stopped for gas if there was anything you needed to get it because we wouldn't be stopping again?"

"Dammit. Yes, now that you repeated it." She paused a moment. "Do you think we made a mistake by not turning around?"

"No. We had no way to fight that many assholes in the middle of nowhere. Two Glocks and an Uzi isn't enough fire power against what we left behind. There's not a fucking thing we could've done. We're about forty-five minutes from the compound, so can you wait?"

"I thought you said I didn't have a choice."

"You don't. I was trying to be nice."

Robert's cell vibrated on the console. Caller ID displayed Billy Wright. When he reached to hit the accept call button, Rita grabbed his wrist. "Wait. Let it go to voicemail." After four rings, she continued. "I just realized; I haven't told you about Billy's alibi. Shit! I'm sorry. Billy must've told Hasan he was traveling with the teens to meet with you."

She gazed out the window, sighed, and continued. "Anyway, long story short, Billy's undercover name is Will Carter. He's probably being forced to call you which means Hasan is in earshot of the conversation. Sebastian told Billy if he crossed into Mexico and ran into any kind of trouble, you could be his way out."

"Alibi for what?"

"I should've told you this morning when we discussed Billy being among the refugees taken. In case I missed any other details, let me back up. Two months ago, we found out that immigrants were being transported from Tijuana east across Mexico but never arrived at their destinations. Sebastian considered you as a possible backup plan then. With you working full time at the shop while Nicholas was on some life changing sabbatical in Florida, you weren't available when we had the meeting."

She reached over and put her hand on his. "It wasn't supposed to happen like this. Billy was never supposed to become part of any kidnapping. I'm sorry this fell through the cracks, but the idea was that if Will Carter happened to cross paths with any potential target, he would be recovering from the loss of his wife. He's supposedly broke. His accounts reflect he has less than a hundred dollars to his name. This is based on the theory that Billy remembered the entire lie."

As Rita explained, Robert's mind drifted back to the first time he met Billy. He had left New Orleans to track Billy down off I-10 near Pascagoula where Billy's supposedly parked his truck and boat when he made trips from the river to drop off his female captives. At the boat launch where Robert found Billy's truck, he remembered seeing Billy fiddling with what appeared to be a phone.

Billy hadn't moved from where someone had dropped him off at the gravel roadway near the boat launch. Robert crouched down and made his way toward the front of Billy's truck and waited. The familiar clicking noise from the prosthetic grew louder with each step the Indian took. As Billy fumbled for his truck key, Robert stood and pointed his .45 across the hood of the F150. *"Stop right there. You're gonna take a ride with m*e." His first statement to the Indian.

When Rita finished explaining, he asked, "So, who am I supposed to be to this penniless drunk?"

"You met him in a bar in Tijuana while on business in Baja. Gave him money and told him if he needed a job, you would give him one. Back story is, he's a carpenter and you're renovating El Rancho restaurant to reopen this summer."

Robert smiled. "I assume Sebastian thought a 'just in case' scenario wouldn't be needed. If Hasan goes downtown, he's gonna know Billy lied. I better call him back. Hasan has probably threatened him. If he made Billy call before he arrives, then he knows someone visited the Gulf property today." He hit the callback button.

"Remember the bastard will be listening."

*****

Hasan ran his hand across the black stubble on his head. "Why didn't you leave a message?"

"I haven't spoken to the man in months."

"Are you worried the man won't confirm your lies? Call again. This time leave a message to call you."

Before he had a chance to hit redial, his phone rang. Caller ID displayed RR. "Hello."

"Hey buddy. Long time, no see," Robert said.

"I know. I've been struggling to get by. Thought it might be a good time to take you up on that offer for a job. Are you still hiring?"

"We've had some issues getting the property released by the city to rebuild. It could be a month or so before we can get started, but I think I can find something on the property for you to do in the interim. When are you headed toward Nuevo Laredo?"

"Should be there sometime tonight. Are you in Mexico?"

"Yes, but not at my house. I had business to take care of at one of my other properties and ran into a few snags. I may not be back until sometime tomorrow. Find a hotel downtown. If you need money, tell them to call me. Hey Will, I'm glad you called. I sure can use a couple of extra hands. Got to go but will call ya' later." Robert clicked off.

Billy glanced over at Hasan. "What the fuck now? I've done what you asked. You gonna let me go?"

"You can forget about any hotel room in town tonight. You will finish the trip in back with the rest of the prisoners. You introduce me to Mr. Reyes, I'll set you free." Hasan called Rico on the radio and told him to stop. "Pull behind the truck in front of us and get out. You make a run for it, and you'll be rewarded with a few holes in your back."

"Why is meeting Mr. Reyes so important to you? He's just a normal businessman."

Hasan smiled slightly. "Let's say that I know the history of the Reyes Cartel and your so-called businessman friend is the son of a dead man, just like me."

Billy didn't respond. His version of being set free and Hasan's version were not the same. Chances were Hasan planned to kill them both. Billy took a deep breath and sighed. When one of the guards opened the driver's door, Billy did as he was told and returned to his place at the end of the bench in the back with the teens. *Robert backed up my story. Sebastian must've told him. Is Robert here to help?* He knew Robert wasn't at the meeting when the discussion came up about a backup plan if he ever crossed the border into Mexico.

The thought gave Billy little relief to his anxiety. He just added Robert to Hasan's hit list. He didn't secure the canvas flaps and neither did the guard. When the truck began to move once again, a light breeze circulated around them. He sat down across from the guerilla wearing fatigues and considered striking up a conversation with the man. He quickly changed his mind when the guard stood and rammed his fist against Billy's jaw.

He rubbed his cheek, wiped a trickle of blood as it dripped from his chin onto his sleeve, then glared at the man. "Fuck you, Asshole."

"You have no weapon, yet you talk like you could whip my ass." The guard held the AK-47 in front of him and pressed the barrel against Billy's forehead. "Who's the fucking asshole now?"

The truck rocked enough to throw the guard off balance. Without thought or hesitation, Billy grabbed the barrel with both hands, stood, and swung it as if he were holding a baseball bat. The damage was done before Billy's reaction registered in his thought process. His homerun swing caused the guard to fall off the truck bed. Billy held the flapping tarp and slung the AK-47 with every ounce of strength he had. Watching the man hit the ground and roll several times brought a smile to his face. Through a burnt-orange haze of sand and dust, Billy concluded the man did not survive. *Driver didn't stop. Hmm…Hasan and his driver didn't notice.*

One down but how many more wait ahead? Are we part of Hasan's plan to destroy Robert's family? How many times has this caravan made this same trek.? When Billy no longer saw the dead man's body, he turned around to find all the teens smiling at him. He considered the possibilities of Hasan hearing him if he banged on the wall behind the cab. The better option would be to wait until the caravan stopped again.

"If you're asked what happened, say the man stood and fell out," Billy said softly.

None of them spoke, but all nodded in agreement then went back to staring at the floor, except one, the young girl raped by Hasan the night before. She managed to straighten her hair some, but the bruises and cut on her cheek had darkened. Blood stains covered her t-shirt and jeans. The rubber flip-flops she wore at the beginning of their trip were gone, along with her innocence and there was nothing Billy could do to fix it.

He slouched slightly. "I'm sorry for what Hasan did to you and your brother. There was nothing…what's your name?"

"Maleah," she said just above a whisper.

"Why did your parents allow you to leave Tijuana?"

"We were told there would be opportunities for work, but only for those under twenty. Our mama caught a fishing boat headed south. My…my Papa was shot a few weeks ago over drugs. My Papa had no drugs. He was honest. A hard worker."

She paused to wipe her eyes with the palms of her dirt-stained hands. "My Mama thought it would be better if we split up. I was going to call her when we settled. Now? I don't know. How can I tell her about Daniel? He…he was only trying to save me." The young girl's tears flowed like tiny streams down her cheek as she turned her head away.

"Who told you about possible job opportunities in Nuevo Laredo?"

"Hasan's partner. Rico Greyson."

"How do you know his name?"

"He told us when he asked for volunteers. Said he used to live there and had connections."

Billy's mind shuffled through images of an old card rolodex. A spindle of name cards given to him when he began working for Swamp Man Stickler to retrieve young girls in the Florida panhandle area nearly five years ago. Yellowed, smoke-stained cards held together on a plastic tray. After Billy trapped the teenage girls, he dropped them off at Stickler's swamp tour business east of New Orleans. The names in the rolodex were to be used in case of emergency any time he needed help. *Does Sebastian keep an emergency rolodex too?*

He closed his eyes and recalled every detail of the card with Rico's name on it. *956 area code. That's not New Orleans. Why stamp the card listing him as dead in red ink and keep it?* Billy wondered if the information had been for Rico's father. Rumors of the incident near Monterrey varied, but all agreed Rico's remains were never found at the crime scene where his two brothers were murdered. *Has Rico worked for Hasan all this time?* The biggest question that weighed heavy on Billy's mind was at what point did Hasan plan to kill him?

Billy gazed out at the barren wasteland as the flaps whipped with the drifting wind. His thoughts soon wandered to brief moments with Kaylee, and little Will. Leaving Kaylee behind for the better life in New Orleans had been a huge mistake.

Hindsight turned that better life into a nightmare. Promises made by Stickler translated to lies. Nicholas and Robert painted the true picture and consequences to the reality of his line of work. *I should've hung onto the AK-47. Dammit. What would be my odds of escape if I killed Hasan and the driver?*

Chapter Fifteen -- Nuevo Laredo, Mexico

Nicholas checked the time on his phone for the third time in less than fifteen minutes. Waiting for something to happen shifted the advantage from offense to defense. He erased what appeared to be an old employee work schedule off the white board hanging on the wall next to the desk in the warehouse office. With the red marker on the tray below the board, he drew a line down the center. On one side he wrote everything they knew. On the other side he wrote all the questions he could think of that needed to be resolved.

The list of unknowns turned out to be twice as long compared to what he knew. Nicholas took a step back and read over the questions. *Abid Hasan is on his way but to where? Here, or the boats waiting at the dock near Abasolo? Waiting for what? Why the river crossing near Hidalgo? Is he bypassing it? Why would he expect it to be open if using the Gulf as his point of exit? How many are with him? Other than the young teens, what else is he transporting across country? What kind of weapons? Bombs? Rocket launchers? Automatic rifles?*

Like shattered glass across a polished floor, there were too many variables to connect the questions to accurate answers. Hasan's final stop could be anywhere. Had Hasan split up the multiple transport trucks? Different cargo, different direction? Nicholas rubbed his chin as if he hadn't shaved his scraggly beard off the day before. His cell phone rang. Nicholas checked caller ID and answered. "Hey Sebastian."

"I don't know if you have talked to Robert yet, but Billy called him. We were able to trace the return call. Hasan is about five hours away from you unless they stop to rest."

"Why did Billy call Robert?"

"Robert was a backup plan for Billy if he crossed into Mexico and found himself in trouble. I spoke to Rita about thirty minutes ago. She will fill you in. Got to go. Catching a flight to Laredo. I should be there by nine," Sebastian said.

Nicholas clicked off. He took the marker and crossed out the first unknown question. *He's definitely headed here. Is five hours enough time to prepare?* His thoughts were interrupted when Robert, Rita, and Diego walked in.

"So, what are we going to do about Hasan's goons in Abasolo? They expected someone to show up," Robert said.

"Chances are there's also a team of minions waiting on both sides of the river where Hasan believes your tunnel crossing is. Could Rico know the exact location?" Nicholas sat behind the desk. Rita and Diego pulled up two chairs while Robert chose to lean against the door.

"Let me give you the abbreviated version on the tunnel's history. It might help." Robert paused to clear his throat. "It took years to finish. My grandfather started digging sometime in the sixties. Back then border officers could be bought. Paw Paw Angelo believed that one day there would be a wall built between the U.S. and Mexico."

He took a deep breath, exhaled, then swallowed the lump rising in his throat. "Wish he had lived to see it happen. Anyway, last I heard construction extending the wall hasn't started near the tunnel. It took almost ten years for my Paw Paw Angelo to complete. A hole that reaches close to fifteen feet below the river at its deepest point. Wood beams, rebar, and concrete. As far as I know, it has never leaked. The tunnel runs about fifty yards beyond the river on each side. Big enough for a small box truck." Robert folded his arms across his chest. "And yes, Rico knows the approximate location."

"I spoke to the DEA agent working with Sebastian. Her name is Sheila Garrett. I believe you two remember her from when she worked for the San Marcos police department."

Back when Robert's father was released from prison after serving thirty years behind bars for the brutal murder of a college student, Sheila was a detective for San Marcos police department and Rita was a DEA agent in the Dallas branch. Carlos Reyes was the top suspect in multiple murders in San Marcos, but when Sheila, Rita and her partner had Carlos trapped. Robert's brother argued the fact that all the murders could be blamed on Carlos's accomplice who was lying dead on the ground a few feet away.

"I do," Robert replied as he took a deep breath and sighed. "She investigated my mom's tragic accident. I made the mistake of listening to my younger brother and let my dad return to Mexico, but you and I both know prison would never take the evil out of my dad." He glanced down at Rita. "You agreed with Juan that day." He paused a moment, walked over to the filing cabinets, and leaned against them. "Garrett also busted up Jack Silverman's operation. Diego, you may not know the name, but Silverman was a small-time distributor for your older brothers and for my dad."

"I will text her number to you. Call her and give her the coordinates on the north side. Tell her to take back-up. If you saw ten at the Gulf property, then tell her to take at least that many border agents with her." Nicholas picked up his phone. "Tell her if anyone gives her any shit, they need to call Sebastian."

Robert's phone dinged alerting him to a text message. "Got it." Robert turned and headed out the door.

*****

A tall, barn-like structure, the warehouse supported a tin roof. A main floor with an office overlooking the entire area and a basement that ran the length of the building. The office was located above the utility room and two bathrooms. A wood deck extended over the main entry doors. Every inch of the building was visible from where Robert stood. Rows of shelving which were once filled with processed and packaged marijuana ready for shipping now supported a thick layer of dust.

Before Robert left for Grapevine, he believed he did all that was necessary for Anita and Diego to take over their property south of Nuevo Laredo. As he gazed across the open space, he pushed aside all the obsessive-compulsive thoughts of what needed to be done, and dialed Sheila's number.

"Agent Garrett, can I help you?"

"Sheila, this is Robert Reyes. Nicholas gave me your number. He thought it would be easier if I gave you the coordinates to where our old tunnel runs under the river."

It took her a few moments to respond. "I apologize. You caught me off guard. I've sat on my ass for two days. After I talked to Nicholas earlier today, I kind of got the feeling that I wouldn't be needed."

"That's okay. Nicholas wants you to make a trip to the Texas side of the tunnel my family built. The openings are steel panels on a rail system. Ropes open and close the doors and can be locked from the inside and outside. We suggested you take at least ten border patrol officers with you. You may very well run into trouble."

"What happened?" Sheila stood and shut down her laptop.

"My family has property near Abasolo, on the east coast. Two deep sea fishing boats were tied off at the dock. Rita counted ten military looking guerillas. They came after us firing AK-47s, but I managed to outrun them. I'll text you the directions."

"I'll see what I can do. I don't really feel welcomed here. The only thing I've been able to come up with is that they must think I'm part of an internal affairs investigation."

"If all the border officers in Laredo are innocent, they shouldn't give a shit why you're there? One more thing. A row of large paddle cactus line up on the east side of the tunnel. That's the only way you'll find it. Remember, don't go alone." Robert checked the time on his watch. "Call me or Nicholas when you reach the tunnel. If you leave now, you should make it before the sun sets."

Robert clicked off and started typing directions. He couldn't remember how many miles it was to the site. Almost twenty years ago, he made the trip at least once a week to deliver his family's illegal drugs to their distributor in San Marcos. A year had come and gone since the last time he checked on the tunnel.

Have I intentionally avoided returning here? The lame excuses I gave Anita for not coming when Rafael was born. Did she know?

He pushed back the memories from his mother's death, the loss of his youngest brother, and his brother-in-law. His Paw Paw Angelo passed away at his Uncle Frank's house in San Marcos, but it didn't erase all the years he lived in Mexico with them. Losses in his life had built a wall around his heart. This hadn't been the first time he had been shot at, but it made him realize life slipped away faster with each passing year.

He closed his eyes for a moment, leaned against the rail, and pictured the exit on the Texas side of the river. Hidalgo was the nearest town on the south side of the border, but what was on the north side. Desolate land. Rough terrain with the long row of cactus his mom had planted. She had told him the prickly plant would be their compass point in the dark. The thought made him smile as he quickly finished the text, then walked back in the office.

"What are you doing?" Robert asked.

Diego cocked his head to the side. "Adding to the list of what we know and don't know."

"Rita caught us up on your conversation with Billy," Nicholas said as he handed the marker to Robert. "I spoke to Sebastian. We know Hasan is maybe five hours away. That gives us something, but not enough. You have anything to add or answer any of the unknowns?"

Robert read down the list of unknowns until he reached the last item. "Who wrote, what time can I have a beer?"

"I did. I wondered if anyone would notice. After being shot at today, I really need one." Rita replied.

Nicholas smiled as he picked up the eraser. Diego got up and opened the mini-refrigerator next to the row of filing cabinets and grabbed four beers.

"Thanks," Rita said as she twisted off the top.

"I told Billy, or maybe we need to use his alias, Will. Anyway, I told him I would not be at the property until tomorrow. I don't know if Hasan will let him call again, but I told Billy to call if he needed a room downtown. We need to hide Rita's SUV and the truck we drove to Abasolo."

Nicholas glanced at the whiteboard. "Let's start there then. I'll drive your truck. You ride with Rita. Diego, you follow us in your Land Rover. We'll eat dinner in town, I'll get a hotel room and we can leave both vehicles in the Colon Plaza Hotel parking lot."

Diego finished his beer. "Rosa left pot roast and potatoes on the stove."

"It should be okay until we return. The visitors may expect dinner. Robert, if you don't hear from Billy again, then we'll take a ride to the south side of the tunnel after we eat. See how many men are there. I need to take care of my two fur buddies and will meet you by the truck in ten minutes. Will that give you enough time, Diego?"

"Yes." Diego tossed his empty bottle in the trash and led the way out the door.

Robert followed Nicholas. "You think Hasan will show up while we're gone?"

"No. For some reason, I think he wants to meet you personally. Do you know why?" Nicholas asked.

"Nope. But whatever his reason is, it can't be good. I don't have that warm, fuzzy feeling about any of this after being a moving target today."

Chapter Sixteen -- Laredo, Texas

Agent Sheila Garrett leaned back in her chair at the long empty table. A repeat of the day before. Nothing to do on the north side of the Rio Grande. Her offers to tag along and help at the bridge were ignored. Now she needed a team. She paused a moment and watched three patrol officers stroll in front of the third-floor conference room glass panes. *Not a single one glanced this way. Why not just stick me in a room with padded walls tied up in a straitjacket?* An unwelcome outsider in a city which appeared as if it had tripled in size since the last time she visited.

Since the day she arrived, the only person she had talked to, was a Lieutenant Lopez. Border Patrol fell under Homeland Security, not DEA. Where were the lines drawn? Which ones had she been assigned to cross? No introductions were made to anyone. How was she supposed to help with the immigration issues and illegal drug problems if she was left alone in the conference room every day?

She took a deep breath and sighed as she twisted her long blonde hair into a butterfly clip. Maybe reviewing the aerial and topographical maps of Laredo she acquired from Lopez one more time might help relieve her stress. The lieutenant appeared to be in his early sixties who struggled to handle his current workload. He was a short, stocky man with gray hair and a thin mustache. *Is he afraid if he lets me help, I will make his team look bad? Hmm?*

She grabbed a red marker and circled the coordinates Robert had texted her. The maps were clear enough for her to make out the long row of cactus. As she wondered if they were in bloom when she glanced up to see Lopez walk in.

"I spoke with Mr. Brad Sebastian. He said that you need a team to search for possible drug activity near a tunnel under the river?"

"Yes. We believe it is about to be accessed, but not by the original people who dug it."

Lopez put his hands on the back of the chair and leaned forward across the table. "I can spare two of my agents and me."

"Did Sebastian tell you the number of suspects is unknown, and they may have automatic weapons?"

"He also said there may be nothing. My understanding is this is just to clear the area on this side of the river."

"I have the approximate coordinates, if you and your men want to follow me."

"Is your vehicle four-wheel drive?"

"No."

"Do you have a motorcycle license?" Lopez asked.

"Yes, why?"

"The area you circled on the map has no public streets or roadways except the dirt road that runs close to the river. The President's wall hasn't reached that area."

"I have the government bridge border crossings marked, but the area in question isn't near any of them," Sheila said.

"I'll meet you downstairs in fifteen minutes," Lopez replied. "We have to wait on my agents to return from their current assignment."

Sheila tucked the maps and her laptop into her brief case as Lopez walked out. She wanted to go by herself. Problem was, this wasn't San Marcos, and she wasn't the detective who once worked her way up the chain of command. It took more than eight years to achieve the rank of detective. She knew every road and every hideout in and around her beat. She wondered if history truly repeated itself. *Would a second round of dealing with members of the Reyes family turn out the same as her previous encounters?*

She hit the down button for the elevator. As she waited, she made mental notes of what she knew about the Reyes family. She had met Robert's brothers, Juan, and Arias. Even though she had no physical evidence, Carlos Reyes had been her primary suspect in several murder cases. Carlos Reyes disappeared almost two years ago. *Did Robert have his father murdered? Does that question matter now? Nope.*

The only way to stop Carlos's long path to revenge was to put him six feet under. She let him go once upon a time but sending the evil man back to prison was never a viable option if the thirty years behind bars didn't fix him the first time. Her mind searched for answers in the Reyes case file. When she reached Juan's plea, the little wheels in her brain stopped.

"Let him go back to Mexico. I will testify that it was Wire who murdered Mack and Mattie. I just lost my mother. I can't lose my dad too."

How many other lives were sacrificed because I listened to Juan and the DEA agents? The lawyer and his girlfriend in Dallas, Amanda Dawson, Silverman, and Dante. No evidence to prove a damn thing. How many were there that we never uncovered? Hmm? Does any of this shit make a difference now? No. Have things really changed south of the border? That's a stupid thought. Robert wouldn't be working for Sebastian now if that was still the case.

There wasn't another soul in the elevator when she stepped on and hit the first-floor button.

Chapter Seventeen -- Hidalgo, Mexico

Nicholas hoped to arrive at the tunnel before dusk. Acquiring a hotel room that would most likely stay empty all night, dinner at Tomatillo's, and the drive took longer than he calculated. Spring breakers were everywhere. If there truly was a pandemic, it appeared no one cared. Diego backed the motorcycle trailer off the road, behind a sand dune. He shut off the engine and headlights. They were still about three miles from the tunnel entrance. A full moon with a scattered array of stars illuminated the sky giving them enough light to see close range. They all got out, stood still, and listened.

"I'm assuming you hid vehicles here before?" Nicholas asked.

"Yes. When this route was traveled on a regular basis, we hid ATVs here in case our trucks broke down. Sand dune used to be a lot bigger, but I think we are far enough from the road to go unnoticed," Robert replied.

"If we can see or hear someone, then they can see and hear us. Robert, can you lead the way? We will fan out behind you?"

"Oh, so I've been nominated to be the expendable one."

"No. By a narrow margin, you've been elected our fearless leader," Nicholas replied with a tone of sarcasm. "Besides, you know exactly where we're going. If Hasan's men expected visitors in Abasolo, then they expect someone to show up here. You do have a vest on under your t-shirt, right?"

Robert smiled and hit his chest with his fist. "Yes, Bwana. You're right."

"Bwana? Where did you hear that big word?"

"John Wayne movie. Means boss."

"I know what the word means, but right now, you're our honorable leader," Nicholas laughed.

"Can you two shut up?" Rita asked and nudged Robert's arm. "Come on. We may be too late."

Robert put on his night vision gear and headed in a northwest direction away from the road. Nicholas grabbed the crossbow and arrows. With them secured across his back, he checked his M107A1 sniper rifle before pulling the strap across his shoulder. He caught up to Diego and Rita as they kept a ten-yard

71

pace behind Robert. All of them were dressed in black. Tucking his hair under the baseball cap, he hoped the light breeze might dry up the sweat beads using his neck as a slide.

Patches of rocks and an assortment of cacti were scattered across the landscape. He listened intently for any out of place sounds while trying to keep Robert in view. Nicholas had worked in many environments, but this was the first time in a desert setting. He recalled the last time he had a reason to visit Nuevo Laredo to track down the man responsible for Casey's death: his Uncle Eric. That job had been a contained operation on Robert's property. Here, they were crossing open country with the snakes and coyotes. He wanted to call Sheila to see if they found anything on the other side of the river, but now wasn't the time. He noticed Robert stop and raise his right hand.

With Diego to his left and Rita to his right, there was no mistaking the sounds echoing from the other side of the river. Gunfire, motorcycles, or maybe a four-wheeler. He glanced both ways and behind them as he wondered if they were too late. Had Hasan outsmarted them and had his men on the other side waiting for border patrol to show up? Did they catch Sheila and her team off guard?

Nicholas ran to catch up with Robert. Rita and Diego were a few feet behind. Less than a minute later, nothing. No engines and no gunfire.

"I'm assuming we are at the tunnel entrance?" Nicholas whispered.

Robert nodded as he searched the river's edge north of the Rio Grande where the gunfire originated. "What are the chances Sheila's team was ambushed? Should we call her?"

"No. She could be alive and hiding. How do you open the tunnel?"

"You see that cluster of rocks next to the cactus? There's a heavy rope buried under the sand. The steel panel slides open. Should've been locked last time someone used it, but I can't swear to that. The door sits on rails like a train on tracks. Same on the other side except for a long hedge of prickly pear cactus. You think we need to cross and check on Sheila?"

"If she ran into a trap then so will we. It's our turn to surprise Hasan. If the gunfire is over, the battle is over. Maybe no one survived. Agent Garrett will text or call as soon as she can if she's alive. Diego, you, and Rita return to the compound and prepare for Hasan's arrival."

Rita crossed her arms. "What are you two going to do?"

"Go for a swim. Diego, leave the motorcycles. Robert and I will ride them back. I need to see if there are any tin soldiers we need to deal with on the other side."

"Well, I think I would be more help here." Her face reddened.

"Do you want to leave Diego with no backup if Hasan arrives before we return?" Robert asked.

Rita's brow furrowed and she stomped her foot on the ground as she grumbled a response. "You're right. Come on, Diego."

"You think that was a good idea?" Robert asked as Diego and Rita disappeared in the darkness.

"You have a better plan?" Nicholas asked.

"Probably not, but right now we are on the wrong side of the river. We don't know who was shooting or who survived. You can thank my Paw Paw Angelo for building a dam below water level. Used to be about three feet deep except near the center. I think the river has worn it down some, but we should still be able to walk across and keep our weapons above the waterline. Bad thing is the current is stronger here because of it. Did you wear swim trunks?"

"No. Did you?" Nicholas asked.

"No. I didn't expect we'd be taking a late-night dip." Robert's brows raised as he smiled. "We could cross in our underwear."

"Okay, I'm not Rita and we're not on a date. Besides, do you want to meet any of Hasan's men in your underwear on the other side?"

"You're right. Just trying to lighten the air. We're going to be swimming ducks on the river. If anyone's watching, we could be target practice."

Chapter Eighteen -- Rio Grande River, Texas

74

Crunch, splat, splat. Insects committed suicide one by one as they collided with Sheila's face shield. The streetlights of Laredo had faded behind her long ago. Before they left the ground transport station, the sun had dropped below the horizon. Sheila thought getting on a motorcycle would be like riding a bike again. Two Christmases had passed since she volunteered to ride in the Thanksgiving parade with the motorcycle division of the San Marcos police department. *I'll have to attend motorcycle school when I return home. What made me think I could do this? Dammit!*

She wanted to question why one of the patrol officers went home sick, but Lopez never gave her a chance. Her instinct told her the officer lied. *Did he have a hot date? Is he married with kids? This would've been a great opportunity for him to earn recognition.* Her wondering ended when she realized that her maneuvering abilities were rusty. She had fallen behind. Lopez and Johnson's taillights were barely visible over the rough terrain ahead of her.

Could this be a waste of time? At least she wasn't stuck in a hotel room again with nothing to do except order room service. She began scanning the landscape along the river for the cactus hedges believing Lopez and Johnson might have missed them even though the two border agents had patrolled this road for years.

Lopez mentioned that if her information was accurate, he knew the exact spot of the tunnel. She intentionally avoided telling Lopez that she received the coordinates from a member of the family that had constructed it. *Will border patrol fill it and shut it down? Has Robert realized that by telling me meant Homeland Security would also know?* When her focus returned to the road ahead, the taillights she'd been following were gone. She checked her speedometer to find she had slowed almost ten miles an hour.

As she began to accelerate, gunfire echoed somewhere ahead of her. Quickly cutting her headlight, she swerved off the road toward a patch of ground brush and rocks. With nothing but open wilderness in front of her, she laid the motorcycle on its side, crouched down, and moved toward a sand mound obscured by cactus. As she fell to the ground, she dropped her helmet. When it stopped rolling, a familiar rattling sound vibrated a few feet away. She quickly glanced to see the coiled creature ready to strike.

Sheila didn't move. She held her breath as a dozen scenarios from a venomous bite in the middle of nowhere zipped through her thought processes. The necessity to check on the two officers suddenly wasn't as great as being in the rattler's striking space. With little light from the stars above, it was hard to tell how long the snake might be. Seconds dragged by before the diamond back slithered away into the darkness. Finally, she exhaled then returned to scanning the immediate area around her. She didn't have night vision equipment with her and hoped the night sky would be enough.

Sheila listened for several minutes then lifted her head enough to see over the rocks surrounding the large cactus. The outline of four figures grew closer. None of them appeared to be as chunky as Lopez and Johnson. She wished she had taken a refresher course in Spanish. Understanding the cuss words from the muffled conversations wasn't enough. Estimating she had less than a minute before they stumbled upon her, Sheila aimed her Glock, but didn't fire. Four against one. *These goons have got to know they're looking for someone else, but how?* Then she heard the lead man speak English.

"Okay, Garrett. I know you're around here somewhere."

She ducked. *Fuck. This must be the officer who didn't go home sick. What the hell was his name? Shit. I can't remember. Come on. I need you a little closer.* Her accuracy at the firing range averaged close to perfect. She glanced over both shoulders and tuned her ears for someone approaching from behind. Out here alone, she wasn't so sure she would survive. Answering would automatically compromise her position. Her calculations put them less than fifty yards away and it appeared they were wearing night vision gear.

Sheila assumed Lopez and Johnson were dead. Thoughts of hopping on the motorcycle and making a run for it diminished with each step the men made in her direction. Her Glock would be the equivalent of a BB gun if all four men had high powered automatic weapons. She raised her head again, leveled her sight, and aimed. As she quickly fired in the direction of her targets, it took three bullets to stop the first one, but the other three raised their weapons.

The ground rumbled beneath her as the men closed in. Bullets passed close enough for her to see the sand kick up around her. She cringed below the rocks and closed her eyes. Any second they would have her surrounded. Chips from the tall cactus next to her fell. Sheila couldn't move. "Shit, shit, shit." she said under her breath. *Where are they? How many bullets do I have left?* She quickly peeked over the rocks. *Now or never. Mexican military? Were these Hasan's men?*

With only seconds to fight back, she aimed to fire, but all three dropped their weapons then wobbled slightly a moment before they fell face down onto the ground a few feet from her. Someone had fired from behind. *Are Lopez and Johnson alive?* She ducked and waited. Her heart raced as if she were running for her life. She could hear the rapid thump, thump, thump, banging like a drum in her ears.

A few minutes passed before Sheila heard approaching footsteps. She waited until all she heard was the sound of the river and the wind before peeking over the rocks once more. Two men stood over the three men before her. One of them rolled the dead men on their backs. More important, the other appeared to be staring in her direction.

"Agent Garrett. It's Nicholas Jacobson and Robert Reyes. Are you okay?"

Sheila took a deep breath and exhaled. "Yes." She stood, brushed sand off her chest and arms, and walked toward them.

Nicholas put his hand out. "Do you know any of these men?"

She shook his hand as she answered, "The one back there." She pointed. "He has a bullet in his head and two somewhere in his chest. He's a corrupt border agent. The other three must work for Hasan."

"You know his name?"

"Won't swear to it, but I think Lopez referred to him as Agent Gilmore. He supposedly became sick and had to go home. Funny what some people consider sick," she replied as she tried to pick cactus thorns out of her hair.

"I'm sure he's running a temperature in Hell by now," Robert said as he shook her hand.

"That's a funny way to rationalize actions of a traitor. Glad to finally meet you both. Why are you soaking wet?"

"We walked across the river. It's a little over waist deep where we crossed. We heard gunshots. The border officers are about two hundred yards behind us. Enough shots at close range to make their faces unrecognizable. Appeared these goons enjoyed using the dead men for up close and personal target practice. We collected their wallets and badges. How come they were so far ahead of you?" Nicholas asked as he handed them to Sheila.

"Thoughts of this being a huge waste time clouded my brain. I expected all the action to be south of the river." She kicked sand over Gilmore's body. "There are no excuses for me falling behind. I should've expected something like this and demanded to lead."

"If so, you'd be dead too. How did these men get out here? Did you hear or see any other vehicles?" Nicholas asked.

"Nope. Too busy kicking myself in the ass."

"We need to find their vehicle. Also, make sure no one's following us when we leave," Robert said as a cell phone rang.

They all glanced down at Gilmore. His shirt pocket lit up. Robert bent over and slid it out enough to see caller ID. "AH. Do we answer?"

"No. Let it go to voicemail. Hasan will eventually realize he has a problem. We need enough time to find their ride and get back to your property. Also, he will know we're on to him if you answer," Nicholas replied.

"What about these dead bodies and the border patrol officers?" Sheila asked.

"We'll call Sebastian when we get back. He may know who he can trust in the Laredo office."

"I hope that list is longer than Lieutenant Lopez."

"Is your bike rideable?" Robert asked.

"Yes," Sheila replied.

Robert picked it up. "I'll push it to the tunnel. If there are more dirty bastards out there, we don't need to let them know we're coming."

"Give me a thirty-yard head start." Nicholas bent down and removed Gilmore's night vision goggles hanging on a strap around his neck and the AK-47 laying on the sand beside him. "He won't need these in Hell."

Chapter Nineteen -- Nuevo Laredo, Mexico

Billy leaned his head back and closed his eyes. All the teens were resting their heads on each other's shoulders. The effects of the heat, lack of water and food had taken its toll. The sun set long ago, yet the hot and humid air remained. Dehydration caused chill bumps to rise on his arms. His mouth felt as dry as the cracked red clay in Death Valley. Testing mind over matter, he devised a mental list of what could be in the back of the other cargo trucks. *Drugs, weapons, or bombs big enough to start a small war somewhere? I need to find out if there's anything I can use.*

As their short convoy came to a stop, Billy recalled what Hasan's soldier had said at their last stop. *Have we reached the final destination? Do I keep my mouth shut and act stupid?* Billy waited for someone to open the flaps and order them to get out, yet no one came. He heard what sounded like Hasan barking orders, but the voices were muffled. Minutes passed. The sudden grinding sound of someone removing the gas cap caused the refugees to sit up straight. No one spoke. Billy kept expecting to see someone as he listened to engines come to life then fade as the trucks left them behind.

Within seconds, a vehicle door shut, an engine came to life, then gradually disappeared as the others before it. He continued to stare at the flaps waiting for them to open. Happy images of the future he once looked forward to with Kaylee and his son had become a blank sheet. With each second that ticked away, his anger grew. Several more minutes passed before the flap opened. It wasn't Hasan.

Rico aimed the Glock at Billy. "Where's Barnabas? Did he get out?"

"If you're referring to the stooge that was back here, he stood to stretch a long time ago and fell out." Billy smiled, put his elbows on his knees, and leaned forward.

Rico's brow furrowed. He glared at Billy then scanned the faces of all the teens. "Did any of you see anything different than what this man just described?"

Billy kept his focus on Rico. No verbal responses. He could only assume the young kids nodded when Rico let go of the canvas flap. Someone else stood outside the truck with Rico. This time he could hear their conversation clearly. The other voice was Hasan. He leaned his head against the tarp, closed his eyes and listened to the men's conversation.

"Who are you calling?"

"Barnabas. Asshole in the back said he fell out."

"Where's his weapon?"

"Didn't find it. Do you believe this Carter dude?" Rico asked.

"Yes. Otherwise, you'd be dead. If Barnabas fell out, he's history. We have another issue. Gilmore's last report was more than an hour ago. He said his team eliminated two border officers patrolling the river road. He believed there might be a third one and was headed to search for them."

"You think they were taken down by one agent?"

"I don't know. We need to assume that they were and go from there. Where's the tunnel?"

"About ten miles from here. I'm not sure in the dark. We'll have to wait until daylight if you've decided to take a chance," Rico said.

"How far are we from the Reyes compound?"

"I think we're less than an hour. It's been a while since I've traveled from this direction. The package is still on schedule for delivery."

"Get Will out. It's time to separate the females."

"Are you going to alert Diego that we are on the way?"

"No."

The flap door opened. "Get out Mr. Carter," Rico demanded. "Your destination has changed."

"Where are we going?"

"None of your fucking business." Rico pulled a Glock from his shoulder holster and aimed toward Billy's head. "Now!"

Billy stood, stretched, and glanced around at the young kids. The fear in their expressions suggested the migrants had lost all hope of survival. Feelings of helplessness weren't emotions he was used to. Hasan wouldn't kill him yet, but he might use another innocent teen to make a point. Billy smiled slightly before stepping out on the bumper.

Rico nudged him with the barrel. "You're riding in the back of that one. If you need to piss, hurry up."

He didn't pass up the opportunity. Still facing Rico, Billy unzipped his pants.

"Piss on me, it'll be your last."

Billy grinned before turning toward the truck tire. From his peripheral view, Hasan stood in front of five men with what appeared to be a map. Rico directed the females to line up first. The gas tanker and three other trucks were gone. *Diversification? Why split up the refugees? Did they need a head start?* While Billy zipped his pants, Rico grabbed his right arm, cuffed his wrist, then did the same with his left. He wanted to chase down the truck leaving with the females, but obstacles mounted. *Can't stretch cuffs. What happened to zip ties?*

"Hasan may trust you, I don't," Billy said as his brows furrowed.

Rico jerked Billy toward one of the other trucks where two of Hasan's guerillas waited. When the canvas was pushed aside, one guard stuffed a rag in his mouth while the other opened a small box, removed a syringe, then stabbed Billy's arm. Billy had no time to argue or resist. Stunned with fear from the cargo being transported, he lost sight of everything happening around him.

"You'll be taking a long siesta. I can only hope you never wake again." Rico held the flap while the two soldiers lifted Billy onto the truck bed.

This time mind over matter wasn't a possibility. His thoughts raced for a solution to stop the effects of the medication. Images of sinking in a pool of quicksand flashed before him. He couldn't move his arms or legs. He stared at three rows of what appeared to be commercial pressure cookers, with a bunch of wires and a cell phone mounted on the top of each as Hasan's men tied him to one of the bench seats. Clouds formed over his eyes like the cotton insulation weaved between the cannisters with a thick foam cushion underneath. He was alone with what appeared to be homemade bombs. *Are these real? Radioactive? Fuck! What the hell....*

Chapter Twenty -- *Nuevo Laredo,* Mexico

Nicholas, Robert, and Sheila searched the area around a four-wheel drive truck. Keys were in the ignition. Black, shiny, and spotless. When they opened the door the unmistakable smell of new leather filled their sinuses, but they decided to leave it.

"Must belong to Gilmore. Is this a perk for working for Hasan?" Robert asked.

"Nope. A booby prize as payment for his life," Nicholas replied.

Robert unlocked the tunnel. Nicholas helped Robert clear the sand around the handles and slide the door open. In less than ten minutes they were on the south side of the river. The trip back to the compound didn't take long on the motorcycles.

After parking all three bikes in the back of the warehouse, Nicholas and Robert covered them with tarps, then moved field equipment and storage boxes around them. When they finished, they found Diego and Rita sitting in the living room of the house that once belonged to the Greyson Cartel. Nicholas quickly introduced Diego to Sheila.

"I remember meeting you when we worked on the Jack Silverman and Carlos Reyes cases. So, what did you find?" Rita asked.

Nicholas surveyed the room as he sat in a recliner across from Sheila, Rita, and Diego. Robert leaned against the wall near the window. He had covered most of the property and surveyed the layout from the towers, but this was the first time he had been inside the old Greyson house. Dark walnut paneling covered the cinderblock walls. The rock fireplace appeared to have never been used. Not a single picture hung on any of the walls. Floors were constructed of solid pine. The floor to ceiling windows next to the door had bullet proof panes.

"Of the four men working for Hasan, Sheila confirmed one was also employed by Laredo's Border Patrol unit," Nicholas said.

Rita stood and walked over to the window next to Robert. "I spoke to Sebastian a few minutes ago. He's in Laredo. He'll cross the border, but only if we need him. Sebastian said that a body was found about two hundred miles from here. Identified as Barnabas Guerrero. He spent ten years in the Texas prison system for drug trafficking. He had been transferred to numerous prisons due to suspicions of killing inmates. No proof was ever found to convict him on any of them. Released three years ago on probation. He's a person of interest in the murder of four Tijuana officers last year but, once again a lack of evidence. So, if this Guerrero guy was with Hasan, then we should expect his arrival sooner rather than later." She pulled the heavy, insulated curtain back enough to peek out.

"Is there anything we need to do to secure the property?" Robert asked crossing his arms across his chest.

Diego stood. "No. Rita and I split up and checked all the buildings. All locked and security alarms set." He started walking toward the door. "I'm going to go climb the northeast tower. Robert, I'll call your cell when I see a vehicle approaching."

"Wait a minute." Nicholas stood. "Hasan told you he expected a meal and a place to sleep. Have you cleared the rooms upstairs?"

"Yes. I told Rosa to lock everything in the wall safe in the master bedroom that was important to them. I planned to sleep in the master bedroom as we discussed." Diego replied. Rosa had been the family housekeeper and cook for more than forty years.

"Okay. Rita, did you have time to set the listening devices?"

"Did you think we've been sitting here watching TV?" She shook her head and smiled.

"Well, no. Twiddling your thumbs maybe. I'm not used to being part of a team."

"Okay. Diego and I will accept that as an apology. Anyway, the receiver is set up in the bunker under the master bedroom. All devices are attached to the ceiling light fixtures. We had to use a ladder, so unless Hasan asks for a ladder, we should be fine."

Diego interrupted. "Y'all figure it out. I'll let you know when I see headlights."

"You might want to sleep with a bullet proof vest on, one eye open, and a shot gun in your hand. Rico may decide to pay you a visit. I doubt it'll be a booty call," Robert said.

"Ha ha! Real funny. I don't plan to close my eyes. I put a loaded Uzi under the mattress on both sides of the bed." Diego shut the door behind him.

"Sheila and I will heat up the roast if you two want to do a final walk through. Also, figure out where you want us to hide," Rita said.

Sheila followed Rita to the kitchen.

Robert peeked behind the curtain. "I guess I'm doing this because I'm damn tired of feeling helpless."

"Do you want to draw straws as to who's going to keep watch all night in one of the towers?" Nicholas asked.

"No. I thought about that. I'll do a quick search upstairs. It's been a year since I finished renovating this place. When I'm done, I'll grab some supplies and go relieve Diego," Robert replied.

"You think I need to put Rita and Sheila together?" Nicholas asked.

"Yes. Rita doesn't know the property layout either, but they'll pretty much be confined to the space under the master bedroom monitoring the listening devices," Robert said.

"I'll watch from the warehouse office. Sound like a plan?"

"Yep. I think you covered all the bases." Robert headed for the stairs.

"Maybe not. Rico knows this house better than me and you put together."

Robert removed a key ring. "The brass one will unlock the warehouse and the office door in case Diego locked them. I will text you the shut-off code."

"Thanks."

Chapter Twenty-One -- Nuevo Laredo, Mexico

Nicholas helped Sheila and Rita test the listening devices. "Have you checked Robert's radio?"

"Yes. He can hear loud and clear. Put yours on and I'll check it now," Rita said.

"Does Diego have one?" Sheila asked.

"No. Hasan and Rico may gang up on him if they believe it's two against one. We can't take a chance on them seeing the connection to the earpiece," Nicholas replied.

"I didn't think about that. So, technically, Diego is our sitting duck?" Sheila asked.

"I hate it, but Hasan works for his two older brothers. If it came down to choosing his family over his new life here, that's a tough call for anyone. Also, I'm not sure Diego can handle Hasan and Rico by himself. Both are big men. It's really going to depend on how Rico responds to the word no. If they get past Diego, you two need to be prepared. Even if I use the golf cart to get here, it'll take me a few minutes."

"We've gathered enough fire power from Diego's assortment of weapons to hold off a small army. Are you sure you want us both here? I can keep tabs on the situation from one of the back towers," Sheila suggested.

"You may be holding off more than a small army if Hasan is using one of the cargo trucks as a Trojan horse," Nicholas said as he heard Robert's voice over the static on the radio.

"Headlights on the way. Diego should walk through the door shortly."

"If I take the tunnel to the warehouse, will I set off the alarm?"

"Keypad to your left before you enter the warehouse. Same code I texted you. You have about two minutes before Hasan is at the gate," Robert said as he ducked behind the four-foot wall in the tower.

Nicholas lifted the floor panel in the master bedroom. It reminded him of the pull-down ladder he had in the closet of his apartment, but this didn't lead to a rooftop oasis above his antique shop in Grapevine. After closing the door behind him, he pushed the cheap slide locks into place on each side of the hatch, then followed behind Rita.

"You two need anything before I head to the warehouse?"

"We're good," Rita replied.

"I'm not sure how long you'll be stuck down here, but if you hear footsteps after everyone's supposed to be in bed notify Robert and me immediately." Nicholas turned and headed toward the main warehouse.

The narrow tunnel ran close to three-hundred yards from the old Greyson house to the warehouse. A strong, musty odor drifted up from the dirt floor and didn't take long to reach his sinuses. Eight by eight railroad ties supported the walls and ceiling. Light cords dangled from hooks connected to long extension cords spaced about forty yards apart emitting enough light not to need a flashlight.

Nicholas ran as fast as he could. By the time he reached the warehouse, sweat drops slid off his hand as he entered the alarm code. He wanted to see Hasan and Rico when they exited the vehicle. Nicholas leaned against the window frame in the upstairs office, took a deep breath and exhaled. He used the binoculars on the desk to scan the front half of the property. Pole lights at the north and southeast towers lit up the front half of the property like stadium lights at a football game.

"You see them?" Robert asked.

"Yes. What's the possibility of finding out what they're carrying?" Nicholas asked.

"You want me to go out the tunnel that opens at the back of the property and check?" Rita asked.

"Let's wait until the driver parks. See what they're gonna do," Robert said.

"Looks like Hasan is driving." Nicholas replied.

After turning in front of the covered porch, Hasan backed up along the south side of the house. The cab door lined up with the porch. *Does he anticipate the need for a fast escape?* Nicholas saw Hasan get out, but lost sight of him when he disappeared behind the truck. He didn't have a clear view of the passenger door.

"I can't see them from here," Nicholas said.

"I can't either. Do you think they're securing the cargo or searching the fields?" Robert asked.

"If I were Hasan, I'd do both."

Almost five minutes passed before both men stepped up on the porch. Rico tried turning the doorknob before knocking. Nicholas wondered if that was out of habit or if he was that bold. These were men he knew little about. As Diego opened the door,

Rico shoved his way in, but Hasan didn't follow. The Somalian leaned against the post near the steps, then appeared to be scanning his surroundings as he lit a cigar.

"Rita, Greyson's in the house. Hasan remained on the porch. He appears to be surveying the landscape. Can you hear them?" Nicholas asked.

"Yes. Rico demanded his half of the property back. Sounds like he pushed Diego onto the couch. Sheila wants to break it up."

"Is Diego fighting back?" Nicolas asked.

"Rico must be pressing something against Diego's throat. He's struggling to respond. I think Diego threatened to call his older brother. He told Rico he was unarmed. He reminded him that the Garcia family owned the property with the Reyes family and the fact that they were second cousins. He apologized that Old Man Greyson never told them the property wasn't theirs. Sounds like Rico backed off and sat down. Diego coughed."

"Don't do anything yet. Robert, stay down. Hasan is walking in your direction. Is your Glock silenced?" Nicholas asked.

"Yes, but at that distance, it will take him a few minutes to get into range. He needs to be a lot closer for me to be accurate. So....?" Robert asked.

"Wait."

Nicholas watched as Hasan took one last puff on the cigar, drop it, then crushed it with his boot. The Somalian stood a moment as if listening. He hadn't walked twenty-five yards toward the northeast tower. He seemed to be staring in the direction of the warehouse window. *He must know he's being watched.* Minutes ticked away before Hasan turned and headed toward the main gate.

"Hasan changed his mind. It appears that he's going to climb the southeast tower. Rita what's the update on Diego and Rico?" Nicholas asked.

"Diego is giving him a tour of the house and told him the food on the stove was still warm. Rico told him that his partner has a proposition. Diego said that he doesn't work for his brothers anymore. Letting him spend the night was one last favor. He explained that he married Anita and partnered with you to raise a family and settle down. A door opened. Sounds like they're coming outside."

"I see them. They're watching Hasan make his way up the southeast tower ladder." Nicholas replied.

Rico furrowed his brow and stared toward his supposed partner. This led Nicholas to believe that Rico didn't know what Hasan was up to. Nicholas paid more attention to Hasan's every move in hopes he would uncover a piece of his intentions before Rico did. *Is he expecting a posse? If so, for what purpose?* Dressed in a black t-shirt, desert fatigues, and jump boots projected the image of a man prepared for battle. *If he came to discuss a business deal with Diego, what's his reason for meeting Robert?*

Seeing Hasan again opened the door to so many more questions. *Why an AK-47 strapped across his back? If this is a so-called peaceful visit, why grenades on his belt next to a pistol? Definitely not a dinner and sleep over. Why lie if he is working for Marlon?* If Diego's brothers and sister were angry with him for moving to Nuevo Laredo and partnering with Robert, that would answer some of the questions, but not all of them. If Hasan decided to go rogue and cut ties with Marlon, that might answer all the questions. It didn't appear that Rico would be that helpful.

"Robert, do you see any lights or hear vehicles approaching?"

The watch towers had thick, plywood walls which were reinforced with steel panels. They were painted a desert sand color to match the block walls. From a distance, it was hard to see where the ground ended, and the wall began. Removable screens kept most of the bugs out, but somehow the small creatures seemed to find their way in between the thin gaps.

"No." Robert replied as he popped a mosquito before it had a chance to bite his arm.

Hasan stopped halfway up the ladder to answer his phone. The call lasted less than ten seconds. He quickly shoved it in his pocket as he descended. Trying to watch Hasan run toward the truck and keep an eye on Rico standing next to Diego on the porch became impossible. Out of habit, Nicholas dropped to his knees then peered over the windowsill. Being bullet proof and tinted supposedly made it impossible for him to be seen by anyone outside according to Robert. Nicholas had his doubts.

"I hear muffled yelling, but I can't make out what Rico's saying," Rita said.

Hasan climbed behind the steering wheel, slammed the door, then started the engine. Rico ran toward the truck, but Hasan drove off without him. Rico wiped sweat off his forehead as he pulled his phone from the back pocket of his BDU pants. Nicholas watched intently as Rico slung his phone as if tossing a frisbee. When Rico jerked his Glock from his shoulder holster and pointed it at Diego, Nicholas stood and headed toward the warehouse office door.

"Robert, is Hasan in sight?"

"His taillights are quickly disappearing. Appears he's headed toward town," Robert replied as he peered through the screen.

"Diego's in trouble, shoot toward Rico but don't kill him. I'm heading downstairs now."

"Wait. Rico expects me to be here at some point. Might as well know that I'm already here." Robert stood, aimed, then fired three shots in Rico's direction. He immediately holstered the gun then headed down the stairs.

All three bullets kicked sand in the air near Rico. They were close enough to divert his attention. Rico hit the ground as he focused on the direction the bullets originated. This gave Diego time to jump off the porch steps with enough momentum to land across Rico's back. He managed to knock the Glock out of Rico's hand. After struggling to hold Rico still, Diego finally jerked hard on of Rico's wrists and held them firmly behind his back.

Nicholas continued to watch the scene unfold from the warehouse window. It reminded him of an old 'Dirty Harry' movie starring Clint Eastwood. From the time Diego fell on Rico, to holding his arms down all seemed to happen in slow motion. *Where's Hasan going? Why did he leave Rico? Who is he meeting?* Expecting the unexpected seemed to be par for the course in this situation. This had to involve more than illegal cocaine and human trafficking.

Nicholas searched his memory for answers. He needed the missing piece that made the puzzle come to life. He recalled the day that he found Hasan in the Bahamas. The straw market appeared to be extremely busy that day. This being his first and only trip to the island, Nicholas wondered if it was that way every day. Street drummers played for tips while vendors haggled with tourists over prices for hair braids, henna tattoos, and straw baskets. The Grey Ghost lived up to his nickname that day when he disappeared into a crowd. *Is Hasan doing the same thing now? He had to know he was being watched. Who did he call?* Nicholas's thoughts were interrupted when Rita spoke.

"Somebody, say something. What's going on?"

"Robert just reached Diego. I'm assuming he's going in the house to find a rope or zip ties. Right now, Diego's doing a pretty good job of holding the fat bastard on the ground. I don't know where Hasan took off to."

"Where are you?"

"Still in the warehouse office."

"Do you think we need to help?"

"Let's wait until they get Rico back into the house. That way you can report to me on their conversation. Call Sebastian. Find out if he has an update on current intel. We need to know if Hasan has planned to meet someone downtown."

Chapter Twenty-Two -- Nuevo Laredo, Mexico

96

Robert held onto Rico's t-shirt as he dragged him across the living room and shoved him face down onto the couch. "Sit up Greyson. I've been told your fucking boss wants to meet me. So, where's he going?"

"Are you fucking blind? He left me. He didn't answer his damn phone, so how the fuck am I supposed to know." Rico rolled to his side. "I need help sitting up since you felt the need to bind my hands and feet."

Diego grabbed Rico's sweat-soaked t-shirt sleeve and jerked him into a sitting position. Rico swung his legs around on top of the coffee table.

"You were fixing to shoot me. What in the hell did you expect?" Diego replied. He sat in a recliner across from Rico with the same Glock Rico had pointed at him. "Nice weapon. If I run the serial number, will it show you as the owner?"

"Yeah, right. Go ahead. While you're at it, trace all the fucking weapons your brothers buy and sell daily." Rico spit toward Diego but missed.

Robert was leaning against the front door, but when Diego lunged toward Rico, he reached Diego in time to grab him by the collar and pull him back. "Calm down. The asshole is intentionally trying to push your buttons. Let me straighten this out."

Robert took two steps toward Rico. He stared at the man a moment and smiled until Rico smiled back. BAM! Robert's fist rammed Rico's jaw like a sledgehammer. He stepped back to the door and waited for Rico to shake it off and refocus.

Rico's brow furrowed. He spit blood on the floor as he glared at Robert. "I was told you wouldn't be here until tomorrow."

"After the shoot-to-kill and don't-ask-questions adventure with your boss's goons at my boat dock in Abasolo, I changed my mind."

"Untie me. Make it a fair fight."

"Why? You've never fought a fair fight in your life. Have you forgotten all the unprovoked attacks your family made on mine a few years back? Demanding to seize our property when you didn't even own the land. The Garcia family allowed you to live here."

"Did Diego tell you that his older brothers stole most of our profits?" Rico leaned forward then spit blood on the floor.

"It doesn't matter. When I cleaned out the storage room under the master bedroom, I found shelving units stacked high with marijuana neatly packaged for shipment along with bundles of cash. Your dear old daddy stole from the man who supplied the roof over his head." Robert looked him up and down. "By the way, it doesn't appear you've ever missed a single meal."

"Fuck you. The inventory and cash belong to me. Where is it?"

"Stolen property has been returned to the original owner. Now, let's get back to why you're really here, and why your so-called boss wants to meet me," Robert said.

"How do you know that?"

"Diego called and told me that you and someone named Abid Hasan were coming here for dinner and to stay one night just to meet me, but then I hear your ETA was supposed to be tomorrow. If I'm wrong, then explain." Robert folded his arms across his chest.

Rico's eyes darted from side to side as if searching for a way out. "Where's my phone."

"In my pocket. Are you expecting an important call?"

"No. I need to find out when Greygo's returning. In answer to your question, yes. He does want to meet you, but he wouldn't tell me why. The lie about our ETA was Greygo, not me."

"Let me get this straight. You're telling me that you and this Greygo dude don't discuss business?"

"Fuck no. You twisted every word I said."

"Diego, do you think I'm twisting his words?" Robert asked.

"Nope."

"Two against one. You're outvoted."

"Fuck you, Smartass."

"I think I have the right since you and your cohort decided to show up early without notice. I have a business to run in Texas. That doesn't include the time I spend overseeing all the stores we have in Colorado and Washington. Plus, we are expanding into California and Florida." Robert put his hands up in the air as he cocked his head slightly. "I'm done with your bull shit. I'll tell you what. Diego can drive your ass downtown and dump you out at Gatos. Wasn't that your favorite hangout?"

"Fuck you."

"I made a trip this morning to Abasolo. Did you have anything to do with the two boats and the dudes firing AK-47s at me?"

"They were told to catch anyone who showed up. I never expected it to be you."

"Why did you feel the need to catch whoever showed up?"

"Leverage, asshole."

"Leverage? For what?"

"Greygo thought it would help sway you to what he needs you to do."

"Which is?"

Moments passed. Robert paced back and forth in front of the coffee table. He watched Rico squirm a little longer before he stopped next to Diego. "I'm waiting. What's the real reason you're here?"

"Fuck you. Give me my fucking phone. I'll take you up on that offer to drive me downtown."

Robert removed Rico's phone from his t-shirt pocket. "What's your passcode?"

"Fuck you."

Robert returned the phone to his pocket then took a step toward Rico. "That's okay. Come on Diego. You hold the bastard. I'll start breaking fingers to see which one unlocks his cell."

"No, No. Okay. Three-eight-two-five," Rico yelled.

"That's convenient. F-U-C-K would be an easy word for you to remember." Robert entered the code and checked recent calls. "Let's see if he answers this time."

Rico continued to jerk his arms as Robert pressed the speaker button. Four rings with no answer. Robert left a message. "Mr. Hasan, this is Robert Reyes. I'm at our family compound. I've been informed by Mr. Rico Greyson, Junior that you would like to meet me. I'm leaving in the morning, so if you expect to see me, you have about an hour before I go to bed." He clicked end and re-pocketed the phone.

"Take my seat. I need a beer."

"Bring me one, too," Robert replied.

"What about me? What happened to your offer to take me downtown?" Rico asked.

"Lost opportunity. You took too long to accept. I'll use you like your boss was going to use whoever showed up on the coast today. How did you put it? Oh, yeah, leverage. If I give you a beer, you might have to piss."

"Now that you mentioned it, I do have to piss. Come on dammit. Cut me loose."

"I didn't trust your ass when you lived next door. I sure as hell don't trust you now."

Diego handed Robert a beer. "Our guest said he needs to pee. Should we be good hosts?"

"Might be here a while. Let me grab my sawed-off shotgun by the bed." Diego turned and headed to the master bedroom.

"Okay. This is how it's going to work. We'll drag you out the front door to the steps. I will cut your hands loose, you piss, then I tie your hands back together. If you do anything, I mean anything to make me think you wanna fight, Diego will shoot you. When your boss returns, we'll let him know you split."

"Fuck you."

"Okay. No deal. I don't really care one way or the other."

Robert glanced up at the clock on the wall as Diego returned. "Your boss has twenty-three minutes left before I unleash Diego on you."

Diego pressed the barrel against the back of Rico's head. The slide and click sounds from a pump action twelve-gauge Remington echoed across the room. "It belonged to my dad. Survival rate at this range will be zero."

"Fuck you. Greygo will call. This mission is too important."

Robert sat in the recliner across from Rico. "I'd prefer not to have your guts spattered all over the room. Rosa has worked for our family since before I was born. I don't want to get on her bad side. So, tell us about your special mission."

"Go to Hell," Rico replied.

"I don't think I care to. Too hot, but Diego's itching to let you go check it out for us. Now, I'm not giving you an option. I'm tired of your bull shit." Robert stood, grabbed Rico's arm, and jerked him up. He bent down, cut the rope, then pulled him toward the front door. "Diego, keep the barrel pointed at his head."

As Robert reached the edge of the porch, he shoved Rico forward. Rico stumbled over the step, then fell face down in the dirt. He quickly rolled over and sat up. "Cut me loose, asshole."

"Diego, shoot."

Diego fired a round about ten feet to right side of Rico. Chunks of sand and dirt spewed across Rico.

"Fuck. Okay. Greygo has twelve homemade bombs. He…he…" Rico wiped his face onto his sleeve, coughed, then spit. I don't know if any of them contain radioactive material."

Before he could say anything else, his phone rang in Robert's shirt pocket. Robert smiled. "It's your lucky day. Saved by the bell." He removed the cell phone then hit the speaker button. "Hello."

"Mr. Reyes. This is Abid Hasan."

"I know who you are. What the fuck do you want?"

"I will be there in twenty minutes. I'm assuming since you have Rico's phone, he is tied up somewhere?"

"You could say that. Diego and I will be waiting on the porch." Robert clicked off and tossed the phone down at Rico's feet. "Have a seat, Diego. We'll wait out here."

Diego kept the shotgun pointed toward Rico as he pulled a rocker closer to the edge of the porch. Robert sat on the step. With the front door open, a cool breeze circulated out through the humid air.

"Okay, Rico. Let's pick up where we left off. What does your boss plan to do with these so-called bombs?"

"Fuck you. Ask Greygo when he gets here."

Robert smiled. "Diego, kill the son-of-a-bitch. We have time to get rid of the body before his ride arrives."

Chapter Twenty-Three -- Nuevo Laredo, Mexico

Nicholas managed to piece together Robert's conversation with Rico as he sent a text to Sebastian. Rita and Sheila had no access to the conversations outside and depended on Nicholas for updates. All they heard were muffled voices from Robert's radio. They still didn't know what happened to the other trucks, much less how many were in the convoy. *What happened to Billy and the refugees? Were they on the back of Hasan's truck with the bombs?*

Hasan added new questions to Nicholas's list when he took off. He turned the desk chair around to where he could sit and watch. As he assessed what they knew, Nicholas wondered if Hasan had found out about the encounter near Hidalgo. Six men dead of which four worked for Hasan. He ignored Sheila and Rita's requests for information as his mind drifted.

Overseeing the construction of the animal sanctuary and his daily conversations with Father Simon changed his life. God had put this man of the cloth in his life for a reason. *Has Father Simon served his purpose? Impossible. God saved him from an eminent death in New Orleans.* Nicholas's thoughts focused on one thing Father Simon had said. *"Have faith that you are doing the right thing. Allow God to carry you through the darkness."*

"What's going' on? Dammit, Nicholas. Are you listening?" Rita's loud tone interrupted his thoughts again. This time he didn't ignore her.

"Rico has refused to tell Robert about the bombs. Robert and Diego are debating on whether they should shoot the bastard. I'm waiting to hear back from Sebastian. I will let you know if I hear anything important." Nicholas's phone vibrated. "Hey Sebastian."

"I'm with the cleanup crew near Hidalgo. Two of Hasan's men are Jon Doe's. The third is Rico's brother-in-law, David Moreno. If Rico finds out, you'll have a bigger problem on your hands. I'm standing at the river's edge and don't see anything moving on the other side. It looks shallow enough to walk across."

"It is. You're near the Reyes tunnel. According to Robert, it used to be shallow enough to drive across. What do you want us to do with Rico? Hasan should be here in the next ten minutes, so we're running out of time."

"Is Rico secured?"

"Yes. Hands are tied. He's sitting on the ground in front of one of the houses on the property near the entrance gate and Diego has a shotgun on him. Robert's weapon is holstered."

"Where are Sheila and Rita?"

"Hiding in the bunker under the master bedroom."

"Have Robert and Diego get Rico downstairs. Rita and Sheila can keep an eye on him. You need to find out what Hasan plans to do with those bombs. Hopefully he's bringing them back with him. I'm leaving a team here just in case more show up on either side."

"What about the boats near Abasolo?

"Got it covered. Coast Guard has been notified to pounce if the rats run. They haven't moved yet, but that's not to say the boats have been abandoned. Didn't you mention they had ground transport? Got to go. Keep me updated." Sebastian clicked off.

"Robert, move Rico to the basement. Do whatever you think is necessary. Get him downstairs to the bunker with Rita and Sheila before Hasan arrives. Rita, unlock the door. A slide lock on each side of the hatch."

"Will do," Rita replied.

Robert didn't answer. Nicholas watched what appeared to be a real-life version of securing a wartime enemy. He could only assume the long list of obscenities that flowed from Rico's mouth until Diego returned with a roll of duct tape. As if Robert were roping a calf for the grand prize at the rodeo finals, he had Rico taped, tied, and was dragging him across the porch stairs in less than thirty seconds.

Nicholas updated Rita and Sheila. "Secure Rico far enough away that he can't hear your conversations."

"Not a problem. I think Robert wrapped half the roll of tape around Rico's bald head. It's going to be a bitch pulling it off. Diego's on his way upstairs. Robert wrapped Rico in a neck to knee cocoon against a support beam near the north tunnel. All we need is firewood," Sheila said.

"He's not a witch. You can't burn him at the stake," Nicholas said.

"You're no fun."

Nicholas heard the women laugh. "Remember, you two are underground. Where would the smoke go?"

"Yeah, yeah, okay. Is Hasan back?"

"Nope, but Robert's sitting on the front steps and Diego is holding a shotgun in the doorway."

Chapter Twenty-Four -- Nuevo Laredo, Mexico

The rubber band tying Robert's hair back had popped long ago. Black strands brushed against his shoulders. He wiped the sweat off his forehead with his sleeve and checked the time on his watch again. Almost forty-five minutes had passed since he spoke to Hasan. With Rico out of the way, he needed to discuss changes in strategy with Nicholas.

"When Hasan returns, what do you want me to tell him?"

"Easy lie. Tell him Rico dropped off the deep end when he left. He pulled his Glock on Diego, and you barely arrived in time to save Diego's life. If Hasan wants to see Rico's dead body, tell him you two dumped the body out behind the west wall. When the wild dogs arrived for dinner, you returned to the house," Nicholas said.

"Great idea. Wish I had thought of that."

"Where's the Glock?"

Robert rested his elbows on his knees. "On the end table next to the couch. What if he asks where I was when they arrived?"

"The warehouse office. I'm pretty sure he knew he was being watched."

"What if Hasan wants to see the body?"

"Say, let's go. I should be able to make it to the northeast tower and take him out before you reach the wall. I know all of this sounds simple in theory, but I doubt it will be. My concerns are, did he meet someone and unload the bombs? And which direction did he send Wright and the refugees?" Nicholas asked.

"Wish I had answers. Why do you think Hasan told me twenty minutes? It's been close to an hour," Robert asked as he stood. Raising up on his toes, he could see lights beaming in the distance. "Wait. From the dust cloud around the vehicle, Hasan should be here shortly."

"His sudden departure along with the length of time he's been gone brings up way too many questions to speculate. If anything goes sideways, kill the bastard. Beating answers out of Rico may be easier."

"Sounds like a plan. Got to go." Robert removed his headset and slid it into his back pocket.

Instead of backing up next to the side of the house, Hasan parked directly in front of them. Robert folded his arms across his chest as he waited for Hasan to shut off the engine and get out. Diego stood next to Robert as Hasan opened the door just enough to jump to the ground before he slammed it shut.

Hasan smiled as he put his hand out. "You must be Robert."

Robert ignored the man's gesture. "What can I do for you?"

Hasan lowered his hand as the smile on his face disappeared. "Where's Rico?"

"When you took off like a bat out of hell, Rico dropped off the deep end. Pulled a Glock on Diego. When I walked up, he pointed it at me, so I shot him between the eyes."

"You did what?" Hasan's tone swelled in anger.

"I didn't stutter. I shot the bastard. You, Mr. Hasan may need a short synopsis of my history with the Greyson family. Goes back to when my Paw Paw Angelo ran our business. Old Man Greyson tried to destroy us. He used a flame throwing catapult weapon which burned crops worth thousands of dollars. The Greyson family wanted to steal our property many times. No way in hell I would give any Greyson the opportunity to fire first."

Robert stepped off the porch closer to Hasan. "I don't give a fuck what Rico told you to make you think I would be interested in a business proposition with you, but he was wrong."

As angry as Robert felt, the man before him seemed to be relaxed as if they were best friends. Hasan reminded him of the occasional vigilante mercenaries that drifted through downtown Nuevo Laredo before it became a popular tourist destination. Hasan was shorter than Robert but made up for it in weight. From his military style haircut to his polished, lace-up jump boots portrayed a man with integrity and honor instead of the sex trafficker and drug runner he was.

"You haven't heard what I have to say." Hasan said as Diego raised the barrel of the sawed-off shotgun. Hasan's focus drifted toward Diego. "I thought you and Rico were cousins."

"Second cousins on my mother's side. He grew up here, I grew up south of Lima. You could say we are unknown distant relatives. A perfect example of a stranger. I know Robert better than I ever knew Rico."

"Why are you pointing that shotgun at me?"

"Why do you have an AK-47 across your back and hand grenades on your belt?" Diego replied.

Hasan raised his hands in the air. "I came here in peace. Not to start a war. Diego, I've been completing contract work for your family a long time. I don't intend to rock that boat. If you lower your weapon, I'll remove my belt and shoulder strap to the ground."

"You do that, I'll pick them up, then Diego will lower the shotgun. Your so-called partner led us to believe otherwise," Robert replied.

Hasan backed up two steps. "You're correct. He's a hot head. I should've told him I had business in town before I left." He unbuckled the grenade belt and removed the AK-47 off his shoulder. Instead of putting them on the ground, he handed them to Robert. "I'm sweating. Can we go inside and speak civilly?"

Robert stepped aside as Diego lowered the shotgun. "After you."

Chapter Twenty-Five -- Nuevo Laredo, Mexico

As soon as Diego closed the front door, Nicholas hurried downstairs to the main warehouse entrance. Locating the bombs became the number one priority. If he took a chance with the four-wheeler used to navigate the underground tunnels to cross three hundred plus yards to Hasan's truck, the floors in the house would vibrate from the engine's loud rumble by the time he reached one of the exits. As he peeked out the door, Nicholas replayed Hasan's reaction to Rico's death in his mind. *Did Hasan expect Rico to jump off the deep end? Did he ask where the body was? No. Was this part of his plan?* An erratic path carrying drugs, refugees, and bombs. Nothing made sense.

"Rita, what are they discussing?" Nicholas asked through the radio headset.

"Nothing yet. Diego fixed Hasan a plate from the pot roast on the stove and opened all of them a beer."

"I'm going to check the back of the truck. Let me know if I need to expect company outside."

Nicholas didn't wait for a response. He took off running toward the shadows of the cafeteria and office building. When he reached the edge of the office he paused and listened. The rest of the way he would be out in the open with nothing to hide behind. His thoughts searched for something he missed. All roads in his mind led to an intersection with no GPS or road signs to guide his way. He recalled something Father Simon had told him one morning while they watched the sun rise from the roof of the church.

"No matter what you do or where you go, God will not leave you alone to weather a storm. He will be there to carry you when you need him most."

"I need to know before the hurricane arrives, not when it's ripping off the roof," Nicholas whispered as if someone was close enough to hear. No matter what Father Simon's words of encouragement were, each one faded as the grains of sand keeping time in the imaginary hourglass in his brain piled higher.

"Rita, what are they discussing? Robert must've shut off his headset."

"It's in his pocket. He didn't want to take a chance on Hasan noticing it. They're in the dining room. Something's got to be wrong with the device we put on the chandelier. There's a lot of static but sounds like someone is pacing the floor. Diego's explaining his departure from the family businesses in South America and the plans he has for the future. Hasan has managed to avoid every question Robert asked. I have a feeling if Hasan keeps on, Robert will explode."

"I'm almost to Hasan's truck. Keep me posted." Nicholas stood behind one of the posts that supported the porch roof for the cinder block and stucco office building and listened for any noise that seemed out of place. Beyond the two bright pole lights, clouds drifted across the sky. Sweat drizzled down his back when he took off running again.

When Nicholas reached the back of the truck, he stopped. The canvas material appeared to be new. Instead of ropes holding the flaps closed, a heavy-duty zipper ran from the metal frame roof to brass snaps located inches above the steel bumper. Was someone behind the zipper? If so, how many? He leaned in close and listened. No conversations or vibrations from the truck bed. He glanced toward the front door and behind him at the main entrance.

He considered updating Rita and Sheila but interrupting them while they listened to the conversation upstairs might be a mistake. Nicholas decided it was time to rip off the bandage. Holding his Glock out in front of him, he popped a snap and forced the zipper open with the barrel of his weapon. With his free hand, he pulled the flap back. A long rope and scattered pieces of either cotton, or some type of insulating material intertwined on the floor was all that remained. He zipped the flaps back together then moved toward the side of the house. Standing still with his back against the stucco wall, he listened intently.

Nicholas holstered his Glock before sending a text to Sebastian with an update. Time ticked away. Half the night wasted with no answers. Instead of feeling like he had moved closer to the finish line, a vortex seemed to suck him deeper into an abyss with no compass or map to lead him to safety. He slid into a squatting position.

"Hey, Rita. No cargo. Whatever was there is gone. Any update on the conversation upstairs?"

"Hasan should run for office the way he can twist Robert's question into a question. Said he received a call and was supposed to meet the buyer for Marlon's drugs in town, but the guy never showed. Sounds like Hasan has finished eating. He asked about a bed to sleep in until morning. Robert has told Hasan he was going to drink another beer and head to his house. He said he would discuss Hasan's proposal in the morning. Footsteps are heading toward the stairs. You should see Robert shortly."

Nicholas heard the door open and close. He stood and peeked around the corner to see Robert walking toward the back of the truck.

"Hey. There's nothing back there."

Robert turned and took a drink of his beer. "If I knew you were out here, I would've brought one for you."

"Did you check to find out if Hasan had a backup weapon? Might not be a good idea to leave Diego alone with him."

"No."

"He has a reputation for being an expert with knives."

"Dammit. He probably has them shoved down in his boots. Sorry. I was too busy trying to figure out why he had grenades clipped on his belt. No excuse for that fuck-up. Diego should be downstairs by now. I'll reset my radio, so if you need anything, let me know." Robert stepped up on the porch and walked away.

Chapter Twenty-Six -- Nuevo Laredo, Mexico

The front door opened. Nicholas peered around the corner as Robert unholstered his Glock. He assumed from the way lights flashed at the door, Diego had turned the television on but must have muted the sound. Nicholas listened.

Robert stood at the doorway and put his weapon away. "Everything okay?"

Diego took a deep breath and sighed. "Yes. Hasan said he needed a shower and would be up by six. I think I'm going to sleep on the couch."

"Good idea. I'll see if I can get some shut eye in the recliner." Robert closed the door behind him.

Nicholas glanced up at the stars peeking in and out between the clouds as he waited. He checked the time when his phone vibrated. Barely midnight. He read Sebastian's response. *Border patrol on alert. Hasan's men gone. No movement at Abasolo. Nothing at tunnel. Bases covered. Update if status changes.*

A light brightened in a small window upstairs. It had to be about two-foot square. Swirled colors of stained glass dimmed the illumination. Only other windows he noticed were the two, floor to ceiling windows next to the front door. Sounds of water running through pipes in the wall reached his ears. *Why did Hasan return if he expected Rico to be dead?* Nicholas contemplated the man's reputation. The nickname, Greygo, short for Grey Ghost was based on Hasan's ability to disappear in plain sight. Was there a hidden stairwell Robert didn't know about? Rico would've told Hasan.

His thoughts were interrupted when he heard a door hinge creak. Nicholas checked the front porch then the safety on his Glock. No one. "Robert, I heard a door open."

"Not me or Diego."

"Is there another way out of the spare bedroom where Hasan is?" Nicholas asked.

"The small window is solid glass. No other windows and one bedroom door leading to the landing upstairs," Robert replied.

"It's me," Sheila said through her radio headset as she approached from the back of the house.

"How did you get out of the tunnel?"

"Snooping around. I opened a door that looked like a closet to find a metal ladder attached to the wall. It's at the back corner of the house. Must be behind the kitchen cabinets."

"Where's Rita?"

"She's headed to find a bathroom. Said the only one she knew of was under the main warehouse."

"And Rico?" Nicholas asked.

Sheila stopped next to Nicholas and smiled. "He kept kicking the support beam. His moaning sounded more like a wounded bull. The bastard had already pissed his pants and the rope Robert wrapped around him ended at his knees. We were afraid that he would vibrate the whole house if he kept on. Rita found a roll of duct tape. We wrapped his ankles to his knees before we untied the rope. When he fell to the floor and tried to sit up, I used my cattle roping skills to immobilize him. We packed him in a utility closet so tiny, that as the saying goes it's like sardines in a can. Rita found two wool blankets to insulate the walls around him. I told him if I heard the slightest peep, he would win a ticket to meet Satan in person."

"Your dad has a ranch up north somewhere?"

116

"Wyoming. He sold the one that I grew up on in Montana when I went to college. Now he has a smaller spread he can handle by himself."

"Why did you come out here?"

"To make sure that we are all on the same page. We know Robert and Diego are both adamant about not selling the property. They both told Hasan that they had no interest in any business partnerships with him or anyone else. So, Rita and I think the only option for Hasan is to call in extra troops, kill Diego and Robert, then disappear."

"Robert, are you listening?" Nicholas asked.

"Heard every word."

"Were you able to figure out what Hasan's transporting?" Nicholas asked.

"Piecing together Diego's conversations with Marlon and what Hasan told Robert and Diego at the table, Rita and I believe that he has two million in cocaine, street value, and half a million in weapons to deliver to a distributor near Brownsville. Marlon knows nothing about the bombs or who Hasan is selling them to. Same with the refugees. Current intel tells us that after Chief Rojas's death, the Garcia family has no contacts in Nuevo Laredo," Sheila said.

"What about Hasan using the property near Abasolo?"

"Yes," Robert replied and continued. "Diego mentioned that Marlon was aware Hasan used the dock. When this is over, next on my list is to put it up for sale. When Hasan brought up the tunnel, I lied. I told him that I hadn't been there in over a year after we heard rumors that Homeland Security began monitoring activity after discovering its existence. There's no evidence as to who built the tunnel. I don't even know who currently owns the land on either side of the river and figured that would cover our tracks over the death of his men."

Nicholas heard clanging in the background. "What are you doing?"

"Getting two bottles of water out of the fridge. Diego said Marlon is terminating Hasan's services after this shipment is complete."

"Sebastian can find out who the property belongs to. Maybe you should take that up with him when this is over." Nicholas glanced up when the light from the upstairs bathroom went out. "Hasan is out of the shower. Robert, do you know if there is an emergency exit or hidden stairwell?"

"I haven't investigated that." Robert paused. "Diego says there is a plywood panel nailed to the closet wall, but he never took the time to check it out. He assumed its purpose was to access pipes in the wall. He said it may be about four-foot square."

"Rita, are you listening?"

"Yes. What do you need me to do?"

"Shut down the equipment. Head to the warehouse," Nicholas said.

"Done."

"What are you thinking?" Robert asked.

"That there's a ladder behind the panel which leads to the tunnel system. If there is, where is the exit?"

"The west tunnel is closed off by a sheetrock wall to the rest of the underground tunnel system. An access door opens to where Rita is. The last time I was down there it was locked. There is an escape hatch at other end that opens at ground level near the southwest security tower."

Sheila interrupted, "The ladder I found in the closet had metal rails that ran the length of the wall. It had a drop ceiling panel as if leading to attic space. I bet that connects to the upstairs bedroom closet."

"How far from Rita?"

"About thirty-five feet. Do we wait here?" Robert replied.

"Yes. Let's see where he goes. Is the passage lit?"

"Not unless he knows where the lights are. All have pull strings. Nothing downstairs is wired to a switch except below our main warehouse."

"Is Diego armed?"

"He retrieved the two Uzis from the master bedroom. He's standing in the shadow of the stairwell. He can shoot Hasan before the man's foot lands on the top step."

"Where are you?" Nicholas asked.

"On my knees behind the couch."

Minutes ticked away as they waited for Hasan to appear from one of the exits. Rita reported that she had made it to the warehouse office. She could see the southwest tower clearly with the binoculars.

"Sheila, did you see anything out of place when you exited the tunnel around back?"

"No, why?"

"I just remembered. When Rico and Hasan first arrived, they walked around to the back of the truck. Disappeared for about five minutes."

"I'll check." Sheila kept her back against the side of the house as she made her way to the back corner of the house.

Nicholas wondered if he should send Robert downstairs or if he was wrong. *Did Hasan do what he said he was going to do*? He leaned his head back, closed his eyes, and recalled the conversation between Robert and Hasan. As if he were dreaming, scenes he imagined many times returned of the battle between David and the Philistines, but this time an explosion created a cloud of dust preventing him from seeing the outcome.

"Run!" Sheila said trying hard not to yell.

Nicholas turned to see Sheila gaining ground toward him. "Robert, you, and Diego get out of the house. Now! Go meet Rita in the warehouse office."

"On our way. I heard Sheila."

Nicholas and Sheila were about a hundred and fifty yards away with Robert and Diego close behind. The explosion rumbled the ground beneath their feet. Nicholas kept running. Nothing he could do to fix the devastation behind them. Pieces of terra cotta roof tiles mixed with splinters of wood and small pieces of shattered glass fell from a blast of dust drifting through the air around them. Slowing down was not an option. He had to reach the northeast tower. *Is the trojan horse on its way?*

Chapter Twenty-Eight -- Nuevo Laredo, Mexico

"Rita, do you see anything?" Nicholas asked with a heavy breath. He still had at least forty more yards to reach the tower ladder.

"No. Not even a dark shadow on the walls. There was a brief period when the bomb exploded where I had to wait for the smoke to clear. Thank God the truck wasn't closer."

"I'll be able to see more soon. Any head lights beyond the wall? He must either expect transportation to arrive or plans to circle around to the truck when the dust clears."

Nicholas headed up the ladder with Sheila close behind. Robert and Diego were on their way toward the warehouse. *Does Hasan intend to use the smoke screen as a diversion?* He stopped mid-way up, held on with one hand, and turned to see what lay behind him. The two-story house appeared to be the result of a well-executed implosion instead of a combustion driven explosion. Scattered flames were giving way to smoldering embers. Wood and cinderblock walls buried the interior furnishings. The front porch support beams for the roof lay where the door once stood. His focus moved toward the south wall.

"What do you see?" Sheila asked standing next to the ladder.

"Dim headlights. I give the vehicle three minutes to be at the front gate."

"Do you see Hasan?"

Nicholas descended the ladder. "No, but if I were him, I'd be waiting right outside against the wall. Come on. Let's join the others. They have a better view than we do."

"What about Rico?" Sheila asked.

"I would be shocked if he survived that cave-in. The problem is, we have a monster on the loose with more of what just took down a two-story house. The bastard tried to kill Diego. Hasan has to be our priority."

Nicholas opened the office door with Sheila at his heels. Robert, Diego, and Rita were standing at the window. Robert had binoculars scanning the area along the south wall searching for Hasan.

"Another transport truck just like the one Hasan drove," Robert commented. "It's slowing down. Diego, you know where the switch is to close the front gate?"

Diego moved toward a breaker box on the wall behind the door. "Yes. Isn't it the red button, un-labeled below the breakers?"

"That's the one." Robert replied.

They watched the iron gate close. "Shut off the pole lights too. Robert, where are your night vision goggles?" Nicolas asked.

"One pair on the desk. More in basement storage if we need them."

Nicholas grabbed the set on the desk along with a cigarette lighter in an empty ashtray. "I'll be back." He turned and headed out the door before anyone asked questions. He picked up a small gas can and rope near the four-wheeler, then opened the door barely enough to see. When Diego flipped the light switch, darkness surrounded the compound except for dim headlights from the truck idling in the distance outside the compound.

He surveyed the area for any motion before moving toward the cafeteria and office buildings. The long bunkhouse blocked his view of the devastation, but his target was Hasan's transportation. Most of the dust had settled around what was left of the house. *Could Rico survive all that?* Any attempt to see would have to wait until the embers cooled. When he reached the edge of the bunkhouses, Nicholas peered around the corner.

He could barely hear the truck's engine. *Why stop?* Nicholas expected it to ram the iron gate any moment. After Diego's older brother rammed through the manual lift gate more than once, Robert replaced the security shack with the motorized, remote-control doors. The new gate eliminated three daily shifts of security guards to raise and lower the wooden arm.

"Does anyone see Hasan?" Nicholas asked.

"No. The truck hasn't moved. I don't know what its waiting on unless Hasan told them to wait," Robert replied.

"What are you going to do?" Rita asked.

"Eliminate Hasan's way out. At least the one we have access to. Shutting off my headset."

Nicholas crouched before running toward the driver's side of Hasan's truck. A faint odor lingered in the air. *Where did Hasan find dynamite? Did he use a combination of nitroglycerin and powder? It had to be someone who knew what they were doing if a stabilizer was added to control damage.* Soviet intelligence used a supplier in South Africa, but Nicholas couldn't recall who. A question his cousin, Mitch, would have to answer.

Images from an old John Wayne movie depicting an explosion which sent a bridge falling into the river below using some of the same basic ingredients drifted through his thoughts. *The War Wagon. The bridge was blown to get rid of the armored stagecoach's security team, but what was Hasan's purpose? Are all the other bombs like this one? Dammit. Where is he?* Nicholas sat the gas can down, leaned his back against the door, and listened. The glow beaming from the truck's headlights gave Nicholas enough light to see without night vision. He let them dangle from the cord around his neck as he reached up and tried the door handle. *Locked.*

He glanced both ways, picked up the small can and moved around the front of the truck to the passenger door. Again, he paused, set the can on the ground before scanning the area once more. The truck still idled in the distance. *Did Hasan have time to hide a second bomb behind the house? Where would he put it?* He reached up and pulled on the handle. This time it opened.

Nicholas eased the door open. Not knowing how loud the screech would be, presented a potential problem. As he glanced down and reached for the gas can, sudden pressure from inside the cab forced the door to swing open. Nicholas lost his grip on the handle. Before he could react, momentum pushed him face down on the ground with something heavy across his back.

Chapter Twenty-Nine -- Nuevo Laredo, Mexico

Cinderblock walls supported the long four by four beams above him. Vibrations shook the rafters. Fine grains of dirt and sand fell between the pressure treated beams. Abid Hasan held his breath in anticipation of the cave-in reaching his end of the tunnel. Sounds of cracking and splitting wood gradually eased as the dust fog dispersed. He could finally breathe again.

His trip from the upstairs bedroom down the closet ladder to the long tunnel ending at the southeast tower were a perfect match to the floorplan drawing Rico had given him. The map that Hasan had committed to memory had come in handy after the explosion blew out the tunnel's electricity. He used the light on his phone to prevent the unwanted approach of creepy crawly bugs and long-legged spiders.

Hasan climbed the aluminum ladder, twisted the brass lock, and lifted the round, hatch door. *The explosion must've knocked out all the power. Should I wait to verify Robert and Diego both died in the blast? No possible way anything survived.* Images of Robert's and Diego's detached body parts crushed under wood beams and cement blocks made him smile.

His focus returned to his surroundings without the use of the light on his phone. He glanced up to see a few stars between drifting clouds. He checked the time on his watch. Breakfast time in Russia, but that would be the easy call compared to the one he needed to make to Marlon Garcia.

He peered around the corner of the southwest wall. His ride waited as instructed. There was no way anyone survived the blast. How and when would he tell Marlon about Diego? Self-defense? Shoot-out with Robert Reyes? Diego turned out to be collateral damage. Hasan wanted to end his relationship with the South American cartel, but not at the expense of adding a price to his own head.

Hasan's mission never varied. Pickup and deliver to specific distributors. The Garcia family demanded positive results. High risk and loss of manpower had risen above his level of comfort. Options to get the cartel's product across U.S. borders diminished with each section of border wall added by the U.S. government. It had been Marlon's suggestion to acquire a central location to store and ship product inventory. Rico promised he would be able to convince Diego to allow them the use of his property. Hasan's last-ditch effort went up in smoke.

If Diego refused Rico's proposal, Marlon told Hasan that the elimination of Rico would become a necessity. Robert Reyes took care of that for him, but it would be Hasan's responsibility to find another suitable location. Marlon's alternative would be as easy as creating an oasis in the middle of the Sahara Desert. A location as safe, secure, and private as the Reyes compound did not exist. His phone vibrated in his hand. Hasan wiped the sweat off his forehead as he answered.

"You're up late," Hasan said.

"You didn't answer my text messages. I was concerned. I haven't received payment for the product you took possession of four days ago. Before I call Diego in the morning, have you discussed the proposal?" Marlon asked.

Hasan hesitated as he pondered which lie to tell. The deaths of Diego and Robert Reyes had to wait.

"Diego and Robert want to sleep on the issue. Your brother mentioned something about raising a family. Also, you don't have to worry about Rico anymore."

"Why?"

"His anger exploded when Diego wouldn't give us an immediate answer. Rico aimed his handgun at Diego and clicked off the safety, so Robert Reyes shot him."

"Shut the fuck up. Payment better be in my account by close of business. I will verify what you have told me with Diego in the morning. Remember, Robert has two brothers that will help hunt you down if you screw with them. They will not be as lenient or as understanding as I."

Hasan stared at his phone. Marlon had hung up on him. Not only did he have Diego's two older brothers on his ass, but Hasan hadn't considered the fact that Robert had younger brothers with as many connections, if not more than he had. He made the delivery of the bombs to Gatos but not per Arie Barobnakov's instructions. A business the SVR Director acquired control of after the death of his longtime partner.

Barobnakov had a way of irritating every nerve in his body. Hasan didn't want to know the history of Gatos, yet Barobnakov insisted on telling him before he left Tijuana. *These things you need to know. Eric Mindelkov and I purchased Gatos from the Torino family. I know you visited this establishment many times when Carmela ran it. With MIndelkov's untimely death, the property is mine. Speak to no one. Manager has been told that you are my assistant and to leave key at bar for you. Store bombs in basement. I will be there next week to arrange disbursement.* He took a deep breath as he pondered his progress. *One down, eleven to go. Too bad I won't be here to see his face when he finds out.*

The bridge between the Garcia Cartel and Barobnakov had burned long ago. Now, Barobnakov expected him to handle all the responsibilities once completed by Mindelkov, but without the same status. Young and stupid, he had made a mistake when he signed the contract with the Garcia Cartel. *How was I to know it included all Barobnakov's demands too? This shit should've ended when Marlon dissolved their relationship. I should own half. Assistant to an asshole I've never seen. Hmm?*

Migrants, sex trafficking, and bombs were not Hasan's cup of tea. The simple life of transporting cocaine once a month no longer existed. There was only one way to get back to a simpler life and reduce his military militia which had grown to twenty-three men. *Dust settled. Time to finish the job and get my ass out of here. Marlon will soon know the truth.* As he peered around the corner one last time, Hasan heard a low, deep growl behind him. All doubts of what Robert told him about Rico's demise disappeared. *Same dog pack? No. These look hungry. How far away are the others?* He slowly eased his hand toward the automatic resting in his shoulder holster.

Chapter Thirty -- Nuevo Laredo, Mexico

Rita asked with a slight irritation in her tone. "What's he doing? I can't see shit. Is there another set of binoculars?"

Robert had taken the binoculars from Rita when he and Diego arrived. "I know the layout better than you."

Rita huffed. "Ugh! Dammit, you don't always have to be right."

All four were lined up in front of the window. Robert stood behind the desk with Diego to his left, Rita to his right, and Sheila at the end between Diego and the row of filing cabinets. A combination of dark tint and bullet proof glass made it difficult to see very far through the solid pane with no lights inside or out. Low flames flickered in the distance, but the only thing clearly visible were the headlights on the truck outside the block walls.

"Not knowing how close or how far Hasan is from the truck, I would've shut my headset off too. Less distraction. Anyway, from what I can tell the driver side door is locked. He's heading around to the passenger side."

Robert watched as Nicholas leaned over. "Shit! Hasan had a dead body in the cab. It just fell out on Nicholas.

*****

Stunned for a moment, Nicholas laid still and listened. *Alive or dead?* He lifted his head enough to wipe sand from his eyes and nose then pushed up on his hands until he maneuvered his way out from under the heavy weight. He stood for a moment and stared at the man. If Rita hadn't filled him in on the fact that Billy cut off all his hair, he would not have recognized the Indian. He reached down to check for a pulse before turning on his radio.

"Robert, Billy Wright's alive. I need help dragging his body. Hasan must've given him an extra strength sleeping medication or a tranquilizer strong enough to knock out a bull." Leaving the passenger door open, Nicholas didn't wait for a response as he turned off his headset once again. He grabbed

129

Wright's hands and began dragging. Nicholas ran at a slow pace toward the warehouse as if he were the horse and Billy the buggy in tow.

He slowed as Diego approached. Before coming to a complete stop, vibrations from the loud boom behind him shook the ground beneath his feet. Diego stopped and seemed to stare beyond him. Time slowed to a crawl as parts of the truck rained down around them. A front bumper, the hood, and chunks of glass fell a few feet from Wright's boots. Diego had balled up on the ground with his arms over his neck by the time the wave of heat reached them. Debris carried by the blast drifted down with the passenger door rolling by like an odd-shaped wagon wheel.

Nicholas turned to see flames billowing from the engine. Metal braces arced. A bent frame clung tight to torn strands of canvas material. The stench of burned rubber filled the air. Nicholas found himself comparing the devastation to movies he had seen depicting the war between the Israelites and the Philistines. Images of flames in the background around a fierce battle between the two armies flashed through his mind. He could almost see David holding the head of Goliath in his hand. All he needed now was for King Saul to show up and ask David who he was. Nicholas's thoughts flipped the pages of the Bible to David's response. *"I am the son of your servant Jesse of Bethlehem."*

Nicholas struggled when it came to blending his past to the recent revelation of who his father was. He tried many times to put himself in David's shoes and say I am the son of your servant Micha of Moscow, but that fact was no longer true. Robert had turned toward the northeast tower, but Sheila, and Rita were running in his direction. He raised a hand hoping they would stop when his focus drifted to the headlights drawing closer to the front gate.

Chapter Thirty-One -- Nuevo Laredo, Mexico

Hasan slipped out his silenced .45 automatic. Before him stood two scraggly dogs. He fired two shots, one in front of each displaying sharp teeth as they continued to growl at him.

"You move any closer and I will kill you both."

Short brown hair with splotches of black, carried his memory back to his childhood. Hacksaw, a mid-size dog with a big dog attitude. His first and only pet had been his protector. His favorite companion for more than six years before he disappeared one night. What Hasan considered a furry friend, someone else considered the animal dinner.

Raised in a poor, hard, and loveless neighborhood, he never found out what happened to Hacksaw. Part of him didn't want to know. Thoughts from his early childhood of an aged, white, one-room building sparked a memory to life. Wood benches on each side, long, narrow stained-glass windows, with an altar at the end of the aisle. Tears streamed down his mother's cheeks as he ran down the aisle and out the solid wood door. The last time he would hear a Catholic priest or anyone else tell him he had to love his neighbor as himself. *The bitch sold Hacksaw.*

His brow furrowed over eyes as black as the night when he fired a third shot between the two dogs. Dirt kicked up in the air sending the wild animals off into the darkness. He took a deep breath and sighed. Torture, rape, even murdering a human in cold blood never caused Hasan to hesitate or lose a night's sleep, but when it came to small animals, he had a soft spot. The day his mother confessed her sins to him was the day he left the only place he ever called home. A paid prostitute who could not swear the man living in their house was his father. The fact that she stopped turning tricks the day he was born did not erase her betrayal.

It was her fault he never married. A woman's purpose became the fulfillment of whatever he needed. His mother's cries, *don't leave, don't leave* seemed to echo in his head as he sent a text to his driver. *Fucking bitch never loved me. Did she believe sitting in a fucking church four days a year would save her from Hell? If she were still alive, I'd skin her alive and feed her to the fucking dogs in Somalia.* Once the truck shifted gears and moved forward, Hasan removed a burn phone from the side pocket of his pants. Having the phone numbers for each bomb in numerical order, he pressed the number two contact then hit send. As the explosion rumbled the ground beneath his feet, Hasan sprinted toward the bright headlights.

By the time he climbed up on the passenger seat, results of the explosion could only be imagined. If the engine fire still burned, it was not visible over the wall. He closed the door, rolled down the window, then removed a driver's license from his wallet. The few stars illuminating the night sky were of no use. High beam headlights reflected off the dirt road ahead, as if he were on a train traveling through a long tunnel, carved out of a mountainside with no way of knowing when it would end. Hasan did not look back.

"Let's get out of here. The two explosions most likely attracted unwanted attention. I don't give-a-shit how far we are from downtown," Hasan said.

Hasan stared at the photo on Will Carter's license. Carter reminded him of someone he had replaced many years ago.

Bowlegs Lewis murdered before my time. No way this man's related. I don't need to hold on to a dead man's ID. He recalled the lies he told Carter as he held the license out the window and let the wind whip it from his fingers. *Carter knew too much.*

Sanchez was Hasan's security chief promoted back to first in command after Rico's death. As Sanchez passed the eight-foot cinderblock wall where a black cloud hovered above the wreckage, Hasan inhaled the stench of burned rubber drifting with the warm breeze and smiled.

He contemplated telling Sanchez to stop and check out the devastation but changed his mind. He pushed back images of Carter's bloody body pieces splattered across the cab, engine, and ground. He wondered if the truck damage equaled the devastation of the two-story house that buried Robert Reyes and Diego Garcia. It didn't matter as long as the only witness left who could tie him to the bombs and three murders became an example of how powerful a small cannister of dynamite and nitroglycerine could be.

Sanchez straightened his black baseball cap. A tall, muscular man in his late fifties, he and Hasan had attended school together in Somalia before they became additions to the dropout statistics during their eighth-grade year. After the murder of Sanchez's father, Sanchez and his mother returned to Miami where she was born and raised. He kept in touch with his school buddy, so when Hasan accepted the contract with the Garcia Cartel, he joined his best friend.

The only thing between Sanchez's shaved head and the few inches to the roof of the cab was his cap. Seatbelts in the old trucks did not include the cross-body strap, nor were they equipped with

133

airbags. He kept the belt tight across his hips to prevent his head from banging the roof every time a pothole came along.

"What's the status of our team in Abasolo?" Hasan asked.

"Awaiting your orders on where to move the females."

"Any sign of the Coast Guard or law enforcement?"

"I don't know. Last time I checked they hadn't seen any vehicles pass by. Coast Guard may be sitting outside radar range. You mentioned the team near Hidalgo hasn't answered."

"Texas side of the river. Rico put his brother-in-law in charge of that clusterfuck. Did you re-direct the trucks with the male migrants?"

"They're camped about an hour from here. Supposed to be near a convenience store. We're going to need gas."

"Good. We'll have to lay low for a while. Rico's fuck-up screwed us all." Hasan rubbed his forehead, took a deep breath, and sighed. "I know what you're thinking. Don't you dare say I told you so."

"In other words, Rico destroyed a dam unleashing a flood of alligators big enough to swallow us whole."

"Sounds about right. Does this trip remind you of a time when we first started working for the Garcia Cartel?"

Sanchez glanced over at Hasan. His eyes narrowed. "You mean the run in with the Coast Guard near the Keys. Lost our entire crew. Lost the drug shipment too. If it hadn't been for the Garcia's connections, we would've been dead men. So, how does

134

that remind you of this job? That was a different place. A different time. We were young and stupid."

"We were. So far this trip, we've lost the border team. I have a feeling we're going to lose the female refugees and the drugs." Hasan put his elbow on the window frame and gazed out at the dark sky.

"Why do you think that?"

"Retracing what happened back at the compound. Pretty sure Diego and Will Carter are dead. Robert Reyes may have left to spend the night in the house he used to live in. I didn't anticipate the fact he might choose to sleep in one of the other houses."

"With you in close proximity I would not let you out of my sight, but I know you too well. You want me to turn around?" Sanchez asked.

"Too late. I avoided every question Reyes and Diego asked while eating dinner. Playing host per Marlon's request, they tried to get me to tell them our plan. They never intended to let us use their property to store and ship products from there. Good thing is, Reyes doesn't have a fucking clue as to what our level of capabilities are. If we consider the fact that the Reyes family still has connections in Nuevo Laredo, I will need to drop you off at the campsite and head to Abasolo. I need to get there before dawn and destroy all evidence that our team has ever been there," Hasan explained.

"I thought they were headed further south to make the transfer?"

"I haven't heard from them. They were told to pick up our team and abandon the boats. I assume there is bad or intermittent reception there."

"What about your contact in Moscow? Can you call him for help?"

"Arie Barobnakov's not a stable man."

"And you are?" Sanchez smiled as he accelerated into the darkness ahead.

"Matter of opinion. Mine being the only one that counts."

Chapter Thirty-Two -- Nuevo Laredo, Mexico

Nicholas leaned against the support beam on the guest house porch. Faint whiffs of burned rubber drifted across the compound. Scattered pieces of the truck littered the area in front of the bunkhouses, cafeteria, and office. Hot flames transitioned to billowing clouds of smoke fading as they rose against the night sky. Sifting through the devastation to find Rico Greyson would have to wait.

He glanced down, took a deep breath, and slowly exhaled. His clothes were covered in grease-soaked grime and dirt. Rips and holes in his t-shirt were too numerous to count. The cuts and burns from the small pieces of engine parts that hit his back and arms were minor. His thoughts were as scattered as the destruction before him. *Logical sense of Hasan's actions isn't adding up.* While overseeing the completion of the animal refuge, Father Simon had taught him the art of memorizing Bible verses. His mind drifted to Psalms, chapter five:

⁸ Lead me, LORD, in your righteousness because of my enemies—make your way straight before me. ⁹ Not a word from their mouth can be trusted; their heart is filled with malice.

I need a distraction to bring Hasan out of hiding. Why remind me of this one? Damn! I need Father Simon's explanations. His thoughts were interrupted when the door opened behind him. "Has Billy awakened?"

Robert handed him a beer and a wet towel. "Diego and I put him in the bathtub and turned on the sprayer. It took a few minutes, but he blinked a couple of times. He mumbled something but impossible to know what he said. Must've been some powerful medication to knock Billy out that hard. I helped Diego get a towel around him and lay him across the bed. I don't think he'll make it downstairs any time soon."

"I appreciate the thought, but this washcloth will be like wiping the side mirror of a mud racing four-wheeler. What I really need is a shower and change of clothes. Where's everybody else?" Nicholas asked as he wiped sand and sweat off his face.

"Sheila's updating Sebastian per your request. Diego is calling Marlon. Rita's getting a bottle of water and aspirins to set next to the bed in case Billy wakes."

"You up for a road trip?"

"Where?"

"Didn't you say you stopped for gas about an hour from here?"

"Yes."

"That big truck is possibly going to need gas before it reaches the coast."

"So, what're you thinking?"

Nicholas checked the time on his watch. "It's almost two. If we wait 'til morning, it'll be too late."

Robert finished his beer. "Then I need a RedBull."

"Get me one too."

Robert left to get the energy drinks and returned with Diego and Sheila.

Nicholas popped the tab. Two long swigs and the can was empty. "Diego, what did Marlon say?"

"I told him chances are Hasan believes we're dead and is trying to figure out how to tell him. I explained in detail and sent pictures of the damage. He's pretty pissed, but I convinced him not to call Hasan tonight. I told him that we need time to find out where the refugees and rest of the bombs went. Marlon said he spoke to Hasan about thirty minutes ago to check on the status of payment for his shipment. Hasan is supposed to call him back in the morning."

"Did he ask Hasan about his location?" Nicholas asked.

"No. Marlon said Hasan told him Rico was dead. That you shot him, and we were going to sleep on Hasan's proposal to use our property as a local headquarters. Now he blames himself for this mess."

"Why?" Robert asked.

"He knew Rico's intentions." Diego stepped off the porch. He began to pace back and forth. "Marlon told Hasan that his contract would end if he failed to find a central location to store and transport inventory."

"What about the fine print at the bottom of your brother's contracts. Doesn't it state that once you sign, you are signing up to work for your family indefinitely?" Robert asked.

"Yep. I've never been involved in the process but depending on circumstances my brothers retain the right to cancel at any time. Marlon considers the contract cancellation with you a while back as his choice, not yours."

Sheila spoke up. "What do you want to do about Rico?"

"He'll have to wait. Finding Hasan is more important," Nicholas replied as Rita walked out on the porch.

Chapter Thirty-Three -- Nuevo Laredo, Mexico

Nicholas laid the hand towel over the porch rail. He removed the band in his hair, ran his fingers through tangled strands, then returned the band. "Diego, do you have another vehicle somewhere on the property?"

Diego stopped pacing. "There's an old Ranger in the back warehouse. It's a stick shift. I haven't started it in a few weeks and wouldn't trust it for long distance driving. We use it to haul trash."

"This is the only thing I can come up with, so if any of you have a better idea, please chime in. Rita, you, and Sheila will drive the truck toward that gas station where you and Robert stopped today. I'm guessing that Hasan will camp somewhere in the vicinity. If you see them, act as if you ran out of gas, pull off the road, and shut off the engine."

"I've never driven a vehicle with a standard transmission," Rita said.

"I can," Sheila added. "I learned on my dad's ranch."

"You want us to get out and raise the hood?" Rita asked.

"If Hasan has guards watching, you won't have to. They'll shoot first then ask questions if you don't die. Prepare to eliminate anyone approaching that has a weapon in hand. We are going to ride in the back. Let's go. We need a blanket or tarp for the back, weapons, and vests," Nicholas said.

"Do we need to call Sebastian?" Rita asked.

"Not yet. Diego, you want to get the truck?" Nicholas asked.

"On my way." Diego took off running toward the back warehouse.

Nicholas turned toward Sheila and Rita. "Robert and I will gather ammunition if you two will check on Billy one more time. I hate leaving him in a strange place when I'm not sure when we'll be back."

Sheila twisted her hair then pulled it through the small opening on the back of her black baseball cap. "Okay. Can't say I would've come up with a better idea, but I'm happy you believe we'll all make it back alive."

Nicholas raised his hand and pointed toward the wreckage. "We survived that. Hasan has to believe Robert and Diego are no longer breathing."

*****

The Ranger looked more like a pair of old, faded blue jeans, with tires supporting thin bands of tread, and a rusted truck bed with holes big enough to put his hand through. Nicholas stared at the truck and wondered how far it would go before they found themselves stranded. He pictured the beat-up vehicle bringing truth to the old saying, '*Found On Road Dead*'.

Two-by-four boards they scavenged from a scrap pile near the workshop area of the warehouse were pieced together. Nicholas helped Robert cover the wood with a plastic tarp then secured it with rope to the end of the tailgate. With the tailgate down, Nicholas wasn't so sure this last-minute effort to construct a brace would keep them from falling off the bed of the truck if Sheila slammed on the brakes, but it was the only way for all three of them to fit.

As tight as sardines in a can, Nicholas, Robert, and Diego lay side by side with binoculars on the truck bed behind their makeshift barrier. Sheila started the truck as Rita climbed in the passenger side. After grinding gears a few times, Sheila headed east.

On a dirt road filled with potholes of various sizes, it was all the three men could do to hold on until Sheila turned onto the two-lane highway. They had about three hours before the sun brightened the eastern skyline. Nicholas wondered if it would it be enough time to track Hasan without a backup plan.

141

He had gambled on this shot in the dark leading them to the jackpot. Ten more bombs and possibly nineteen refugees lost. Questions as to where Hasan left the bombs crossed his mind. *Are the teens and bombs in the same place? Will there be one big explosion or ten different locations? No.* He realized there was one possibility. "Diego, who is Marlon's current partner in Gatos Bar?"

Diego cocked his head as his brow furrowed. "Why?"

"I'm trying to figure out where Hasan went when he left Diego earlier. Was it Arie?"

"Yes, until the SVR director and Mindelkov bought my family's interest. Happened when Mindelkov fucked up the search for his son. Marlon blamed Mindelkov for the death of Marcus. How did you know?"

"Mindelkov was once considered to be part of my family. When he died a few months ago, everything he owned reverted to the SVR Director. That has to be where Hasan took the bombs." Nicholas raised up on his elbows, let the binoculars dangle from his neck, then pulled his phone from his back pocket.

Nicholas listened to four rings before Sebastian answered. "Hello."

"Sorry to wake you, but I think the bombs are at Gatos Bar. Do you have any kind of relationship with the new police chief?"

Sounds of bedsheets being shoved out of the way could be heard in the background as Sebastian responded. "Let me see what I can do. Where are you?"

"Trying to find a ghost in the dark. Got to go." Nicholas clicked off.

The bumpy ride to MEX-2 took almost an hour. Rita scanned the area from the passenger seat, Diego searched the north side, Robert, the south side, and Nicholas switched back and forth. If Rita missed seeing something out of place in the darkness, it fell to one of them to find. Nicholas heard a crackling sound from his earpiece before Rita spoke.

"I see what looks like smoke from a campfire. Don't see any trucks. Damn pitch dark and too far."

"Where?" Robert asked.

"About two o'clock and at least seventy-five yards from the road. You should be able to see now," Rita replied.

"Got it."

"Cut the engine and coast onto the gravel," Nicholas said.

"No movement, but it looks like there are three trucks. All appear to be the same as the others."

Nicholas climbed out, crouched down next to the tailgate, then scanned the entire area. Cactus, rocks, and desert brush provided nothing big enough for them to hide behind except the trucks.

"Make sure the overhead light is out. You two slip out the driver's side. Diego will follow close behind. You three fan out around the east side. We need to find out what's on the truck beds before we shoot too close."

143

"Yeah. I'd hate to open fire and find out the bombs and migrants are here," Sheila said as she opened the door and got out.

"These antique radios aren't going to work out here. Guess we'll have to deal with whatever comes along," Rita said.

"Unless you have a better idea, Robert and I will drop down and approach from the west side. Rita, you hang back a few yards in case they have security keeping an eye on the perimeter."

Chapter Thirty-Four -- Nuevo Laredo, Mexico

Nicholas waited with Robert behind him until Rita disappeared into the darkness ahead. "We forgot the night vision goggles."

"Yep, but I think we got a good enough view of the area. We'll see them as soon as they see us. It will depend on who has the fastest draw. So, Quick Draw McGraw, lead the way," Robert chuckled.

Nicholas smiled. Images of a white horse wearing a gun belt, tall western hat, and star on his chest standing on his back legs next to a short sidekick flashed across his thoughts. "I assume you chose to be Baba Looey?"

"Fuck, no. He's following Sheila and Rita."

Robert crouched behind Nicholas following close in his footsteps. They kept their eye on the campsite ahead. When they were about thirty yards away, Nicholas dropped to his knees. Robert moved a few feet to the right and did the same. Nicholas grabbed the binoculars dangling from his neck to survey the target area.

Eight sleeping bags were lined up in a row between the trucks and ash remains from a dying fire. Three men sitting near the trucks on fold-up chairs were passing what was left of a clear glass bottle. Dressed in desert camouflage pants, black t-shirts, and lace-up boots, each soldier had an AK-47 propped next to them. No one else in sight. Were there only three? If not, where were the others?

"There's got to be more of Hasan's men somewhere. We get any closer and they'll see us. How's your aim…?" Nicholas didn't finish his question. Gunfire echoed beyond their view. Carrying silenced weapons meant the gunfire was not Rita, Sheila, or Diego.

The man holding the bottle slung it toward the flickering embers as all three jumped to their feet. Too little, too late. Nicholas and Robert were able to aim and fire before Hasan's men had time to reach their weapons. Nicholas waited for the men to hit the ground before he took off running toward the sleeping bags. Robert followed close behind him until they reached the campsite.

Moving his arm from left to right with Glock in hand, Robert cleared the area as he made his way closer to the men face down on the ground. He bent down to check for a pulse. Blood puddled around them. Pieces of brain and blood spattered across the canvas material of the truck directly behind the folding chairs. After he slung their weapons over his shoulder, Robert walked over to where Nicholas stood next to the refugees. The sound had caused the young boys to pull their sleeping bags over their heads.

With only a clear view of their fingers holding tight to the edge, Nicholas kneeled, swapped the clip in his pistol, and spoke just above a whisper. "It's okay. We're here to rescue you, but you must hurry."

The boy closest to Nicholas peeked out. Curly black hair fell across his forehead. "Where will we go?"

"Run toward the highway." Nicholas raised his arm and pointed. "You will see a blue Ranger on the side of the road. Stay down next to the passenger side and wait."

The boy nodded as he gently pushed on the sleeping bag next to him. They quickly headed out in single file leaving the sleeping bags on the ground. None of them looked back. The gunfire ceased. Three cargo trucks were in a semi-circle in front of them. After the boys disappeared out of sight, Nicholas said, "You go right, I'll go left."

Chapter Thirty-Five -- Nuevo Laredo, Mexico

Sheila assumed point about fifteen feet in front of Diego. With Rita about twenty feet to her left, Sheila kept the Uzi shoulder level in front of her. Clouds covered most of the stars above leaving them in almost total darkness. A bird squawked in the distance as if warning others of a looming danger. Sheila's pace slowed as she tried to keep an eye on the ground while maintaining a focus on the campsite ahead.

The occasional mosquito bite didn't seem so bad when compared to the chance of crossing paths with another rattler. Prickly needles on the cactus let her know she had invaded their space with each step she took. Her denim jeans and lace-up boots failed miserably to do their job. Questions stacked up like a long line of dominos. If she could answer one, would the domino effect apply? Right now, the only thing she wanted to know was how many innocent refugees might be in their line of fire when they came face to face with Hasan's overgrown minions.

Without stopping to contemplate these issues, her brain continued in overdrive. *Is Hasan even here? Is this where the bombs were delivered? Who's on the other side?* Her attention reverted to the smoke drifting between two of the trucks ahead. They were quickly approaching the small convoy. She checked the safety on her Glock. Her eyes and hands moved in unison as she searched for movement from the engine of the first truck to the last one's bumper.

Are Diego and Rita enough backup to save all of us? There had been no time to lay out a plan of attack. Three approaching from one side and two from the other may have been a mistake. *Where is Robert and Nicholas? Are they hostages?* Sheila recalled the first time she met Rita Livingston. Back then she carried a detective badge for the San Marcos police department. Rita was a DEA agent assigned to the Dallas office. An investigation that brought them together changed both their lives. Rita and her partner at the time recommended Sheila for a vacancy with the DEA. When Rita changed her career path from DEA to FBI, Sheila transitioned from her one-bedroom apartment to a new complex on the north side of San Antonio.

A new life, a new job, and hopes of a long-term relationship with the man she was dating at the time were on her horizon. Her only downfall turned out to be her career. Jake Remington tired quickly playing second fiddle to her long hours at work. A wedge between them seemed to become too deep to overcome. Sheila and Jake went from night-time lovers to day-time friends in less than a year, but he still cared enough to cat-sit her orange fur ball when she was out of town.

Sheila's thoughts re-focused on what lay ahead. Something seemed off until muzzle flashes from gunfire came into view. The outline of two large men running toward her caused her to lose track of Rita and Diego. The ground rumbled under her feet. From her peripheral vision she caught a glimpse of Rita about ten feet to her left. Rita had fallen to her knees with her Glock out in front of her firing at the two moving targets. Sheila went down on one knee. Losing track of her team members locations was unacceptable. She started as lead on the approach. First shots should have been fired by her.

Where's Diego? Has he been hit? Did Rita unload every bullet in her clip before I fired the first shot? Using one of Diego's Uzis Sheila opened fire. She thought she put enough holes in both men to kill a giant until she saw the monster behind what was left of his human shields standing a few feet from her. In one swift motion the giant let the dead bodies fall and aimed the nose of the AK-47 at her forehead before she blinked once.

The man reminded her of a bald and slimmer version of Andre the Giant. Wrestling was something her dad liked to watch back in the eighties. Andre died in 1993, but this giant had her dead to rights. *Where are Rita and Diego?* The thought of praying crossed her mind, but quickly faded. No prayer on earth would make this mess vanish. *Will Nicholas and Robert have to dig me out of another hole?* As the man stared down at her, something about him seemed familiar.

The figure before her was taller than any person she had ever seen. He had to be more than seven feet tall. Tattooed arms from shoulder to wrist were more like tree limbs. A black baseball cap covered his bald head. He was dressed in desert camouflage with lace-up jump style boots. Even in the dark his skin tone appeared to be a medium shade of brown. She had slowly raised her left arm as she lowered the Uzi to the ground with her right. She was out of bullets and no time to replace the clip.

"Drop it or end up like these two."

"Don't shoot. I broke down on the side of the road. I saw your trucks in the distance." Sheila raised her right arm as if surrendering.

"What is a decent looking woman like you with a weapon like that doing out here this early in the morning?"

"My weapon of choice. Light and accurate." She paused a moment to wipe sweat off her forehead with the back of her hand. "Heading to the coast. My phone app said this was the shortest way."

"You're American?"

"Yes."

She watched him scan the area around them. "Are you alone?"

"Yes."

"I don't believe you." His brow furrowed as he took a step closer and surveyed the area behind her once more. "Okay. Let's say I'm curious. So, before I drag your ass back to camp and beat the truth out of you and then let the rest of my men use you for a play toy, convince me you're not lying."

In no position to tell the truth or lie, maybe a half-truth could be believable. She broke his glare to glance at the dead bodies at his feet. Drenched as if they had taken a bath in their own blood made it impossible for even their mother to recognize them. She sighed. "Can I get off my knees. The clip is empty."

He stared at her for a long moment. "You make any move out of line, I'm done and you're dead. Und…."

Four quick poof sounds came from Sheila's left and two flew passed her on the right. The first two hit the man's forehead, one cut through his throat and the last hit his shoulder. He stumbled back a couple of steps, wobbled, then fell forward, face down. Sheila jumped backward. Rita came running up with Diego not far behind.

"You okay?" Rita asked.

Sheila bent over and picked up the Uzi. "If the thorn scratches from various cactus plants don't count then I'm good."

"As soon as I saw the muzzle flash, I fell flat on the ground about fifty yards back. You were directly in my line of fire," Diego said.

"The bullets you fired flew by my ear close enough for me to feel the force of the wind."

Rita holstered her Glock. "When they started firing toward you, I crouched behind a cactus bush and returned fire in the direction I saw the muzzle flashes. When I ran out of ammunition, I laid flat on the ground. The goons seemed to be focused on you, but I couldn't understand why the bastards didn't fall. Now I see why."

The tall giant landed on top of the two crumpled bodies. Diego picked up the AK-47. He slid the strap across his shoulder before checking the man's back pockets. "This is Hasan's righthand man." He reached down and pushed the man on his back. "Hasan has to be around here somewhere."

"What's his name?" Rita asked.

Diego handed a phone and wallet to Sheila. "He goes by Sanchez. I've never heard his full name."

"According to his Florida license, his first name is Darrell. That's how I know the name. I brought down a drug ring a few years ago in San Marcos. Sanchez's name was listed as a person of interest, but our warrants and APBs never turned up a damn thing."

"We need to find Robert and Nicholas. I'll lead this time," Rita said.

Sheila took a deep breath and sighed. Rita didn't have to tell her she had compromised the team by not paying attention to what was most important. *Has lack of sleep caused my mind to drift again? No acceptable excuse. First time saved my ass. Rita covered it this time.* As her ego deflated to zero, she fell in line behind Diego.

Chapter Thirty-Six -- Nuevo Laredo, Mexico

Using the center truck's back tire as a shield, from a squatting position, Nicholas peered under the bed of the truck. He used the binoculars to survey the vast desert behind the campsite. When Rita came into focus, Nicholas said, "You okay?"

"Yes. Sheila and Diego are circling around to my left and right to make sure there are no more of Hasan's men wondering around."

Rita passed between the vehicles and walked toward the sleeping bags. "Where's Robert?"

"On the last truck bed." He pointed to the three lumps in front of the folding chairs. "They were sleeping, so easy targets. There should be eight male refugees at the truck."

"What about Hasan?"

"Not here," Robert replied as he walked up to where Rita and Nicholas stood next to the campfire. Sheila and Diego were not far behind. "Nothing but supplies on the last truck bed. Several boxes of MREs, a tent, cots, and more sleeping bags. There is one Honda motorcycle, but no key. Enough space and dirt marks to suggest Hasan left on two wheels. Tracks lead east. Keys for trucks are in the ignitions."

Sheila handed Sanchez's wallet to Robert. "Do you know this man? He's dead next to two more of Hasan's men. Sanchez used the other two as personal body armor, so not much left to identify."

"Yes. He was on Jack Silverman's payroll. Must've been the middleman between Hasan and Silverman. I met him one time when I stopped by to see how things were going. Must've been about five or six years ago. From what I can remember, Silverman assured me Sanchez had nothing to do with moving my family's product." Robert handed the wallet to Nicholas.

"I haven't seen him before," Nicholas said.

Diego spoke up. "I guess you could say that he was the General of Hasan's tiny army depending on what title Hasan gave Rico. I still don't get how Hasan could've trusted Rico."

"I agree, except we still haven't located Hasan, the bombs, or the female refugees."

"Is it time to update Sebastian?" Rita asked as she pulled out her cell phone.

"No, unless you want him on this side of the river."

"Nope," Rita replied.

"Robert, do the trucks have automatic transmissions?" Nicholas asked.

"Yes."

"Rita, you, Sheila, and Diego drive these back to Nuevo Laredo. Robert and I are going to take the Ranger and head toward Abasolo."

"If they camped here, then we may not have enough gas to make it back."

"Then drive them until you run out of gas. Take the eight teens with you. Diego, can the boys stay in the bunkhouse until we figure out what Sebastian wants to do with them?"

"The bunkhouses have been closed up for a long time, but it's got to be better than where they've been."

"Okay. Once you get them settled, I want all three of you to check out Gatos. No matter how honest the local police chief is, if he drags his feet, we may be too late. That is the only possibility I can come up with where Hasan might have dumped the rest of the bombs." He checked the time on his watch. "It's three forty-five. We only have a couple of hours before daylight."

Sheila kicked dirt on the dead men's boots. "What about these bodies?"

"I'll send Sebastian a text when we reach the compound," Rita said as she turned toward the lead truck. "Sheila, can you stop and pick up the boys?"

"On my way." Sheila climbed in the cab of the middle truck, then cranked the engine. The passenger window was open. "Gas gauge shows almost a half tank." She shifted gears and followed Rita.

"Drop us off at your Ranger," Nicholas said to Diego as he climbed on the back of the third truck with Robert.

Chapter Thirty-Seven -- Nuevo Laredo, Mexico

After a short, bumpy ride, Rita parked on the side of the road. She quickly explained the situation to the young men then helped them climb into the back of Sheila's truck. Within five minutes the short convoy was on its way west. When Robert and Nicholas could no longer see the taillights of Diego's truck, Robert climbed behind the wheel of the Ranger as Nicholas closed the passenger door.

The old Ranger had no air conditioning. With the windows rolled down, Nicholas propped his elbow on the door. Hasan's men were stacking up. Questions as to why the Somalian would leave the protection of the caravan led to one answer.

"Hasan's on the run. If he truly thinks you and Diego are dead, he finally realized the ramifications of his actions."

"Yep. You thinking he's headed to the fishing boats?"

"No. If I were him, I'd use them as a smoke screen. He either knows a way across the border near Brownsville, or he's catching a boat further south."

"I would head south. How far ahead of us do you think he is?"

"Depends on how long he hung out at the camp. It would've been nice if Sanchez had survived."

Robert smiled. "I don't think so. The man stood seven-foot two. When I met him years ago, he had biceps that would rival Schwarzenegger during his early body building days. For Sanchez, it would be a kill or be killed scenario. Rita said the giant used the other two as human shields. He was just a few feet in front of Sheila before he dropped the remains and pointed the AK-47 at her head. Them bastards he used as a bullet proof vest had to weigh close to five hundred pounds together."

"This is the biggest shot in the dark I've ever taken. The thing that concerns me the most is the young females may already be on their way to some foreign country."

Robert pushed the gas pedal until the frontend vibrated. Slowing down was not an option. If there had been a race between the 1985 Ranger and a Honda 300, the motorcycle would win every time. "He's making mistakes he's never made before. He's got to be listening to someone else. Screwing the Garcia brothers and the SVR director leaves him few places to hide."

Nicholas let his hand ride the wind as if it were a surfboard skimming the Gulf waves near the beaches of South Walton. Feeling the warm breeze against his skin was something he enjoyed as a child. A time when life seemed uncomplicated. Back then, he had no knowledge of what his father did to support their family. KGB and SVR were letters in the American alphabet. It was not until his mom told him of Micha's death, that he understood the sacrifices his parents made were for the sole purpose of protecting him. Micha would always be his dad no matter whose blood ran through his veins.

Nicholas's thoughts drifted to a snowy winter day when he and his father were huddled close together high above the ground in a tree stand. The damp breeze had made a whistling sound between the tall pines that day as they pointed their rifles toward an open field covered with a blanket of snow. He didn't remember how old he was or whose property they were hunting on. He did recall the words Micha whispered as a buck wandered out into the open.

"Keep your focus on the target in front of you as you reflect on your knowledge of the past. There's nothing you can do about what you left behind, but it can guide you beyond the obstacles on broken roads ahead."

His father fired one shot. Micha knew exactly where the bullet needed to hit to save the animal from an agonizing death. The deer never knew what hit him. Nicholas's thoughts returned to the darkness ahead of them. A two-lane highway with no buildings in sight. Cactus, tumbleweeds, and rocks as far as he could see. The sun would be riding the horizon by the time they reached Abasolo. *If the boats are still rocking with the waves next to the dock, how many of Hasan's soldiers will be waiting? Will the two*

156

AK-47s, one sniper rifle, and two handguns be enough?
Contemplating what Hasan might do hit the imaginary target in his mind between difficult and impossible.

"Are you testing the wind for the possibility of flying to Abasolo?" Robert laughed.

Nicholas pulled his arm back in the truck. "No, but I have wondered, with all the technology that's become reality from the original *Star Trek* series, why can't we push a button and instantly be transported to the coast?"

"Good question. *'Beam me up Scotty'*. Have you considered the fact that if Hasan's men are still at the property, they'll see us coming?"

"Yes. When we get about a quarter mile out, I'll get out and ride in the back. When you slow down at the intersection, I can slide off without being spotted. They'll think you're alone."

"What are the odds we'll be able to find Hasan?"

"What's the old saying? Between slim and none?"

"Yep, but I picture you as Wile E Coyote and Hasan as the Road Runner. You get some off the wall mail order Acme contraption and hunt the ugly bird down one more time," Robert said.

Chapter Thirty-Eight -- Nuevo Laredo, Mexico

Once all three trucks were parked inside the compound, Rita lined up the eight teens from oldest to youngest while Diego went to get the keys for the bunkhouse. Sheila searched the supply truck after Diego turned the flood lights on. It didn't take long to find a box with several spiral notebooks, pens, and a solar powered calculator. The notebook on top had schedules and notes, but none made any sense to her. She tucked it under her arm, grabbed a blank notebook, a pen to write with, and hurried to join Rita.

Most of the boys were wearing dirty jeans with at least one rip or hole in them. All wore t-shirts but each varied in color. Only five of them had some form of footwear. If this scene had appeared in a commercial, requesting charitable donations, she wouldn't hesitate to give. Rita took a couple of steps back as the pungent smell of dried urine and stale body sweat rose high enough to reach her sinuses. Their expressions suggested all chances for a future life of freedom would equal finding the golden ticket at '*Willy Wonka's Chocolate Factory*'. Her mind searched for what she could say to give them hope, but with strict immigration laws, her promises were no better than a fairy tale.

Rita tucked strands of hair behind her ear as sweat drizzled down her back. None of the refugees had spoken. They had either nodded their heads or blindly followed orders. "Do any of you speak English?"

The oldest spoke up. "We all do. Some better than others."

"What's your name?" Rita asked.

"Gabriel." He slid his bare foot back and forth through the sand but never met her gaze.

Sheila stepped closer and handed the notebook to him. "Please print your first and last name then pass the book down the line."

"Do any of you know where Hasan was going? Did he leave on a motorcycle?" Sheila asked.

Gabriel passed the notebook and pen to the boy next to him. "Yes. He took a motorcycle. I heard something about a boat before sunrise, but that was all."

"How long before we arrived did Hasan leave?" Rita asked as she pulled her phone out of her back pocket.

"Maybe a half hour? He made a phone call, but we were too far away to hear. After he left, I heard three of the guards sit in chairs and open a bottle of liquor. If we moved, the guards would take turns kicking us."

"They won't be doing that again." Rita noticed all the boys except Gabriel stared at the ground. "You're all okay. We're not going to hurt you. We were sent to help. Diego's going to let you shower and sleep in his bunkhouses. We must leave, but the bald man with a beard that was with you is here." This comment seemed to make them all a little more at ease.

Sheila turned toward Rita. "Billy knows who you are. I'm assuming that's Diego heading this way in his pickup. So, do you want to go check on Billy while we get these kids settled? I saw a stack of bags and suitcases on the supply truck bed. There's got to be clean clothes in them that these young men can change into. We're running out of time. We've got to get downtown as soon as possible."

Rita checked her watch. "Pick me up in front of the house in fifteen minutes. We'll leave then." Rita took off running. Three hundred plus yards wasn't going to be a short sprint.

Rita stood silently in the doorway. From the silhouette of Billy's body across the bed, she assumed the man hadn't moved. With his head turned to the side, he slept on his stomach with a white towel draped across the lower part of his back. She hadn't seen Billy without his prosthetic and prayed she didn't have to help the man get dressed.

"Billy." She noticed his artificial leg leaning against the wall as she flipped the light switch. "Billy," Rita yelled as she walked around to where he could see her when he opened his eyes. She reached down and pushed on his shoulder. "Billy, you've got to wake up."

He groaned but didn't move.

She knelt. "Come on Billy. Wake up, dammit," she said louder.

She shook and pushed on his shoulder until his eyes opened wide. His eyes narrowed as a crease formed between them. He stared but didn't speak. Without warning, his hand grabbed her throat and jerked her closer. She gasped as her arm swung into defense mode. Once she broke his grip, she pulled back and fell to the hardwood floor.

She rubbed her throat until her panting eased. She took a deep breath and sighed, "Billy, it's me, Rita. Don't you recognize me?" She slowly stood and placed her hands on her knees. "Dammit. You're staring at me like you don't know who I am."

He moved as if to roll over. Rita panicked. She put her hands out and waived. "Wait, wait, wait. Diego helped you bathe, you have no clothes on, and your prosthetic is against the wall behind you." She reached over and gently slid the towel to where he could reach it.

His eye lids fluttered a few times. "What the fuck? How long have I been asleep?"

"I can't answer that, but it's after four in the morning. I'm going to see if Robert has a pair of pants and shirt that will fit you."

Rita hurried out of the room. She dug a pair of jeans, underwear, and a pull-over shirt out of Robert's suitcase. By the time she returned, Billy had managed to sit on the edge of the bed. She waited at the doorway while he finished off the bottle of water.

"I can't say I know how you feel, but I've been given a strong tranquilizer medication before. In fact, the last time I was drugged was by you."

"Sorry about that." Billy coughed then cleared his throat. "Another place, another time. I'm not that man anymore." He wiped his mouth with the back of his hand. "Where am I."

"Diego and Robert's property south of Nuevo Laredo. We rescued eight boys and desperately need you to stay with them. I don't know how much you remember, but Hasan has dropped off the bombs somewhere and Nicholas has an idea of where they might be. Do you need me to help you get dressed?"

Billy sat up a little straighter as he cocked his head in her direction.

"Let me rephrase that. You may be weak when you try to stand. You want to put this pair of underwear on first?" She placed the clothes on the edge of the bed. "I'll run downstairs and grab you another bottle of water."

By the time she returned, Billy had the underwear on, and he was in the process of fastening the prosthetic in place. As he stood to pull up the jeans, he reached out and put his hand on the nightstand.

"You okay?"

"A little dizzy. Caught me off-guard." He rubbed his forehead. "I really hope the shit I gave you wasn't as bad as whatever Hasan gave me. It feels like there's a spelunker pounding on a drum as hard and as fast as he can in my head."

"The aspirins next to you will help. You need your shoes?" She checked the bathroom and found his boots under the stack of dirty clothes.

"I guess it's a good thing Robert and I are about the same size."

Rita walked over next to him. "Come on. Put your arm over my shoulder. I want to make sure you make it down the stairs first. I'll explain what we need you to do on the way out." She slid her arm around his waist.

Chapter Forty -- Nuevo Laredo, Mexico

An expression of relief appeared on the teens' faces when Billy walked in the bunk house with Diego.

'Rita rolled the passenger window down. "Come on Diego. We've got to go."

"I'm coming." Diego turned toward Billy. "If you need anything, this is the key to the house you were in. There's food in the fridge. Sheila unloaded a bunch of the MRE meals. They're in the kitchenette down the main hall." He shook Billy's hand then hurried over to the open driver's side door.

*****

Located on the outskirts of downtown, Gatos appeared to be a bed and breakfast house at the entrance to a large subdivision. Unlike the houses that surrounded it, the entertainment establishment catered to men. A two-story frame house with a swing on the front porch. In the back, a rickety, wood staircase considered to be the fire escape, led to the former owner's old room.

A rusted dumpster with no lid overflowed. Beer bottles, cans and liquor boxes littered the ground. Diego drove passed the trash bin, then pulled off the road onto the gravel easement. Residential houses lined both sides of the street. None of the streetlights were on and only a few of the houses had their porch light on. Rita counted three older model cars and two pickup trucks in the parking lot. All were lined up at the back corner of the lot.

Diego turned off the engine. "What was the decision on notifying Chief Vito?"

"Sebastian said he was working on a search warrant. Chief Vito may not be on the take, but that doesn't mean the judicial system here is as honest as he is," Rita replied as she opened the glove box in search of pen and paper. "Who's in charge of this place now?"

"I don't have a clue. Unlike my older brothers, I've never been inside."

"We can't wait on a maybe search warrant. Okay, this is what we're gonna do." Rita handed each of them a pair of disposable gloves. "Since I can't seem to find something to write on, Sheila, can you take pictures of the vehicle plates and text them to Sebastian?"

Sheila slid off the seat behind Diego. "On it."

"Diego, you armed?"

"Yes."

Rita scanned the area around them. "I don't see anyone up and out yet. Take a stroll down the road about fifty yards and we will all meet back here. I'll see if I can find anything out of place on the front side of this fine establishment."

They all took off in different directions. Clouds drifted across the sky hiding what was left of a starry night. With the sun just below the horizon, they didn't need flashlights. Gatos's entrance faced the main road leading to downtown. Rita hurried passed the dumpster as she held her breath. Rats scurried behind it when her shoes hit the gravel lot. Rita paused at the back corner of Gatos. Sheila finished taking pictures of the vehicle plates faster than Rita anticipated.

"All done and sent. Sebastian said he would let us know if any of them come back stolen. So, if the bombs are here, where do you think they would be?" Rita caught a glimpse of headlights headed their way before she saw the vehicle. "Duck!" She said in a low whisper.

They leaned against the back side of the building and then slid into a squatting position. Never having the opportunity to see a real brothel before, Rita knew enough not to expect the glamour and glitter portrayed in '*The Best Little Whore House in Texas.*' A humorous musical based what happened at the Chicken Ranch in La Grange, Texas. While attending college in Austin, she had chosen to write her final history paper about it.

The Chicken Ranch originally opened in 1844; the house of prostitution had been shut down by the Yankees during the Civil War. In 1905 it re-opened under the guidance of Miss Jessie. With prostitution considered illegal in the state of Texas, the brothel closed permanently in 1973. Having an appearance of a local farmhouse, the brothel acquired its name during the Great Depression by charging one chicken in return for one sexual favor.

Images of the original chicken ranch faded from her thoughts as the vehicle disappeared behind her. She peeked around the corner. The pickup stopped at the intersection, then turned left. When Diego returned, they both stood.

"That didn't take long." Rita peered around the corner one more time. "Anyone outside yet?"

"Nope, but the street will be busy soon. Lights were coming on when I started back this way. We're running out of time."

Rita glanced over at the staircase. "If this is their fire escape, I think I would take my chances making it through the ground floor flames before attempting to descend this one. Sheila, you look like you weigh less than we do. You think you can make it to the top without falling through?"

"So, I'm the guinea pig?" Sheila smiled. "I'll give it a try. A question to ponder. Why only one window?" She paused as her eyebrows rose. "I assume this leads to the infamous bedroom?"

"So, you've heard the rumors?" Rita unholstered her Glock.

"Yes. I connected the dots while following the murder cases mentioning Carlos Reyes as a possible suspect after his release from Huntsville. Too damn bad, no evidence." Sheila surveyed the area beyond the staircase as she removed the Uzi Diego had given her from her shoulder holster. She headed toward the stairs with the weapon aimed at the landing.

"Have you checked the front?" Diego asked as he watched Sheila make her way up the stairs.

"Not yet."

"I'll call my brother. He may be able to give us a rough idea of the floor plan," Diego whispered.

Rita watched Diego keep his back to the wall as he stayed inside the shadows until he reached front porch. She recalled the detailed stories Robert had told her about the room at the top of the stairs. It belonged to Carmela Torino, but her friends called her Cat. A few days after Robert's father returned after spending thirty years in the Texas prison system, Cat turned up dead. *No proof but Robert said his dad was the only possible suspect.* Images of the woman being shot with the barrel of a silenced .45 shoved up her vagina while leaning over her dressing table were beyond Rita's comprehension.

She cringed slightly until her thoughts moved on to the murder of Rafael. Robert's late brother-in-law. From what Robert managed to piece together, Anita had been held hostage in Cat's old room by the former police chief, Tito Rojas. When Rafael found her, Rojas shot him in the back of the head before moving his body to El Rancho. His remains were discovered in the fire pit behind the restaurant.

Rita glanced around the corner to check on Diego. *Shit! Did he go in without us?* When she glanced up, Sheila stood on the landing with her hand on the doorknob. Rita raised her Glock as she eased closer to the stairs. Sheila nodded to confirm the door was locked. It was now or never. She couldn't let Sheila enter without backup. Rita quickly searched their perimeter before running up the stairs. Holding on to the rail as she kept to the outside edge. The tip of her shoes hit every other step just enough to propel her forward.

"You think you can bust it open with one hard kick, or do you think we both need to throw our weight against it?" Sheila whispered.

Rita took a deep breath and exhaled. She studied the landing. The four-foot by four-foot rotting planks supported an unstable rail. The wood posts leaned outward slightly. Rusted nails were visible between the deck and the door. No option for a running start. She surveyed the door then moved closer.

Rita pressed gently on the frame. "It's as rotten as the wood we're standing on. Step back a little."

"Where's Diego?" Sheila moved to top step as she held tight to the rail.

"Around front somewhere. Probably still talking to Marlon. You know if this damn thing gives way, that piece of wood you're holding onto for dear life won't save you," Rita smiled.

"It makes me feel safer."

"Rational answer." Rita grabbed the silencer from her back pocket. "This may keep the neighbors from hearing, but if someone's inside and happens to be a light sleeper, they're going to hear us coming." She stepped back, aimed, and then fired three shots. Aged, white paint flaked away as splintered wood pieces fell to the threshold.

The gap at the lock gave Rita enough easement to push the door open a few inches. She paused and listened. Peering through a narrow crack, the room appeared to be pitch black. She removed a small flashlight from her pocket. Shining it on the window turned out to be a waste of time. Plywood sealed it closed.

"What do you think?" Sheila whispered.

"I'm calling Diego. I hope to hell he didn't go in the front door by himself." Rita removed her phone from her pocket, found Diego in her contacts then hit the call button. She listened to four rings before hanging up. "No answer."

"He may have silenced it. That boy definitely had a sheltered life."

"Come on. Help me pull away enough of the frame to get in without breaking the door. Don't want to alert anyone inside."

Creaks and cracking were minimal from the outside. Rita hoped the same level of noise echoed inside. She held the door in place and listened. Sheila slipped through first. Rita closed the door behind her. When she turned around, Sheila had the flashlight shining on the bed.

As if they just stepped back in time to a roaring twenties, untouched crime scene, Rita gasped and tried to breathe through her mouth. The four poster, queen size bed, stripped of bed linens showed more stains than they had time to analyze. Blood spattered lace curtains hung over the plywood. When something moved, they both glanced toward a trash can next to the dressing table.

Overflowing with molded food wrappers and beer bottles, two rats disappeared beyond a hole in the baseboard. Sheila moved the flashlight around the room. Discolored smoke stains on a bright pink wall marked the places pictures once resided. A gold tone rack supported a long row of frilly, feathered gowns next to the dressing table. Dried stains from spilled makeup and perfume bottles diminished the once fairy tale style white laminate, with gold trim surface. A shattered oval mirror reflected the damage.

It did not take long for their attention to reach a large, black spot on the wood floor next to the bed. All indications of being dried blood. The mixture of odors reminded Rita of rancid vomit. She swallowed hard to keep from contributing her stomach's contents to the horror scene. Behind her, she found an open bathroom door. Rita reached around the door frame and flipped on the light switch. Nothing happened. *Maybe it's better if we don't see.*

Images of Anita being tied to the bed, drugged, and raped numerous times before Nicholas and Robert saved her, stirred

Rita's anger. Compassion washed over her as she considered Rafael's last memories. The woman he loved lay bruised and battered before him only seconds before the back of the head was blown away. The empathy, the sense of helplessness had shut out the danger around him. Dying and never knowing that Anita was pregnant with their first child. Tears welled in her eyes until footsteps outside the bedroom door next to the vanity were close enough to vibrate the floor beneath her feet.

Sheila shut off the flashlight as Rita motioned for her to move behind the door leading to the hallway. Rita kept her silenced Glock aimed at the door as her heart raced. *Hasan? Impossible. More of his goons?* She held her breath as the knob turned. When she saw the person opening the door, she holstered her weapon and exhaled.

"Dammit Diego, what the hell?" Rita asked.

Sheila did the same then closed the door behind him. "How did you get in?"

"I talked to Marlon. He had a key hidden in a rock among the cactus plants near the porch. He told me exactly where to find it and gave me the alarm code. The alarm wasn't set which seemed strange."

"Did you see anyone?" Rita asked.

"No. There's no one here. I checked the bedrooms, closets, and downstairs storage rooms."

"Hmm. Sheila, have you heard back from Sebastian on the tags?"

"No."

"Something's not adding up. Why wouldn't the live-in work staff not be in their beds? I can only assume those vehicles out back belong to someone who works here. Can either of you think of anything?"

"Sounds to me like Hasan plans to blow this place and told everybody to get out. Question is, why would he want to piss off Barobnakov?" Diego asked.

"Stupidity comes to mind, but why would he take the chance of telling anyone his plan? If I were in their place, I'd immediately call the SVR director. Someone here must have a direct line to the man. I'm sure he expects updates," Rita said.

"Okay. We have less than an hour before the sun rises. Diego, do you know the layout of this place? Is there a basement?"

"Yes. The strange thing is that the downstairs is cleaner than my house except for a few glasses and beer bottles on the bar. I doubt the bombs are here. Beds were made, rooms neat, and clean. Unlike this one." Diego sighed as he scanned the room. "Anita described what she could remember. It appears that she had no clue of reality. There's crime scene tape across the other side of the door."

"Where's the basement?" Rita asked.

"Entrance is under the fire escape."

"Did you check everything downstairs?"

"Just areas big enough to hold the bombs Rico described."

"Let's go. My stomach can't take this stench any longer. If there's nothing in the basement, we'll split up and check a second time." Rita turned and led the way.

Chapter Forty-One -- Nuevo Laredo, Mexico

Diego unlocked the door with the same key that fit the front door. He switched on the light then stepped out of the way to let Rita lead. Cement steps ended at a dirt floor. Florescent lights, hanging from the rafters lit the front half of the space. A haze of dirt and dust seemed to float like a cloud when she reached the last step with Diego and Sheila behind her.

Eight by eight-inch square support beams, butted against one another, appeared to be coated with some type of fire-retardant coating. Rita assumed the room ran the length and width of the house above. Plumbing and possibly gas pipes were visible next to insulated air conditioning ducts fastened to the rafters. Heavy duty shelves lined up against block walls as far as she could see.

Rita turned on her phone flashlight. Moving the light clockwise down the wall to her left, shelves were filled with boxes of various types of liquors. Along the back wall were nine sealed stainless-steel canisters with cell phones wired to the top of each. Cataloging every detail of the basement ended when Rita's gaze drifted beyond the canisters. She counted eleven women and two men.

The females were naked. One man at each end of the line wore boxer shorts soaked with their own blood. She could only assume an automatic weapon had been used to put so many holes across the men's abdomen region. The blood on their legs had dried but small puddles remained at their feet.

Each woman had a hole at their right temple with tiny lines of dried blood on their cheeks. Rita moved close enough to the woman in the center to examine the wound. "Whoever did this, took the time to stand next to each woman, hold a handgun against their temple. Maybe a small. .22 caliber. No exit wound. Blood is dry."

When the smell of death reached her sinuses, Rita took a step back then shown the flashlight on the large black letters on each victim's chest. Like a row of chainsaws dangling on chains from the roof of an abandoned barn, this scene had to be staged.

"You are too late," Rita read out loud as she covered her nose and mouth. "Shit. Too late for what? Did Hasan expect someone to find the bodies before the bombs blew this place and half the block with it?"

Diego moved closer and kicked a paint can against the wall. "Fuck. Why would he pull a stunt like this? It's beyond every kind of psycho act I can imagine."

Sheila squatted to examine the bombs. "It appears that he went to extreme measures with the assumption that someone would show up. If this place is still owned by Barobnakov, what point is Hasan trying to prove? Fuck you Mr. SVR Director?" She paused as she stood. "He had help. The approximate two hours he disappeared last night wouldn't be enough time for one person to do this. If he dials any one of these phones while we're standing here, it's too late for all of us."

"I have a scrambler on my phone. It'll temporarily block the signal." Rita pulled her phone out of her back pocket. "Shit! I have no signal down here."

"Well, if you don't have any bars, then none of those cheap burn phones do either." Sheila said.

"I've never used the damn thing. Never dreamed I'd have to. I would feel safer if all signals were blocked. I'll be back." Rita turned and ran up the stairs.

*****

Sheila took out her phone and began taking pictures. No blood on the stairs or drag marks across the dirt floor. The victim's arms were tied behind their backs. She gently turned the bodies of each, took pictures of their backs, then their arms even though none of the needle scars she noticed appeared to be recent. Each of them had neatly brushed hair. Underneath the lines of blood on the side of their faces, it appeared someone had touched up their makeup. Both men had clean shaven heads.

"No bruising or marks to suggest the women were beaten or raped. Hasan staged this but why? Did he use the same tranquilizer on them as he used on Billy?" Sheila asked but didn't get a response. Then she noticed the tiny red spot behind the ear of the male bodies hanging at the end with a capital E on his chest. "There's probably DNA all over this place, but we don't have an investigation kit."

"You think Sanchez and some of his fat bastard crew helped? Timeline suggests they had the time. No way he was alone," Diego said as he began taking pictures with his phone.

Sheila turned when she saw the flash behind her. "What are you doing?"

"Need to send these to my brother."

174

"Hell no. No, you can't." She held out her hand like she needed to stop an eighteen-wheeler rapidly approaching an intersection.

Diego frowned. "Why?"

"For one thing, when Rita finishes turning on her scrambler, our phones will be useless until she turns it off. We can't take the chance of anyone outside this room finding out about this until we disconnect the phones and find Hasan. I hate to say this, but at this point, I don't trust your brothers. Besides, they sold their ownership to Barobnakov. Now, see if you can find a pair of wire cutters."

"Do you know which one to cut?"

"The only one to the phone, I hope. It doesn't appear that any of them have a backup timer if the wrong wire is cut," Sheila replied.

Diego passed Rita on his way upstairs. "Where are you going?"

"Sheila needs wire cutters."

"Do another walk through. If there were twelve bombs, one is missing."

"Will do."

Rita walked over to where Sheila stood. "Block set. I left my phone right outside the door. I don't know much about it or how long we have," Rita said as she removed a pocketknife from her back pocket.

"Diego snapped pictures of everything. He wanted to send them to his brother."

"What did you tell him?"

"Hell no. We can't let anyone outside the three of us know about this until we figure out what Hasan plans to do. I would really prefer that no one knew we were ever here unless you'd like to stay and answer questions as to why we didn't call the local police before entering the premises."

"You're right. I know Diego just wants to help. Maybe he can find the missing bomb upstairs." Rita found an empty, cardboard liquor box. "You want the privilege?"

Sheila smiled. "Nope. You got this. Hand me the box."

Wires between the lid and cannister connected to a black, plastic box with metal brackets securing them to the lid. Only one connected the cell phones to the box. "As I cut the red wire, gently loosen the tape to remove the phone."

"What do you think is in the box on top?" Sheila asked as she tucked her phone in her back pocket.

"C-4 would be my guess. It would blow the lid off this thing and ignite whatever's inside the cannister. We've witnessed the damage one causes. You know this should be done by a bomb specialist instead of me and you."

"I agree but we can't leave knowing they could go off at any second. I took pictures of everything. Hopefully, we'll have time to piece this massacre to the senseless road of destruction between here and Tijuana."

"I agree. If Hasan's working on an exit strategy, why not take the Garcia's drugs and the immigrants somewhere along Mexico's west coast? Leave the country, see a plastic surgeon, and disappear permanently. Isn't his nickname attributed to his ability to disappear? Do you think these were the employees that worked here?" Rita asked.

"Yes, and yes. And all reasons for us to stay and investigate further even though, it's not our jurisdiction. I really hate to leave a crime scene like this, but we have no choice."

"I agree."

They were done and heading up the stairs when Diego appeared in the doorway. "Found some needle nose pliers. Will they work?"

"Thanks, but I had a knife. Did you find another bomb?" Sheila asked.

"No, but I only checked spots one would easily fit into."

"What about the dishwasher and stove?" Rita asked.

"No. You want me to go back?"

"We don't have time now to go back. Let's get out of here before someone spots your truck. We'll head back to the property until we can get in touch with Nicholas and Robert," Rita said as she turned off the signal block. "I guess we don't know if it works or if we were just lucky enough to disarm them before Hasan called one of the numbers."

Diego locked the door behind them. He tucked the key in his pocket and followed behind Sheila. "It'll be daylight by the time we get home."

"I need two shots of expresso," Rita said.

"Got a machine at home if you can figure out how to use it," Diego said.

"So, I'm assuming you're not domestically inclined?" Rita laughed.

"I had maids and a nanny. My older brothers never let me do anything."

"Do you have something that will erase the horrific scene of what happened to those innocent people in the basement?" Sheila asked.

"I wish," Diego replied.

Sheila put the box of phones on the seat then slid in next to them. Rita opened the passenger side door as Diego sat behind the wheel. When Diego started the truck, all three of them turned their attention to the phone ringing in the box.

"Don't answer it," Rita yelled. "We don't know where Hasan is or if he has someone watching this place. Hurry up, Diego. Let's get the fuck out of here."

Chapter Forty-Two -- Abasolo, Mexico

Nicholas slid off the truck bed when Robert slowed to a crawl at the intersection. Nothing in site except for the two boats tied next to the dock rocking with the tide. No trolls from Hasan's

178

small army and no Jeep. Robert parked close to the dock and got out. He walked a few yards down along the beach where the damp, compressed sand made a path along the water's edge.

Nicholas cut back to the north before circling around toward the dock. After Robert shut off the Ranger's engine, Nicholas thought he heard another vehicle but with the splash of the waves, he couldn't tell the direction it originated from. By the time he reached the dock, the sound had disappeared. Within a few moments, Robert returned.

"I know this property pretty well even though it's been a few years since I've walked it. I noticed a set fresh set of tire marks cutting across to the south a few yards from here. I'm assuming you heard a vehicle in the distance?" Robert asked.

"I thought so, but with the waves splashing against the rocks, it was hard to tell. I'll check the dock and boats if you want to see where the tracks lead," Nicholas replied.

Nicholas made his way toward the dock. He dropped to his knees, placed his palms on the sand, then leaned down enough to peer underneath the weathered structure. No visible wires and nothing tied to the planks. Waves broke against the pylons as he stood and gazed beyond the ocean. The sun peeked above the horizon displaying a beautiful array of orange, pink and yellow shades. He brushed the sand off his jeans, then slowly walked toward the end of the dock.

Salt air filled his sinuses. Two days and he already missed his beach house in Florida. The murky brown water here lacked the beauty of the clear, emerald-blue water he was used to. A heavy layer of dark stains on the splintered boards were prominent around more bullet holes than Nicholas could count.

He quickly understood Robert's abrupt departure as he recalled the story about the death of his youngest brother, Miguel. This had to be the first time Robert had set foot on the property this close to where his youngest brother was murdered. Carlos, Robert's father had brought Miguel to the property late one night to save him from a blackmail scheme with Miguel's girlfriend and her three brothers. Carlos had expected too much out of his youngest son by placing him in the direct line of fire.

Carlos told Robert that he had buried Miguel at sea. Nicholas stopped at the end of the dock and stared at his reflection on the water. He had no brothers or sisters. Only his cousin, Mitch, but the loss of someone you loved no matter who it might be takes a piece of your life with them. Nicholas had lost his mother, father, and the woman he loved. As he stood there his mind drifted to a verse in Proverbs 27.

19 As water reflects the face, so one's life reflects the heart.

So, Lord, if my life reflects what is held within my heart, the compassion and love I hold now has not always been there. This night has turned out to be a long and broken road to a ghost. Not just a man who can disappear in thin air, but an evil, dangerous man. There are so many who count on me to have the answers. Will I be able to piece it...? Nicholas's prayer trailed off when he gazed beyond his reflection on the surface of the water.

Even at low tide the water appeared to be about four feet deep at the end of the dock. Sediment settled around a large object. He squatted to get a closer look at the motorcycle lying on its side.

Confusion filled his thoughts when he noticed the absence of sand on the wheels and handlebars. Purposely placed instead of being pushed off the end of the dock. Something that big and heavy would disrupt the sand when it fell. Deep in thought he didn't realize Robert was standing next to one of the boats.

"Have you checked the cabins yet?"

Nicholas stood straight up and turned. "No. Don't touch them." In one swift motion, Nicholas pushed off the end plank and leaped. Robert's foot was already in motion. He had leaned toward the deck of the boat when Nicholas hit his chest as if tackling a receiver running toward an end zone on a football field. Planks made a cracking sound when Robert landed on his back with Nicholas across him. Stunned, they both laid still for a moment and listened.

"The boats are wired to blow." Nicholas pushed up on his hands and knees. He took a deep breath, exhaled, then stood before reaching down to give Robert a hand. "Hurry. Let's get the hell out of here."

"Shit. That hurt. You're stronger than you look." Robert turned and followed Nicholas.

Before they reached the end of the dock, the explosion blew them off their feet. As Nicholas hit the shallow, rippling waves, he turned his head to see shattered pieces from the back section of the boat Robert almost stepped on, spray across the water. The second he hit the water's surface Nicholas scrambled to get his feet on solid ground.

Soaking wet, Nicholas trudged toward shore. Quickly scanning the beach area, he spotted Robert face down, not moving.

Nicholas landed in the water on the north side of the dock. Robert ended up on south side where a jetty rock barrier lined the beach and extended out into the water. When he reached Robert, he rolled him on his back. He wasn't breathing and he had a small gash on his forehead.

Without hesitation, Nicholas began resuscitation measures. "Don't you dare fucking die on me. Wake your ass up," Nicholas yelled as he continued to press on Robert's chest. After a few seconds with no change, Nicholas grabbed Robert's shoulders. Once he had him in a sitting position leaning forward, Nicholas used the palm of his hand to hit Robert between his shoulder blades.

Robert coughed, spit water, then gasped for air. Nicholas continued to brace him until Robert moved his hands to the sand. After several breaths Robert cocked his head and said, "Fuck! What happened?"

The sun balanced like an orange slice on the horizon leading the way to a clear, blue sky. White smoke billowed from the bow. Pieces of the dock washed up on shore along with planks from the boat. The boat on the north side, still secured to two posts rocked with the tide. Jagged, broken boards held tight to what remained of the frame.

Nicholas stood as he brushed sand off his knees. "Come on. I'll explain on the way to Monterrey."

"Why Monterrey? Don't we need to find the rest of the refugees?"

"What would make Hasan leave a path of devastation and screw two people who have enough contacts to torture him worse than any terrorist?"

It took a moment for Robert to respond. "A woman."

"Right. Rico's sister, Arlene lives there. Hasan's going to extremes to create a mirage to disappear permanently. We're losing time. That explosion had to be big enough for the Coast Guard and Federal Police in Matamoros to see. I'll drive." Nicholas took off his t-shirt. He squeezed out as much water as possible before shaking it in the wind then slipping it back on.

"Okay, okay, but I'm pretty sure I just died, so give me a second."

"Yeah? Okay. That means I saved your ass."

"I might need stitches for this cut on my head." Robert dabbed it with his shirt tail as he stood.

"Really? Suck it up and get in." Nicholas smiled as he opened the driver's side door.

BOOM! The ground rumbled beneath their feet as Robert ducked down beside the passenger side door. Nicholas used the truck door as a shield. Flames shot high in the air. Shattered boards fell across the hood of the truck and littered the ground around them.

After the debris settled, Nicholas slid behind the steering wheel. "That was no simple homemade bomb. It had to be C-4. Hasan would've been able to set it with a timer. If my theory's correct, Hasan's still close enough to catch."

"Why did you blow the other boat? Robert Reyes had time to board the boat from the time we saw him." Arlene asked as she turned to see smoke appear in her rearview mirror."

Hasan smiled. "Getting rid of all possible evidence."

"Then why take so long to place the motorcycle at the end of the dock?"

"That was a distraction. If Reyes had walked to the end of the dock and looked down to see the bike so perfectly placed, his mind would be preoccupied when he tripped the timer wire. Sixty seconds gave him time to find the package under the instrument dash, but not enough time to get off. You saw him. He was alone when he parked. That's all I needed to know."

"Are you sure he was alone? Why didn't we stay? I wanted to see body parts scattered across the beach for what his family did to mine."

"In that tiny piece of shit truck? No way. Besides, the Coast Guard's too close. I want to be as far away from here as possible before they have time to notify the local authorities. I told you, your anger should be directed at the Garcia Cartel. They owned the property you grew up on, not your father."

Arlene moaned. "He shot the only family I had left. If it hadn't been for Rico, I wouldn't have met you."

"You know how hot headed your brother was. Aiming his .45 at Robert was a stupid mistake."

She sighed. "You're right. He was that way even when we were kids if he didn't get his way. Don't we need to check on the destruction of Gatos?"

"When none of the phones worked in the basement, it triggered a memory from the first time I met Marlon there. He mentioned the basement is soundproof. No wireless service. While you created your movie scene downstairs, I wired two of your blocks of C-4 to the coffee pot timer as a backup plan. We'll see the results on the news."

"You expected Robert to go there first?"

"No. He would do the same thing I would. Notify the police chief. Vito starts his day at five. Your brother said he was a few years ahead of him in school. Rico said Vito showed up every day at the exact same time as if he were a programmed robot. He had Vito's email address. So, your brother scheduled an email two days ago to be delivered at five fifteen this morning. An anonymous tip about a possible hostage situation. It would give Vito just enough time to arrive before six. Why all these questions now?"

"We haven't had five minutes alone together in a week that hasn't been filled with phone calls, meetings, or inventing this extravagant illusion to cover our tracks."

"That sounds about right. Running from the Garcia family is one thing. Creating a broken path Arie will spend years wandering among a massive maze of mirrors trying to figure out which direction I chose had to be extensive. Did Rico know about us?"

"No. Why?" Arlene asked.

185

"Then neither do the Garcia's or the SVR director. How long until we reach Monterrey?"

"Three hours. We should pass the rest of the trucks soon. When is Sanchez supposed to catch up?"

"I'll call him when we reach your house. I need a short nap. Wake me when we arrive."

Hasan reclined the passenger seat of the Mercedes GLA. He closed his eyes and wondered how one married woman could turn his life upside down. He swore off all women the day he left Somalia. *Is it her beauty? Her idea to retire?* The plan to setup her husband, David turned out to be easier than Hasan had anticipated. The death of Rico was not part of their original plan, but it created one less potential issue he had to worry about.

He was performing his final disappearing act. Not even the SVR director would be able to find him. Using Marlon's money for the drugs to pay for plastic surgery had been Arlene's suggestion. The rest would provide them with a comfortable living for a long time. He had finally found a woman who was as evil as he was. *Will she eventually cheat on me?* He fell asleep.

Chapter Forty-Four -- MEX-40D To Monterrey, Mexico

Nicholas dialed Sebastian's number. He listened to three rings before Sebastian answered. "I know where Hasan's headed."

"Where?" Sebastian asked.

"Monterrey. I think he's hooked up with Arlene Moreno. She hid her brother Rico from the Garcia family. We need to get there before they do."

"I just got off the phone with my contact with the Coast Guard. They're near Brownsville and saw the explosions. He is working with the Federal Police in Matamoros to investigate the scene. What about the refugees?"

"Found six of Hasan's men and eight teenage boys about an hour east of Nuevo Laredo. Rita, Sheila, and Diego were taking the boys back to Robert's property and then going to check on Gatos. I haven't heard from them yet."

"Give me your coordinates and I will get a chopper to you. It'll take them about three hours to drive."

"Robert's texting them to you now. You may want to send a cleanup crew to retrieve Hasan's men. Among the bodies, you'll find David Sanchez, Hasan's righthand man. They're about thirty to forty yards from the road and there's a gas station across the street. I need an address for Arlene if you can find out. I don't believe that will be their final destination," Nicholas said.

"I'll handle Hasan's men and text you Moreno's address when I find out." Sebastian clicked off without waiting on a response.

Nicholas parked on the side of the road then turned off the engine. "So, we wait."

"Why here?" Robert asked.

"How many bars do you have on your phone?"

"Three."

"That answers your question. I had one bar on my cell at your property. When I spoke to Sebastian, he faded in and out. So, when I picked up better reception, I figured this was as good a place to wait as any."

"How long you think we'll have to wait?" Robert asked as he opened the truck door and got out.

"Sebastian said he would have emergency transport on alert."

"Then he called Bandit. I gave him the name and number for a high school buddy who went to work for the Federal Police in Matamoros. I haven't talked to him in more than five years, but if Sebastian was able to get in touch with him then we're good to go. So, let's say Hasan teamed up with Arlene to steal the Garcia Cartel's drugs, there's nowhere on Earth they can hide."

"All it takes is plastic surgery and new identities. For all we know they've been planning this escapade for a long time. Do you know anything about where she lives?"

"Yes, if she still lives in the same place. Let me give you a short background on the woman. Just over two years ago, she came to visit her dad and brothers. She came over to talk to my mom and Uncle Frank and offered to distribute our products through central Monterrey for twice our cost at the time. Mom didn't trust her then and we definitely shouldn't trust her now. Back then, she lived in a rural area about forty miles outside the nearest residential subdivisions and commercialized, tourist areas. Something like we have, except on a much smaller scale. Arlene's more like a coordinator to move shipments."

"What about her husband? Do you think she and Hasan collaborated to set him up as an easy target?"

Robert glanced over at Nicholas. "Not until you mentioned it, no. Makes sense if you think they're headed to Monterrey."

Chapter Forty-Five -- Nuevo Laredo, Mexico

An explosion miles away vibrated the windows of Diego's truck. Rita and Sheila turned to see a smoke cloud in the general direction of Gatos.

Rita glanced at the time on the dash. "Six o'clock. Did either of you see wires connected to a timer?"

"I examined them all. The wire to the cell phone you cut and three wires from the black box that connected the explosives inside the canisters," Sheila replied.

"Should we go back?" Diego asked.

"Hell no. We'll check local news reports to see if it was Gatos. I just hope Chief Vito didn't send any of his men there," Rita said as she hit the speed dial button for Nicholas. "Hey. I have you on speaker."

"Good. Did you find anything at Gatos?" Nicholas asked.

"We left about fifteen minutes ago. It may be in a million pieces by now. Just felt the vibrations from an explosion in that general direction. Hasan expected someone to show up. It was a horrific staged scene. There were eleven naked women with small bullet holes at their temples and two men with several holes across their abdomens in the basement. One man at each end and all were hanging from rafters by a noose. Nine bombs were lined up in front of the bodies, but those didn't cause the explosion unless there was something we overlooked. We removed the burn phones and cut the wires to the black box on top. Black spray paint was used to spell out, '*You are too late*'. One letter on the chest of each victim. The men's heads were shaved. The women's hair appeared to be brushed and make-up touched up after their death."

"Hmm. The question is who did the psycho expect? And why go to that extreme?"

"Exactly."

"What about the boats?"

"Hasan had them both wired to blow about five minutes apart. If you found nine, then maybe he used the last one here. The motorcycle he rode was purposely placed at the end of the dock almost like putting it on display. So, my thought is it was just a distraction to keep whoever showed up on the dock long enough for Hasan to blow up the boat. This scenario would work for Gatos too. He may be travelling alone in the Jeep that was here earlier. Diego, can you drive to Monterrey? We need more ammunition for the AK-47s."

"Yes."

"We believe that is where Hasan is headed. Sebastian arranged a chopper for us so we can get there before he does. I've got to go. I hear our ride approaching," Nicholas said as the whirling sound of chopper blades grew louder.

Rita stared at the blank screen. "So, Rico's sister is Hasan's back-up plan. I wonder if he knows that Sanchez is dead yet?"

"It will buy us some time if he doesn't," Diego replied. "We've got to hurry. It's a good two-hour drive from here." His phone vibrated on the console. "It's Marlon."

Rita grabbed the phone and said, "You can't tell him yet. He needs to wait a few more hours."

"My brother's aren't patient men."

"I know. We've had this discussion. I'm not either, but we can't take the chance on losing Hasan. If he disappears, we'll lose every chance of finding the rest of the refugees. I'll hold on to your phone for now."

Diego's brow furrow as he cocked his head toward her. "You don't trust me?"

"Yes, I trust you. I don't trust your automatic reflex to answer a ringing phone."

The silence in the cab of Diego's truck created an air of tension until Sheila spoke. "Diego, Rita's right. If Marlon finds out that Hasan blew up Gatos, he won't wait. He'll try to call him and when Hasan doesn't answer, Marlon will call Barobnakov. I know your family no longer shares ownership in Gatos, but I'm sure that won't stop Marlon from calling his ex-business partner. Hasan will find out one way or the other and then do the math. He'll realize you're not dead."

Diego took a deep breath and exhaled. "Fuck! Okay, okay. Being the youngest with three older brothers and a sister, I've never had anything taken away from me. I'm just say'n I don't like it." He paused and sighed. "But I guess I understand."

He drove around what was left of the cargo truck. The devastation appeared to be a war zone with the sun's brilliant colors in the background. Even with the window up, the strong smell of burned rubber made its way in. He stopped in front of the warehouse and shifted to park. "All three of us don't need to go downstairs to the weapons room."

"I need to pee if we have a two-hour drive ahead of us. I'll leave this box of phones in the office. Can you bring me a couple more clips for this Uzi?" Sheila asked.

"Okay. Do you think we need to check on Billy?" Diego asked.

"No." Rita and Sheila said in unison.

Chapter Forty-Six -- *Valle Alto, Mexico*

Between a winding band of trees and a mountain range was an open field. The medical chopper hovered about six feet off the ground long enough to let Nicholas and Robert jump out. Within seconds it disappeared over the mountain range west of Valle Alto. Beyond the wooded strip of land, a golf course separated them from an exclusive section of Monterrey. From their ariel view before they were dropped off, the upper class, residential neighborhoods appeared to be more than five miles to the east. Arlene's fortress was closer to ten miles further south.

"A landing strip for the rich?" Nicholas asked.

"More like a touch and go for drug smugglers," Robert laughed. "According to Rita's last call, they're about an hour away."

"Have you dried off?"

"Just about, but my head feels like someone wacked me across the forehead with a baseball bat," Robert replied.

"Good thing our ride was a flying clinic. Do we know if Arlene has armed security guards?"

"No. According to local gossip when I still lived in Mexico, her husband worked for the Federal Police before he met her. After they married, he used his contacts to have their house secured as if it were a prison in the middle of nowhere. Ten-foot brick walls are lined with razor wire. Land mines along the interior perimeter. Living off the grid, power comes from solar panels and generators. There's a natural gas tank somewhere on the property and water is from a well."

Nicholas found a narrow trail beyond the tree line close enough to see the open ground between them and the mountains. The well-worn path had a few twists and turns. A dirt road cut across the middle of the long clearing. He could only assume the road was maintained for site seeing tourists. Wind rustled the tall pines. Other than the occasional flutter of bird's wings above, their peaceful walk ended when his stomach grumbled. More than twelve hours passed since dinner the night before.

"Man. That was loud enough for me to hear," Robert said.

Nicholas didn't reply as he stopped short of the road. No cars in sight. He figured it must be a scenic route through the mountains. He paused and glanced both ways. The trail continued across the road, but with several different options instead of just one. "So, what do you think?" Nicholas asked as his phone vibrated.

He read aloud Rita's text message below the aerial photo. "This is the approximate location of Arlene's property. Drone shots from a few months ago. Sebastian acquired from someone named Bandit. Federal Police have had the place under surveillance for about six months. Arlene is their number one suspect in the murder of a Monterrey officer, but they haven't been able to catch her. Hope your instincts are right."

Nicholas turned toward Robert. "Shit. What if I'm wrong?"

"Let's go. Either way, we've got to find out."

Chapter Forty-Seven -- Valle Alto, Mexico

"Wake up." Arlene reached over and nudged Hasan's shoulder.

"Are we there already?" Hasan grumbled.

"Fuck no. Traffic's at a standstill. I need you to get your ass out to see if there's a roadblock ahead."

Calle al Rancho las Palmas was the only paved road that came close to Arlene's property. She could see the box trucks about seven vehicles in front of her but nothing beyond that point. Vehicles were flying passed her in the opposite direction. Beyond a grassy easement, trees lined both sides of the road. If she abandoned her SUV, they could cut through the woods, but the walk would be slow and long. They were out in the open with a cloud free sky, but there was more than one temperature on the rise. Frustration fumed from the pit of her stomach as if lava rose to the top of an erupting volcano.

Hasan raised the seat, rubbed his eyes, then surveyed their surroundings. "How far from here?"

"More than eight miles."

He checked his phone. No missed calls and no reception. "What the fuck? No service."

"The mountain range, trees, and we're out of range to the nearest cell tower. Take your fucking pick," Arlene snapped.

"Your anger will solve no problems. If there's a roadblock, I need to redirect the trucks and the tanker. Do they know we're behind them?"

"If you don't have phone service, what makes you think I do?"

"Yelling at me needs to stop. Now!" Hasan hit the dash with his fist as he cocked his head toward Arlene. "What the fuck have you done? It's no coincidence they're this close to your property."

She squeezed the steering wheel until her knuckles turned white. Arlene took a deep, breath then exhaled. "Not a damn thing. Remember, I've been doing your fucking grunt work for the past few months preparing for this. You need to make them split up. Have them return to the downtown area. They'll have more options to lay low until dark. You're in command. Walk your ass up to the trucks. Do your damn job."

"Why are they ahead of us? You said we would pass them."

"I stopped for gas and something to eat. The drive-thru line took longer than I expected."

Hasan got out and slammed the door. She watched him disappear beyond her view. How was she going to tell him that the police were looking for her? Killing the officer in broad daylight had turned out to be bad judgement on her part. If the Monterrey traffic officer had searched her vehicle, she would already be behind bars. The driver in a passing truck had turned in her vehicle information before she had time to eliminate the tattle tale.

No witness, no proof, but somehow, she didn't feel like she had gotten away with the murder scot-free. The last six months had been hell trying to hide her affair with Hasan from her husband. Slipping in through the underground entrance would have been another problem if David had come home once. *Is it too late to tell him? Is there another witness out there?* Her thoughts were interrupted when Hasan opened the passenger door.

"The fuel truck is in front. There looks to be about twenty vehicles ahead of it. I told him to turn around when the vehicles in front of him move up. Joe will block both lanes to appear like he has an engine issue so the other three can turn around. As soon as you have room, you need to figure out a better route."

"This is it. The only other option is to ditch the Mercedes and cut a path through the woods."

"Fuck."

"You've been here before. You know how isolated my property is. It's either the woods and fly out of here or drive further south and hope we can find a charter that won't ask questions."

"What about the cash and weapons?"

"Wins, losses. Is it worth it to you?" She kept her focus on the vehicles ahead avoiding his stare.

Hasan's brow furrowed. "A million dollars. I'm done riding."

Arlene waited for the first box truck to pass. When the truck in front of her eased forward, she made a quick U-turn. When she glanced at the rearview mirror, other vehicles were doing the same thing. She breathed a sigh of relief when she glanced over at Hasan. He had tilted his head back and closed his eyes. When she saw a break in the trees, she pulled off the road, cut across the grass, and didn't stop until she neared the tree line.

"Let's go. We've got nine miles ahead of us."

Hasan didn't respond. He took off running as she grabbed her purse and .45 automatic. In the console she found a lighter and a hand full of fast-food restaurant napkins. After wiping her prints off the steering wheel and door handles, she twisted the napkins. Her only concern was removing all evidence she had ever been there.

When the police traced the SUV's registration, they would find it belonged to a Rene Rogers in Mexico City. Paying cash at point of sale with one of her five alias packets containing a driver's license, passport, and credit cards made it easy for her to disappear. They were well beyond view of the vehicle when she heard the explosion.

Chapter Forty-Eight -- Monterrey, Mexico

When the forest ended Nicholas and Robert emerged to find a large clearing. A fairly, new wood structure sat outside the ten-foot brick wall. Well-worn truck tracks ended in front of the two sliding hangar doors. From where they stood, the tracks wound around the south side of the house. Nicholas opened his text message from Rita with the aerial photo. Terra-cotta tiles covered the roof of a ranch style house. A large screened in back porch opened at the back gate with a narrow path between the wall and the house. Concrete pavers covered the front yard. An area big enough to hold four large vehicles. Tall prickly pear cactus lined the wall on all sides with gaps for the gates.

"What now?" Robert asked.

"We are at the northwest corner of the property. I don't think anyone's here, but the dirt road leading to her property is on the other side. You think that warehouse is big enough to hold a plane?"

"Yep. A prop plane would easily fit with room to spare."

"That's why they're coming here. We'll split up. How much ammo do you have?"

"A full clip in my .45 and maybe half in the AK-47."

Nicholas checked his Glock. "I have about the same. You go around front. Check the gate and meet me at the building in the back."

"Okay. Are you thinking they'll arrive from the dirt road?"

"Yes. Run back this way if you hear anything."

He waited for Robert to disappear beyond the northeast wall then ran across the open field to the red brick wall. He paused and listened. Nothing except the rustling of tree limbs with the occasional warm breeze. *Are the rest of the missing trucks on their way here too? How many men does Hasan have left? Does he plan to take Marlon's drugs somewhere for delivery? Where are the female refugees?*

Nicholas shut down the questions he had no answers for. With his back against the warm bricks, he sidestepped until he reached the iron gate. He quickly searched the area. The mountains were less than a hundred yards away. If Arlene had lived here most of her adult life, she would know every possible path of escape.

As he started toward the building, he noticed a door at the south corner. The closer to the door he came, he noticed it stood slightly ajar. The dark stained door blended with the siding perfectly. If it hadn't been partially open, he would've never noticed it. When he heard footsteps approach from behind, Nicholas put a finger to his lips. He removed the Glock from his shoulder holster, then eased closer. Robert lined up behind him. Nicholas paused with his back flat against the frame and listened. A loud clanging sound as if metal against metal echoed through the narrow gap before a whiff of jet fuel reached their noses.

Nicholas whispered, "I'll go right, you go left."

He crouched then moved close enough to swing the door wide open. It hit the wall and returned to its original position before Nicholas opened the door. As he eased right of the frame, Robert went left with the AK-47 in hand. From the instant Robert crossed the threshold, he fanned the muzzle clockwise unloading what was left in the magazine. When it was empty, he slung it across the floor before dropping to a squatting position.

Seconds passed as they waited for the dust to settle. Nicholas blinked a few times before his eyes adjusted to the dim lighting. Nothing moved. The only light streamed in from the gap between the door and frame between them. A wet spot under the plane formed. As it increased in size, so did the jet fuel, fumes. The wide spray of ammunition hit the gas can next to a TBM 900 turbo prop, but no human movement in sight. The back wall had an array of lawn and mechanical tools hanging from hooks above a long worktable. Next to the table was a riding lawnmower. Both front tires were flat.

Nicholas kept his weapon out in front and his back to the wall behind him as he moved toward the front of the plane. He wondered how both his targets disappeared until the sound of a shotgun being cocked reached his ears. He turned to see Robert with the barrel of a twelve-gauge shotgun against the side of his head as the outline of a woman's figure emerged from the dark corner.

"Drop your weapon or he dies," Arlene said. She kicked the door open and stepped into the light.

Behind her were an assortment of rakes, shovels, and brooms. Her long, black hair hung in a braid across her shoulder. Wearing a black polo, black jeans, and black knee-high boots, she easily blended in.

"If I drop my weapon, we both die."

"You have five seconds. One…"

Without taking his eyes off her, Nicholas swung his arm around and fired before she said two. The bullet hit near her collar bone next to the butt of the shotgun. Nicholas didn't stop to assess the situation. He lunged, knocked Robert off his feet, out of the line of fire, and then jerked the twelve-gauge from Arlene's tight grip. After letting go, she grabbed her shoulder, and fell back a couple of steps before landing against the sharp corner of the worktable.

She groaned and struggled to keep her balance. Robert had his hands around her ankles as she reached for the .45 automatic in her shoulder holster. When her back landed against the cement floor, the Smith and Wesson slid across the smooth, concrete surface. Nicholas kicked it out of her reach as he pivoted around with the shotgun in one hand and his Glock in the other. He ducked between the riding lawnmower and the table when the plane wobbled slightly.

"Get her the hell out of here." Nicholas quickly scanned the top of the table. He tossed a braided rope toward Robert. "Get her as far away from here as possible. Hasan's on the plane."

"The fucking bastard's leaving me. Let me go. I'll help you."

"I don't need your kind of help," Robert replied.

"You're supposed to be dead. You son-of-a-bitch, I'm bleeding."

She jerked back and forth desperately trying to free herself. As the sliding doors began to open, Nicholas followed the cable connection to a large battery unit resting on a shelf near the rafters above. Too far away. No time to take out the power source.

Blowing out the tires would not prevent take off, but if Hasan had a parachute, he could jump anywhere and disappear. Nicholas ran to the doorway. He paused long enough to fire the shotgun once at the puddle of fuel. Within a few seconds he was back at the north corner of the brick wall enclosing Arlene's house.

Robert had Arlene against the wall on her stomach securing her hands and ankles. Nicholas peeked around the corner in time to see Hasan emerge from the hangar doors on a four-wheeler ATV. Hasan paused long enough to toss something inside the hangar. All Arlene's screams and pleas to Hasan were no incentive for the man to turn around.

"Hand grenade. Duck," Nicholas yelled as he crouched down shielding his neck and back of his head with his arms.

BOOM. After pieces of debris from the warehouse stopped falling around them, Nicholas stood. From what he could tell, the damage appeared to be contained to a corner of the hangar. A damaged workbench, the hangar doors on the ground, and a portion of the wall, but the main structure still intact. As he moved closer, puffs of white smoke drifted over an empty water bottle next to the gas can. In the distance the sound of an engine drifted further away with each passing second.

Nicholas walked over to where Arlene continued to scream. He gently pressed his running shoe against her bloody shoulder. "Shut the fuck up or I press harder. Do you have a vehicle inside this compound?"

"You're hurting me. I need medical attention."

"A clean shot. Entry and exit wounds. You'll live. Now, answer my question." He took his foot off, squatted then rolled her onto her back.

"Fuck you." Arlene spat at him.

He put the muzzle of his Glock against her abdomen as he wiped saliva off his cheek with the back of his hand. "You know a gut shot is a slow and painful and death. You've run out of time. I've run out of patience."

"Yes…yes."

"Robert, help me drag this worthless piece of shit to the front gate."

"Happy to."

They each grabbed an arm and pulled Arlene between them to the front gate. Nicholas punched in the code as she recited six digits. He pushed open the iron gate. A Corvette, Ram truck, and Jaguar XE were lined up in front of the covered porch.

"Where's the key for the Jag?"

"Untie me and I'll drive."

"Not happening. So, die here or start talking."

"In the console."

"Robert, you drive. I'll secure her in the trunk."

"Got it."

Robert opened the trunk then climbed behind the wheel while Nicholas picked Arlene up and shoved her in the trunk. By the time Robert had the car in reverse, almost ten minutes had slipped away. Hasan could be anywhere, but on a four-wheeler, his directions were limited. Nicholas tapped on the trunk three times, stepped back, and watched Robert drive away.

Chapter Forty-Nine -- Monterrey, Mexico

After Robert headed west down the only road that accessed Arlene's property, Nicholas dialed Rita's cell number. After the first ring she answered.

"Where are you?" Nicholas asked.

"Following the three box trucks. We turned around after they passed us heading back toward downtown Monterrey. Sebastian's working with Robert's friend to coordinate the Federal Police to intercept. I'm afraid if we lose sight of them, they'll vanish downtown somewhere. You got Hasan?"

"He managed to get away on a four-wheeler. My guess is he'll return for the plane. From what I can recall, this dirt road ends at Cerro de la Silla. Robert will wait for you there."

"Got to go. Sebastian's calling. I'll call Robert when we're headed that way," Rita said.

Nicholas clicked off. He muted his phone then put it in his t-shirt pocket. He walked up on the front porch and listened. The front gate stood wide open, but the only sound reaching his ears was the soft rustling of tree limbs. The brick walls were too tall to see over. He pondered whether, or not Hasan would dump the four-wheeler and return on foot.

Tall, green prickly cacti lined the wall's interior perimeter. With barely two feet between the house and the thorny plants, he kept close to the house until he reached the back gate. Whether or not there were land mines was not a fact he cared to verify. He unlocked the door then opened it wide enough to see the warehouse door. About twenty-five feet of open ground with no place to hide. As he stared at the bare path between him and the warehouse door, his mind drifted back to the words his dad had said one cold winter day they spent in a tree stand.

"Keep your focus on the target in front of you as you reflect on your knowledge of the road behind you. There's nothing you can do about what you left behind, but it can help guide you beyond the obstacles on the path ahead."

Knowledge of the past. Knowledge of the past. Hmm? My past or Hasan's past? A ghost that can disappear in a crowd. A man desperate and on the run. If I were him, I'd return, take the plane, and return to Somalia. Nicholas scanned the area around him. He needed to see more of the area before crossing the open field. As he held onto the gate, he recalled the front gate opened outward.

Nicholas left the door slightly ajar and started running. He ran out the front gate, stayed close to the wall until he reached the northeast corner. A clear, open field and no sound of an ATV approaching. He ran as fast as he could to the front of the warehouse where the huge aluminum doors lay on the ground. No sign of any movement. Seconds ticked away as he searched the warehouse. Nothing. The grenade explosion had created Hasan's smoke screen but that was gone. Nicholas stepped up to the open door on the turbo prop with his Glock ready to fire.

Chapter Fifty -- Monterrey, Mexico

Hasan left the dirt road behind when he found a break between two large pines. It didn't take long before he found himself at a dead end. Trees became too wide and too close together to maneuver any further. He checked the bars on his cell. No service. Desperation sent his mind searching for one direction out. *How did a foolproof plan fall completely apart?* He climbed off and walked toward the road.

Arlene double-crossed him, but that didn't matter anymore. As he walked back to the tree line, he recalled the moment she confessed her teenage crush. At fourteen, she had quit school when Robert Reyes graduated high school. Watching Robert supervise field workers had seemed more important at the time. Arlene's detailed description of how his sweat glistened like sparkling diamonds as it drizzled down his bare back turned his stomach. Her aspirations of becoming part of the Reyes family one day came to a crashing halt when he told her he would shoot her out of the security tower next time he caught her stalking him.

Did she really cry for weeks? Did she lie about his rebuttal? A strong woman would never let any man threaten her like that. No way two men would overtake her that easy. If she colluded with Reyes to make me the fall man with the Garcia family, she can rot in Hell. Who was the other man? Where did he come from? Must be one of her transporters. Hasan's thoughts drifted when he heard a vehicle approach. He reached the tree line in time to see Arlene's Jaguar zoom by.

Hasan had a million dollars in his backpack, two grenades on his belt, and an AK-47 strapped across his shoulder. He returned to the ATV. Arlene's two biggest mistakes were trusting him and underestimating his ability to disappear. *Leaving the refugees and drugs behind was her deception and decision, so I can blame all this on her. She worked with Reyes will make a believable alibi. I can blame Reyes for Rico and Diego's deaths. The destruction of Gatos was done by her without my knowledge.*

He backed up and returned to the dirt road. Confident that he had a new plan and a rock-solid alibi, he realized he just compared Arlene to his mother. His love for both women blinded him to their lies, deceit, and betrayal. As he approached the open field between the back of Arlene's house and the warehouse, he stopped and shut off the engine. Walls were closing in, and he needed to get as far away from Monterrey as possible.

He checked his phone once again to find the same results. *Is there wireless service for the satellite phone on the plane?* He kicked himself for not thinking of that before. *Where is Sanchez? Stuck in the traffic jam?* Hasan searched the area as he listened for anything out of place. The front gate stood wide open, but he expected that. He started the ATV and headed toward the plane.

*****

The TBM900 door opened at the pilot's seat. The six-passenger turbo prop equipped with the Garman G1000 avionics integrated system had a perfect view of the grassy runway ahead. The cockpit still had a new leather smell. Nicholas removed the rubber band from his hair and ran his fingers through it. Using the tail of his t-shirt, he wiped sweat off his face. Two days with no sleep. Counting on backup to arrive in time wasn't a viable option. Hasan would return sooner more so than later.

Sebastian wanted Hasan alive but the odds on that happening were dropping faster by the minute. Setting up his sniper rifle from a roof top or a perch in a nearby tree would require too much time. The only information he needed out of the Somalian was the location of the young teens. *If there were only twelve bombs, then all are accounted for if the last one was used at Gatos or on one of the boats. Why use all of them? How much were they worth on the black market? Were the bombs for Barobnakov?*

A small cooler sat between the two bucket seats. He checked the contents to find four bottles of water. He opened one, poured half the bottle over his face then drank the rest. He scanned the plane for an optimal hiding spot, but Hasan would detect his presence before boarding. He climbed out and checked the immediate area around him. The rafters above were his only option. From the top of the plane, they were in reach without a ladder.

Taking a chance on calling Robert, Rita, or even Sheila would be too risky. Nicholas closed his eyes and started to pray for guidance when he heard an engine rumble. Hasan had a keen sense of danger, but if he assumed the danger left in the Jaguar and suffered from a lack of sleep, then maybe Nicholas had a slight advantage. He holstered his Glock, slipped the strap holding the AK-47 off his shoulder, and balanced the barrel between two metal rafters.

The sun's glare bounced off the shiny aluminum doors on the ground ahead. He contemplated several scenarios as to the outcome of this long battle as he waited. Nicholas readied for the final round. *Tic tock, tic tock.* Seconds seemed to drag out in slow motion as the four-wheeler appeared within his site.

Before Hasan came to a complete stop, Nicholas fired twice. One bullet hit Hasan's right hand on the handlebar, the other grazed his left shoulder. Hasan slid off the four-wheeler and ducked behind it. With his bleeding hand, Hasan removed the .45 automatic from his shoulder holster and returned fire, but Nicholas had left the AK-47 hanging between the beams and dropped to the roof of the plane. As he jumped off the wing, he fired once striking the gas tank, but it was too late. Hasan was on the move and out of sight.

Hasan scrambled to his feet heading toward the back gate of Arlene's house. He didn't look back as flames engulfed the ATV. Nicholas followed. Before Hasan opened the iron gate, Nicholas fired again hitting Hasan's thigh. As he fell, Hasan lost his grip on the handgun then jerked one of the grenades off his belt as he hit the ground. Before he removed the pin, Nicholas snatched it from his hand and threw it as hard as he could across the open field. Within seconds, he kicked the .45 out of Hasan's immediate reach.

When Nicholas put a knee on Hasan's chest and aimed his Glock, Hasan swung his arm, missed his face by inches but knocked the gun from his hand. Nicholas quickly regained the advantage when he grabbed Hasan's wrist and twisted it with both hands until Hasan's left arm popped out of its socket.

Hasan exhaled a loud moan when Nicholas dropped the limp arm. "Move again and die here." He bent over and removed the last grenade then tossed it near the other one. After he pulled Hasan into a sitting position, then proceeded to drag him through the gate and around to the front of the house by his collar.

"Who the fuck are you?"

"Nicholas Jacobson."

"I'm bleeding and in pain. Fuck! Will you stop?" Hasan groaned.

"No." He continued to drag Hasan until they reached the front yard. Nicholas dropped Hasan between the porch and the red Corvette. After removing his Glock and pointing it directly at Hasan, he backed up to the porch steps and sat down.

Hasan took several deep breaths. The backpack strapped to his shoulders like a parachute added pressure to both shoulders. Not only was his left shoulder dislocated, one of Nicholas's bullets had removed a small chunk of flesh out of it. He used his right hand to adjust his left arm enough to relieve some of the pressure.

"Can I stand long enough to pop my shoulder back in place?" Hasan lifted his right hand enough to assess the bleeding gap below his thumb knuckle.

"Your pain doesn't' concern me. Unfortunately, your wounds are not bad enough for you to bleed to death. I wanted to make sure you were adequately distracted."

"Smart man, Mr. Jacobson. I understand your lack of trust. Can I adjust my sitting position?"

"Make any stupid moves, accidental or not, I shoot to kill."

Hasan grunted several times as he leaned the backpack against the front of the Corvette. Sweat dripped from his jawline as he returned Nicholas's stare. "Do I know you?"

"We've never met."

"Who do you work for?"

"No one. I'm helping a friend."

"Your friend's name?"

"Billy Wright." Nicholas could almost see the gears churning in Hasan's head.

"Son of Billy Bowlegs Osceola Lewis?"

"Yep."

"I was told Wright worked with a team in New Orleans. Someone by the name of Stickler? He lives somewhere around Tampa. Had long hair and a scar on his face last time I saw him."

"No. Last time you saw him, you drugged him and left him to die in the cab of a cargo truck propped up next to a bomb. By the time the bomb exploded, you were catching a ride with your high school buddy, Sanchez."

Hasan's eyes widened. "How do you know?"

"I was the one who pulled Wright to safety before you blew the truck into a million pieces." He watched Hasan's eyes dart left and right then stop on his boots. "Don't even think of trying to reach the knives in your boots. You'll be dead before you lean forward."

Hasan's focus drifted back to Nicholas. "I was right. Robert Reyes is alive."

"Yes."

"How did you know I would come here?"

"Process of elimination. You intentionally placed Arlene's husband in Texas knowing the border patrol would show up. Then you tried and failed to kill Robert and Diego."

"No proof."

"Keep believing that. Robert will return shortly. Your girlfriend is in the trunk of the Jaguar." Nicholas smiled. "I'd be willing to bet she'll turn State's evidence and sing like a bird to shorten her time behind bars."

Nicholas kept his gaze on Hasan. One tiny diversion could shift the table of control. He steadied his Glock as he put his elbows on his knees. An uncomfortable silence lingered. He wondered if the Somalian was contemplating his options like tearing down the web of a spider one thread at a time.

Chapter Fifty-One -- Monterrey, Mexico

"If you get any closer to the back of that tanker and he slams on his brakes, we'll be the marshmallows at a bon-fire." Rita hung on tight to the passenger door.

Diego let up slightly on the gas pedal. "You think you can do a better job?"

She took a deep breath and sighed. "No. Sorry for snapping. I have control issues."

"I've noticed," Sheila interjected from the back seat. I hear sirens approaching. Sounds like both directions." She turned to see four police vehicles gaining ground.

Diego had kept up with the short convoy of trucks when they caught up to them near Calle al Rancho las Palmas. Now, less than five miles from the exit ramps leading to the busy city streets, they were running out of pavement. If the trucks exited the ramp, they could disappear within seconds unless Monterrey's finest had the next two exits covered.

Rita's phone rang. She didn't recognize the number but answered. "Hello."

"Ms. Livingston, this is Bandit. Mr. Sebastian gave me your number. You can back off now. I've been told my comrades have enough manpower behind you and in front of you to take over."

"Thank you and please keep me updated on the status. I'm afraid there are several innocent girls in the back of one of the trucks."

"Yes ma'am. Will do." Bandit clicked off.

Rita tucked her phone back in her shirt pocket. "Okay Diego, turn around and head back to Arlene's. Robert's waiting on us."

"Have you talked to him?" Diego asked as he transitioned to the right lane and exited the highway.

"I tried. Goes directly to voicemail. He probably has no reception."

"You know I hate not being able to be there when the police surround the trucks. I feel like we did all the work and will never see the final showdown," Sheila said.

"Me too, but they have jurisdiction, we don't," Rita said.

"It's like playing the whole football game as quarterback until the coach puts in the second-string quarterback after the two-minute warning," Diego said.

"Sounds like you speak from experience," Sheila replied.

"Yep. The guy got credit for winning the game. I quit the team after that. Coach was pissed. Said I was being childish."

"I would've done the same thing," Rita said as she gazed out the window.

Traffic leaving the city wasn't half as bad as the number of vehicles heading toward the tall skyscrapers. They had been a step behind Hasan and his team for almost two days. She wondered if Nicholas and Robert had captured him or if Hasan managed to disappear again. *What will happen to the innocent kids? Sex trafficking along all the border states and Mexico has got to be way higher than what's reported. Will they fall through the so-called cracks somewhere along the bureaucratic process?*

The two days seemed more like a month with all that had happened. The chance of finding Rico alive under all the rubble grew closer to impossible with each passing hour. Rita glanced over at Diego. *He's not the youngest brother of a large cocaine cartel anymore. He's a father, a husband, and now a friend.* Her thoughts were interrupted when she heard Sheila snoring in the back. Rita peeked around the headrest and smiled. Sheila's head lay against the window with her mouth wide open.

Diego laughed. "She sounds like a grunting pig."

"Good thing she's not awake to hear you say that. How are you feeling? Need me to drive?"

"I'm good. Drank one of those high-octane Monster drinks when we stopped for gas. We're getting close to the dirt road where Robert's supposed to be. What do we do if he's not there?"

"Assume the backup plan is to end up at Arlene's house. I know that as long as it's been, I would've grown tired of waiting," Rita said.

"I can relate. There's another energy drink in the console if you want it."

"Thanks."

Chapter Fifty-Two -- Monterrey, Mexico

Robert slowed and veered off the dirt road onto the grass about halfway to Calle al Rancho las Palmas. He checked his phone. No service. Listening to the banging in the trunk, he wondered how she could make so much noise. The braided rope wrapped around her ankles were double knotted with the opposite end binding her wrists together the same way. *She barely has a foot of leeway between her feet and hands. Did she figure out a way to untie the knots? A knife, but where?*

Robert yelled, "Shut the fuck up." He pointed his .45 toward where her kicking appeared to vibrate the seat and fired. Silence at last. She stopped kicking. "If you kick the seat one more time, I will add several more holes to your body before I open the trunk to see if you survived."

He opened the door and got out. After a few deep breaths of air, he leaned against the passenger door. He had forgotten how peaceful and beautiful this area of Mexico was. He recalled the Parque Ecologico Chipinque. It had to be less than fifty miles north of where he stood. A fond memory of his mom taking four kids camping for a summer vacation. No smog, no city traffic, and no Abid Hasan. With his father, Carlos Reyes serving a life sentence at Huntsville State Prison, and being the oldest, he picked up the slack.

He lost track of how long it had been since he left Nicholas alone at Arlene's house. *Has lack of sleep affected my memory? No. If Bandit handled coordination with Monterrey law enforcement, Diego should be headed this way. Open the trunk and check on Arlene? No.* Robert allowed his thoughts to drift. Seeing Rita with no real alone time together made him ache inside. The one night at the compound, they were both too tired to even cuddle. He inhaled the fresh air as if he could almost smell her perfume. *What would she say if I ask her to marry me? Does she still need more time?*

When the loud banging noise returned, Robert glanced both ways down the road then sat behind the wheel. He returned the silenced .45 to his shoulder holster then started the engine. He had to do something, and waiting wasn't it. Nicholas might need help with Hasan if the Somalian had returned.

*****

Nicholas stood and leaned against the post supporting the roof covering the porch. Hasan appeared to be assessing his wounds. One bullet remained in his thigh, but his greatest pain had to be the dislocated shoulder. Nicholas noticed Hasan wince every time he moved. He compared the man he located for the Garcia family many years ago to the worthless lump on the ground. Hasan's short military style hair cut had sprouts of grey as did his mustache and beard.

Hasan broke the silence. "Arlene is an employee. She is not my girlfriend. Anything she says will be lies. She has no evidence or eyewitnesses to confirm."

"Maybe not, but I'm sure Billy can put you away for life. I heard Mexico's prison system makes U.S. prisons look like bed and breakfast inns."

"I will never go to prison. Marlon will make sure of that."

"When Diego tells his brothers that you tried to kill him combined with the fact you blew up the old Greyson house…I doubt it."

Hasan glared at Nicholas. "How do you know so much about the Garcia Cartel?"

"A long time ago, I completed contract work for their older brother, Marcus. I hunted you down for them. I assumed back then that you sensed danger when you disappeared among the straw market vendors."

Hasan groaned. A chunk of skin missing from under his right thumb knuckle and shoulder, a dislocated left shoulder, and a bullet lodged in his thigh had to be painful. Nicholas recalled a conversation he had with his dad one night when Micha returned from a long assignment. His father always made a point to stop in his room, no matter what time to kiss Nicholas on the forehead and tell him he loved him. This time Micha's hand was bandaged.

"Minor scratch. You know son, pain is controlled by the brain. If you believe it hurts, then it does. If you shut the pain away and concentrate on something more important, like the ones you love, the pain subsides. That's where the term, mind over matter came from. You don't feel the pain of a cut until you see the blood. Then your brain tells you it should hurt."

Nicholas smiled at the thought until the sound of a vehicle getting closer reached his ears. Keeping the Glock aimed at Hasan's forehead, he stepped off the porch.

Chapter Fifty-Three -- Monterrey, Mexico

"I see you caught the bastard," Robert said as he shut the car door.

"Yep. What's the banging noise?"

"Arlene."

Nicholas used the Glock to point toward Hasan's feet. "I'm pretty sure he has knives in his boots. I'll feel safer if you will remove them while I make sure he doesn't do anything stupid."

Robert kneeled at Hasan's feet. He removed two six-inch switch blades from each boot, one from his BDU pants side pockets and a small .22. "Saving these for later? Maybe if you had answered my questions last night, you wouldn't be this deep in dog shit."

As he stood, Robert tucked the knives and .22 in his back pockets. "What about Arlene? I think she has a knife. By the pounding she's been making, she could've cut the rope around her ankles. Don't know about her wrists."

218

"Leave her until the others get here. Even if she busts out, bringing a knife to a gunfight never works." Nicholas removed his cell from his pocket and tossed it to Robert.

Robert laughed. "Glad to see you still have a since of humor."

"This one is the one Sebastian gave me. It should have service. Call Rita and find out ETA."

Hasan cocked his head. "I recognize that name. He's FBI. You have no jurisdiction here."

"Let's just say, we're giving the Federal Police a helping hand for the benefit of both countries. The refugees may not be American, but the two vans you decided to set on fire with the drivers strapped to the steering wheels were on loan by Border Patrol," Nicholas replied.

Robert sent Rita a text and waited for a response. "According to her Waze app, about fifteen minutes."

The banging from the Jaguar's trunk stopped. Robert's and Nicholas's gaze drifted to the trunk. As it opened, a weapon was fired from inside, Nicholas moved toward the front of the vehicle. Before Robert moved, Hasan grabbed his leg with his right-hand knocking Robert off his feet. Arlene had climbed out of the trunk, ducked, and moved to the far side of the Corvette before Nicholas located her position. She fired two more shots in his direction then moved next to Hasan. She aimed her Browning automatic at Robert.

"Okay whoever you are, toss your weapon over here or I'll shoot Mr. Reyes," Arlene said.

Nicholas stood with his Glock pointed at Arlene's head. He stepped off the porch then backed up a couple of steps without dropping his stare. "Same scenario as before. I can only assume you forgot. I give you my weapon, you kill us both. If you fire one more bullet, I'll do the same." He kept his eyes locked on her. One split second is all he needed for her to look away. The bullet wound to her shoulder no longer showed signs of bleeding, but it had to hurt.

"How did you get a weapon?" Robert asked.

"I'm a drug distributor, Asshole. I have weapons hid in all my vehicles including the switchblade I used to cut the fucking rope. Now, remove that .45 from your holster nice and slow then toss it toward Hasan." Arlene continued to stare at Nicholas. She never glanced down at Robert.

"My left shoulder is disjointed. Give me a hand," Hasan demanded.

"I'm injured too, but have you asked how I'm doing? No. I should leave your ass here the way you took off and left me."

"Unlike me, I knew they wouldn't kill you. I had a plan. I came back to get you. Assessing the situation from a distance seemed to be the smart thing to do."

"Yeah? Okay. He's lying," Robert said as he sat up but didn't remove his .45.

Arlene didn't waiver her stare as she swapped the Browning to her left hand. She held out her right. Hasan pulled himself into a standing position, limped over to the porch, then banged his arm against the post. He let out a loud moan took a deep breath and did it again. Nicholas counted on Hasan's injuries to slow him down, but Arlene's shoulder wound didn't appear to affect her at all. Nicholas wondered if her anger toward Hasan made her forget Robert had a .45. *Hasan doesn't have a weapon, so why didn't he grab it when he stood?*

"We're at a standoff. So, we're taking him with us. Stand up Robert."

Hasan opened the driver's side door on the Corvette. As he sat behind the wheel, he said, "Get in. Let's get out of here. FBI reinforcements are on the way."

The second Arlene's focus shifted to open the passenger side door her aim toward Robert's forehead dropped. Nicholas fired then ducked. As the Corvette roared to life, Robert jumped to his feet, but Hasan already shifted to reverse. With a bullet between her eyes, Arlene slid off the hood as Hasan backed up. Nicholas unloaded his Glock at the moving target. His bullets ricocheted off the bulletproof glass as if they were tiny brass pellets from a BB gun. When the back wheels hit dirt, Hasan created a huge dust cloud allowing the back wheels to spin in place before releasing the brake. Instead of heading west down the road, Nicholas and Robert listened as Hasan circled toward the rear of the house.

Chapter Fifty-Four -- Monterrey, Mexico

Nicholas opened the driver's door to the Jaguar and climbed behind the wheel. Arlene lay in a crumpled pile on her side with a tight grip to the Browning in her left hand. Robert pulled the handgun from Arlene's grip then rushed to get in the passenger seat before Nicholas shifted to reverse. By the time they reached the plane, the Corvette had disappeared. They followed the fresh tracks toward a gap in the woods. When they reached the abandoned Corvette, the driver's side door had been left open. Nicholas shut off the engine and they both got out.

"You hear anything?"

"Not a damn thing," Robert replied.

"If I were him, I would head toward the mountain range. I'm sure he feels the walls closing in. The gashes on his right hand and shoulder are minor, but the bullet in his thigh will need to be removed."

"You want to chase him?"

"No. Too many opportunities for him to hide. He has the advantage here. We'd be dead before we see him. Underbrush around here is really thick," Nicholas removed his phone. He sent Sebastian their current coordinates and his guess of Hasan's direction.

"That's probably why we don't hear him now. I'll follow you in the Vette. No sense in leaving it here for him to return to." Robert checked the ignition. "Never mind. The bastard took the keys."

"Don't you have a knife or two in your pocket?"

"Lack of sleep. My brain's a little fuzzy," Robert replied as he removed one from his back pocket. He jabbed holes in the front and back driver's side tires. "What about the plane? You think he's trying to outrun us?"

"Yes. Next on my list. Let's go." Nicholas got behind the wheel of the Jaguar and started the engine." By the time he reached open field, the turbo prop was rolling toward the grassy runway. Nicholas pressed the gas pedal to the floor.

"Fuck! So much for heading to the mountains on foot. The bastard backtracked while we debated on what to do."

Robert rolled down the window, aimed in the direction of the turbo prop, then proceeded to empty the clip. They were too far away. Nicholas stopped as Hasan set out over the trees toward the mountains. After sending Sebastian the tail number, he returned to Arlene's house.

"Backup plan, to backup plan, to flying out of here by the seat of his pants. The fucking Somalian is still one backup plan ahead of us." Nicholas took a deep breath of air and sighed.

Chapter Fifty-Five -- Monterrey, Mexico

Diego leaned against the support beam on the porch. Sheila and Rita sat on the steps next to him as Nicholas parked in front of them. They had left Arlene on the ground.

"We watched your ghost fly away," Diego said as Nicholas and Robert walked up.

"He has nowhere to hide. Sebastian will find him. So, I'm assuming Monterrey's finest took over?" Nicholas asked.

"Yes. Robert's friend, Bandit called to let us know they would assume pursuit. What does Sebastian want us to do now?" Rita asked.

"I haven't spoken to him. Just sent him the tail number for the prop. Diego, have you spoken to Marlon?"

"No. When I had a chance, I had no reception."

"You said you had pictures of Gatos?"

Rita turned to Sheila sitting next to her. "You want to show them while I refresh their memories?"

"Good idea," Sheila replied as she removed her cell and walked over to where Robert and Nicholas stood.

"By the time we got there, it was too late. Nine bombs were rigged to blow. Eleven naked women between two men with their guts hanging out over their underwear. All were strung up from their neck and dangled from the rafters. Estimated T.O.D. will most likely coincide with Hasan's disappearance last night. The women had been meticulously shot. Barrel flush against their temple. Makeup and hair touched up after the fact. The men's heads were shaved."

"I found a .22 in Hasan's pocket," Robert said.

"My guess is that's the murder weapon. He didn't do it alone. We're assuming Sanchez and his team assisted before we found them. Sheila and I disconnected the phones from the bombs, put them in a box before leaving the scene as it was. That's about it. Except, shortly after we left Gatos, the phones started ringing. We didn't answer them, but Hasan must've had something wired upstairs."

"What do the painted letters mean?" Robert asked.

"Hasan expected someone to show up," Rita replied.

Nicholas's phone dinged. He read the text out loud. "Have a chopper on its way. Need you, Robert, Sheila, and Rita to catch a ride. Keeping track of Hasan. Tell Diego to head home."

Before he finished the sound of whirling chopper blades grew closer. "Diego, when you get home, help Billy and the boys search for Rico. There may be a dim chance he survived. Sheila and Rita stuffed him in the storage closet under the master bedroom. You will have a better idea of where to start."

"Shit. I forgot about him. What are we going to do about his sister?"

"Monterrey's problem. Let's check the trunks on both these vehicles. I'm out of ammunition. Did you bring some?"

"Yes. A Browning, two AK-47s with extra clips, and clips for the Uzi's." As Diego drove away, the four of them loaded onto the chopper and headed west. The same pilot, Bailey brought provisions with him. Water, energy drinks and power bars. More important, he had extra ammunition for their Glocks.

"Your friend Bandit had a drone pick up your target's tail. Plane has been ditched beyond the mountain range. Mr. Reyes, Bandit is sending you the last coordinates of where contact with the drone was lost. I'm to drop you there," Bailey said.

After the short flight over the mountains, they found scattered pieces of black plastic near the empty turbo prop. Nicholas glanced inside the open, pilot's door. The bottles of water were gone. Robert, Rita, and Sheila searched the immediate area around them. Robert found fresh boot prints in sandy patches surrounded by weeds leading toward a band of trees. Thick underbrush intertwined among the tall pines. Not much different from the landscape around Arlene's house.

Nicholas jumped off the wing. "I'm assuming all these pieces of plastic belong to the drone Bailey mentioned. Looks like Hasan shot it down then stomped on it."

"It appears the man has anger issues," Robert said.

"The way Hasan protected his backpack I'm guessing it's filled with cash and provisions. It was packed solid. He's added three sixteen-ounce bottles of water. With the bullet in his thigh, we may have a chance to catch him. Robert, you and Rita, head south. See if you can pick up his trail. He may be looking to hitch a ride from a passing tourist on the main road. Sheila and I will check north. Rita, text if you find him. I'll do the same."

Chapter Fifty-Six -- Monterrey, Mexico

Hasan leaned against a boulder, let the backpack slide off his shoulders to the ground, and removed a bottle of water and a pair of binoculars. Between the limbs of two trees, he watched the chopper hover long enough for Robert, the FBI agent, some woman he didn't recognize, and the so-called friend of Billy Wright. *Blondie must work with Livingston.*

When two went north of him, and two ran south, he took a deep breath and exhaled. He was almost a mile from the road that cut through the mountain range. The bullet lodged deep in his thigh throbbed, but at least the pain from his dislocated shoulder had subsided. He tried to retrace his steps as to where his plan turned sideways. Questions began to bombard his brain. *How did a clean-*

cut guy like Jacobson become friends with Wright? Why did Wright end up on that van? His lies were perfect.

The nagging jolts of pain from his thigh wound remained tolerable. He checked the gash between his knuckles. The bleeding had stopped. Flying the turbo prop had been a mistake. Returning to Tijuana on a quarter tank of gas wasn't possible. He had no bars on his phone, no help coming, and needed a viable escape option. *Arlene had contacts here, I don't.*

He climbed up on the boulder. Rocks on both sides and a mountain behind him offered little protection. If all four of his pursuers surrounded him, he would run out of ammunition before they did. For the first time his opponents had him cornered. Eventually, the Federales would show up.

Hasan removed his baseball cap and ran his hand across the short stubbles on his head. If he had to, he could climb the massive stones to reach the top. He checked his perimeter through the binoculars once more then let them dangle from his neck. Soaked in sweat with the tree canopies sheltering him from the noonday sun, a chill washed over him. *Is it from the damp breeze or fear of losing?*

He could only recall one loss that broke his heart and that was his dog. Hasan propped the backpack against the rock behind him. His million-dollar pillow would be of no use if he failed to disappear as easily as he did many times before. *This was supposed to be my last job. Retirement with Arlene on an island somewhere. She double-crossed me. Did Rico help? Is he really dead? My broken roads never failed. Why now? Where did the dots connect?* All questions with no answer would have to wait. He leaned his

227

head back, closed his eyes, and listened. Nothing. No one approaching from either direction.

Hasan let his thoughts drift back two days. When they surrounded the two vans, Rico said his Tijuana connection assured him they would not be followed. Tying the drivers to the steering wheels then setting the vans on fire destroyed all evidence of them being there. Taking the refugees to Nuevo Laredo had been Rico's idea. His plan to send the refugees directly to Monterrey. *Sanchez was right. Trusting Rico is the dot that connects Arlene, and the Garcia family. They're all related. Falling in love with a married woman tipped my scale in the wrong direction. Doesn't matter now.*

His senses switched to high alert when he heard the crackling of twigs, and something fall from a nearby tree. He wanted to groan out loud. He grabbed the binoculars, sat up straight, and listened. Stiffness in his bones had set in while he rested. Hasan scanned the area around him to find two squirrels chasing each other from tree to tree. This was a sign he needed to get lost where no one would find him. He slipped the backpack over his shoulders, stood, then started climbing. *I can make it to the road on the other side by dark.*

Chapter Fifty-Seven -- Monterrey, Mexico

Nicholas reached the tree line where boot prints turned to the right with Sheila close behind. Robert and Rita had already disappeared on a path beyond the trees. He stopped and glanced both ways then stared straight ahead. *Hasan hid in plain sight. Not left or right.*

"What's the matter? Tracks head that way," Sheila said as she struggled to catch her breath.

"Look closely at the boot prints. They end eight steps away. I bet if we walk that way, we'll see several obvious damaged limbs." Nicholas pointed at the tracks. "Original track is slightly disturbed compared to the prints across the field. Most people wouldn't notice."

"Now that you mention it."

"Hasan's got to be using the rocks at the base of the mountain to hide. See the freshly broken limbs? Appears he failed to cover his tracks as well as he used to. My guess is he's watching us. Come on," Nicholas whispered.

Instead of trudging straight ahead, Nicholas headed north in search of a hiking trail. When he found a well-worn path, he stopped and sent Rita a text. This gave Sheila time to catch up again.

She leaned over and put her palms on her knees. "Dammit. I didn't realize I was so out of shape. You think Hasan made it over to this trail instead of cutting through the woods?"

"He's taking the short, more difficult route. Being injured, the overgrown landscape will give him options to hide. I told Rita and Robert to try and find a hiking path near the road and let us know when they reach the top. You need a minute?"

"I'm good. My body's telling me it knows I've been cheating on exercise with someone called '*Tito's*'." She twisted her ponytail under her baseball cap.

"I can relate. Let's go."

The mid-day sun took its toll. He wished he had time to enjoy the scenery, listen to the birds sing, and walk up the winding path, but they were almost there. The bottle of water he had before jumping off the chopper transformed into the sweat on his t-shirt. His fast pace slowed to a jog with the steep incline. He glanced back to make sure Sheila was close behind. Still in sight but closer to fifty yards behind him now.

As he slowed to a walk to let her catch up, his mind drifted to a conversation he had with Father Simon on the roof of Saint Vincent's Church. During the time he spent at the church supervising the construction of the animal sanctuary across the street, Nicholas ran every morning. When he returned, he climbed the bell tower to watch the sun rise before breakfast with the children from the orphanage next door. The old priest would eventually join him on the roof, but that was long before Father Simon told him who his real father was.

Father Simon had leaned against the wall next to him and said, *"How do you think your life would've turned out if God spared Casey from that tragic explosion? The loss of not only her, but five others including her mom and dad. God carried you through the tragedy because of the big picture. Staying ahead of Satan's undermining can't be an easy job. What most people don't stop and consider is the completed puzzle. While Casey's death was devastating, did you consider your path? Would your cousin be where he is? Would your Uncle Eric still be in the U.S. stirring up evil? Would God send the Archangel Michael to see you? Even bigger picture, would you be here now? What you're doing for the animal sanctuary across the street will not only save their lives, but has shown our children, that there is hope still left in the*

230

world. God has a plan bigger than all of us and needs your help. While Satan wins a battle now and then, God plans to win the war."

"How does Father Simon make sense when nothing else does? God, what is the bigger picture now? Am I where you need me to be? Will Hasan manage to pull off some last-ditch magic trick?" Nicholas mumbled to himself as he heard footsteps approaching.

Sheila jogged up next to him. "How much further do you think?" She asked as she wiped the sweat off her forehead with her sleeve.

"Can't be much further. A fast walk from here. You need to stay close to the trees in case we need cover. This trail has drifted south toward the mountain's peak where I believe Hasan will be forced to emerge if his intention is to disappear on the other side."

"If you were Hasan, would you have chosen the mountain over circling back to the road and hitching a ride?"

"Look at it from his perspective. He stomped one drone into a million pieces. He will assume there will be more. Trees give him hiding options. If he waits 'til dark, he could head back to the road, leaving us waiting up here."

"Okay Mr. Sunshine, I need you to be a little more positive."

Nicholas smiled. He nudged Sheila toward the tree line as they reached an open clearing at the top. He squatted next to her behind a large pine, removed his cell from his t-shirt pocket, then sent a quick text to Rita advising her of their approximate location.

They had a complete view of the field. A few patches of rocks arranged in circles around ashy remains from old campfires, but none appeared to be recent. He wondered when spring break season started here. They hadn't passed a single hiker. Then he remembered the pandemic.

If I were still in Florida, this would be the first weekend for college kids to show up on the beaches unless COVID-19 changed that too. Has Bucky continued to show up for a bowl of fish scraps? A tinge of guilt set in at the thought the pelican might go hungry. *Bucky will have to fend for himself and hope the college kids show a little compassion until I return.* His thoughts were distracted when his phone vibrated.

He held his phone where Sheila could read it too. "On the other side. We can see you with the binoculars Robert snitched off the chopper, but we don't see Hasan yet. We are directly across the field from you at about eleven o'clock." Nicholas glanced in their direction as the reflection of the sun bounced off the binocular's lens. He let Rita know if he could locate them, then so could Hasan.

Chapter Fifty-Eight -- Monterrey, Mexico

More than an hour crawled by as they sat in silence waiting for something to happen. Nothing, not even a whisper. A light breeze combined with shade from the trees helped relieve the heat. Nicholas began to wonder if he miscalculated Hasan's plan of escape. He started to stand. As he removed his phone from his pocket, he heard what sounded like limbs rustle in the distance. Someone or something gained ground closer to them.

Nicholas slipped his Glock out of his shoulder holster. He dropped to his knees, aimed, and waited. Sheila stood, pressed her body against the tree, and aimed toward the approaching footsteps. Suddenly, the rustling and footsteps stopped, but nothing appeared outside the tree line. *Were the noises from Hasan or a wild animal? It can't be more than twenty-five feet away. Have we been spotted?*

Minutes ticked off the clock with no movement. Nicholas honed-in on the spot he believed the last footsteps fell. He stepped away from the tree trunk into the open field. He closed his eyes and pictured his target. He aimed then emptied the clip in the general direction. Before he finished, a loud thud sent a slight vibration across the ground under his feet. With Sheila in motion Nicholas fell in behind her.

When they reached Hasan, he was still alive, but struggling to stop the blood flow coming from a hole in his chest. Propped up against his backpack, Hasan had fallen against a tree. Out of the seventeen 9mm rounds fired, two ended up in Hasan's chest less than an inch of each other. Without thought Sheila opened his backpack, removed a bottle of water and a bound stack of twenty-dollar bills. She put the money over the two wounds and told him to press hard. She opened the bottle of water and poured it over the money and Hasan's hands.

"The money should stick together almost like a thick bandage."

Robert and Rita appeared as Nicholas dialed Sebastian's number. He didn't give Sebastian time to speak when the phone stopped ringing. "We got Hasan. He has two bullet wounds to the chest and needs medical help immediately. There's a clearing on the top of the mountain." He clicked off without waiting for a response.

Sheila continued to kneel next to Hasan. She helped hold the money and apply pressure.

Hasan glanced up at Nicholas. "How did you know where I was?"

"Trained by an expert at a young age. You may not recognize my name, but my father was Micha Gustovich. His half-brother was Eric Mindelkov."

Hasan's eyes widened. "You're...you're Christian Gustovich."

"Once upon a time."

Hasan's eyes closed and his head fell to his shoulder. "He has a pulse, but it's weak," Sheila said.

Robert turned to Nicholas. "I hear our ride. It's gonna take all four of us to carry him. Sheila needs to continue to keep pressure to the wound, me and Rita will grab his arms, if you will grab his ankles."

Chapter Fifty-Nine -- Monterrey, Mexico

Two federal police officers waited with a medical team on the roof of Hospital San Jose. After the emergency technicians put Hasan on a gurney and lifted him off the chopper, Bailey flew the four of them back to Nuevo Laredo airport. Exhausted, they barely spoke. Rita and Sheila's eyes were closed, mouths wide open, and snoring as soon as Bailey lifted off the helipad.

Robert put his elbows on his knees as he leaned forward. "What did Sebastian say?"

"We're done. We can go back to our normal lives. Hasan is Mexico's problem now."

"You think he'll make it to prison?"

"No. When Diego tells Marlon about Gatos and the confiscation of his drug shipment, Hasan will mysteriously disappear for the last time."

"What is your take on the homemade bombs?" Robert asked.

"After assembling all the aspects on this…hmm? What can we call it? Ah! I know. A broken road to a ghost. Abid Hasan, otherwise known as Greygo had a rare ability to disappear when his enemies grew close. The bombs and refugees were supposed to be shipped somewhere for Barobnakov. I doubt Arie would have had anything to do with the destruction of Gatos since he assumed controlling interest when my uncle died. Hasan's untouchable attitude became his downfall. Trying to make a statement with Marlon and Arie, his second mistake, then falling for Arlene, his third."

"Why a broken road? I can understand the ghost part."

"Hasan traveled from somewhere near Tijuana to Monterrey by an erratic path across Mexico through Nuevo Laredo, Abasolo, and several little towns along the way. I don't even think we could play 'Connect the Dots' from where he started to where he ended up. Why not go straight from Tijuana to Monterrey and let his minions handle the rest? I figure he wanted to prove he was untouchable by people who could find a needle in a haystack."

"What's your plans from here?" Robert asked.

Nicholas leaned back, took a deep breath, and exhaled. "Haven't thought that far in advance. I do have a couple things I need to take care of before returning to Grapevine. What about you?"

"George and Ellen will be heading back to McAllen on Thursday, so I want to be back at the shop by Wednesday afternoon. Tomatillos for dinner?" Robert asked.

George and Ellen had been Nicholas's first employees when he opened the wine and antique shop in Grapevine. When they retired, Nicholas bought them a house in McAllen as a retirement gift. The couple volunteered at the sanctuary and continued to lend a helping hand when needed at the shop in Grapevine.

"Salted cardboard sounds good at this point." He lifted his arm and sniffed. "I don't know if any restaurant will let us in. We smell like pigs in slop."

"What do you mean we? Speak for yourself. You have a mouse in your pocket, Quick Draw?"

"Quick Draw didn't have pockets. Maybe his gun belt." Nicholas laughed. "Sniff your t-shirt and tell me you don't smell like stale sweat."

"Nope. Smells like roses," Robert replied.

"Roses buried in horseshit."

Chapter Sixty -- Nuevo Laredo, Mexico

By the time they made it back to the Reyes compound, the eight boys, Billy and Diego were working to dig Rico out from under a pile of wood and debris. Billy had a bent, stainless-steel sink in hand, Diego, had ceramic pieces from what appeared to be the remains of a toilet, and the teens were moving support beams. Diego and Billy dropped what they were carrying onto a trash pile as Robert parked his truck. Rita pulled in behind him.

"Is he alive?" Nicholas asked as he closed the passenger door.

"Pretty sure he is. We heard a banging noise." Diego turned and pointed. "Where the boys are working, there is a gap big enough to supply air to the basement.

Rita and Sheila walked up next to Nicholas. Sheila put out her hand. "My name is Sheila Garrett."

Billy shook her hand. "Diego's told me about your adventure today. If it hadn't been for you four, I would be dead by now."

"Have you eaten?" Diego asked.

"Stopped in town before we picked up the vehicles from the hotel," Robert replied.

Nicholas turned toward Diego. "Did you talk to Marlon?"

"Yes. Twice. He's pretty pissed about Gatos even though he sold our family ownership to Arie. Chief Vito was on his way to

Gatos when the explosion occurred. Since the basement had thick concrete walls and soundproof panels, the C-4 attached to a coffeemaker timer caused Gatos to collapse as if intentionally imploded. News showed the bombs and body bags being pulled from the basement. There wasn't enough C-4 to cause the floor to cave. Funny thing is my brother knows Hasan made it through surgery and what hospital he was taken to."

"Thanks for the update. We hadn't heard that yet. Someone's got to tell Sebastian he's falling down on the job and it's not going to be me. Does Marlon know about Rico?" Rita asked.

"Yes. Marlon's sending a plane to pick him up tomorrow. Plans to give Rico the option to work in Lima for him or die. This option is offered because of his relation to our mom."

"Saves us from having to deal with his ass. What about tonight? Do you trust Rico to be loose while we all sleep?" Sheila asked.

"Fuck no. Rico gets a shower and a MRE for dinner. He's staying in the bunkhouse. He'll be chained to the bed with enough leeway to reach the toilet. I gave the oldest two a .38 special to make sure Rico stays in line."

"Sounds reasonable to me." Robert smiled. "We don't have much daylight left. Maybe if we help the boys, we can have Rico out by dark."

Chapter Sixty-One -- Nuevo Laredo, Mexico

Rescuing Rico didn't take long. Uninjured, but filthy and furious for being left so long under the rubble. "Fuck all of you. I'm filing a complaint of abuse and mistreatment."

"Go right ahead. Marlon will appreciate your complaints. While your complaining, explain how you tried to murder Diego. You're damn lucky I don't let these boys treat you the way you treated them. Let me remind you about the young refugee burned alive for trying to save his sister from Hasan's brutal rape. Maybe you deserve the same," Billy said as he slapped the duct tape back over Rico's lips.

Billy and the young teens gladly took over. Robert, Rita, and Sheila set out in search of a shower. Nicholas left the others to check on Shadow and Coal, his two furball companions. Their food bowl had been licked clean and they were back where he left them. Curled up together in the center of the bed. When he sat next to them, they both stretched, moved closer, and sniffed. Coal put his nose in the air and opened his mouth.

"I know I smell bad. You don't have to remind me."

He petted them a few minutes. When he finished taking care of his cats, he put all his dirty clothes in a trash bag. All the death and destruction from past twenty-four hours somehow had to be ingrained in every fiber. As the warm water beat against his head and shoulders, he wondered what he would say to Father Simon. The priest always knew exactly what to say as if he knew him all his life. Father Simon had known him. He married his parents. He was his mom's confidant. He was there when she lay on her death bed. He helped Sebastian by sharing his knowledge about the drug cartels in the area.

Every bone in his body ached, but somehow it didn't matter. The satisfaction of eliminating evil off the face of the earth seemed to wash the pain down the drain with the dirty water. He was exhausted but not sleepy by the time he dressed. He noticed Robert's bedroom light on as he made his way to the refrigerator. Nicholas didn't disturb them. Instead, he grabbed a beer, and walked out on the front porch. The lights were on in the bunkhouse. Checking on the status of Rico wasn't at the top of his to-do list.

The smell of burned rubber still lingered in the air. As he sat on the rail, he heard a door open and close from Diego's house next door. He tucked strands of hair behind his ear and watched as Sheila pulled her hair back with a butterfly clip. She reminded him of Casey with her long blonde hair and blue eyes, but Sheila was different. *Strong, independent, and hard working. Raised by her dad after her mom was hit by a drunk driver.* His comparisons were cut short when she stepped off the porch and headed his way.

"I had a feeling I wasn't alone. Can't sleep?" Sheila asked as she leaned against the support beam.

"If I can shut my brain off long enough, then maybe. I have two furballs that are better than an alarm clock."

"That's funny. I have an orange tabby that does the same when I'm home."

"Are you returning to San Antonio tomorrow?"

"No. I spoke to Robert and Rita after you wandered off. Since I crossed the river to get here, to make things easier, he and Rita are going to drop me off at the tunnel. I can ride the motorcycle back to Laredo. The less people who know I crossed

240

without my passport the better. The Laredo border patrol office has asked if I could stay a few weeks until they hire replacements for the three officers lost. They want outside supervision to make sure Robert's family tunnel is sealed permanently and the river dredged to keep anyone else from being able to just walk across. Since it's basically DEA related, my supervisor approved the extension. What about you? Grapevine or Florida?"

"McAllen. I want to check on the animal sanctuary. After that, home. Florida will have to wait until after spring break. With the pandemic and social distancing, I heard rumors the Governor is considering closing the beaches for a while. Plus, charity organizers cancelled the South Walton Wine Festival this year."

"Not rumors. It's inevitable." She paused a moment and smiled. "For years I heard about the caricature drawings showing up at a next of kin's house a few days after the loss of a black sheep member in the family. The artwork was rumored to be done by the assassin who eliminated the victim. The victim being a worthless, son-of-a-bitch, murderer, drug dealer, or combination of all the above. Funny thing is I never would've guessed the artist to be you."

"As they say, looks can be deceiving."

"Doing the right thing, whether it was for the right people or the wrong people, taking the time to leave the ones who loved the victim a happy image to remind them of the good person sucked up into a life of crime, shows true compassion," Sheila said.

"My past has been littered with pain and evil. My luck is God realized I needed a life rope. I believe he put Father Simon in my life to show me."

"Do you still draw?"

"Every chance I get, but no longer for the victim's families. I do it as an escape. Most of my drawings lately have been ocean scenes."

Sheila turned to leave. "You know, it's been a while since I've been to Fort Worth. There's a great Mexican restaurant that serves ghost pepper cheese dip near the Stockyards. Next time I'm up that way, want to join me?"

"Are you asking me on a date?" Nicholas smiled.

"Okay. Yeah, you could call it that. If I wait on you, life might get in the way, or the pandemic may kill us all."

"Sure. I would like that."

Nicholas watched her until she closed the front door to Diego's house. The past four months he spent hiding from life. Stuck in limbo between what he believed to be true and the actual truth about his parents. Facing reality and moving on meant he had to put one foot in front of the other. Sebastian sent Robert and Rita at the right time to solicit his help. Coincidence? No. Once again, Sebastian had been his life raft.

Chapter Sixty-Two -- Nuevo Laredo, Mexico

Without fail, Shadow and Coal, were taking turns walking on him or nudging their cold, wet noses against his cheek to let him know it was time to get up. *How do they know when it's six?* He slipped his arm from under the covers and held it out for them to rub against. Seven hours sleep didn't feel like it was enough, but it was time to get back to the real world and his shop in Grapevine.

While Shadow and Coal were eating their breakfast, he packed. Certainly, someone else was up by now. Robert's bedroom door was slightly ajar as he passed by on his way to the front porch. When he opened the front door, Robert and Diego were standing next to a black SUV parked in front of the bunkhouse. Two burly men he recognized to be long-time security guards for the Garcia family. Rico's hands and feet were shackled and cuffed. The two men were dragging him toward the open passenger door.

One less piece of shit he didn't have to deal with. The two men shook Robert's and Diego's hands, got in the SUV, then drove away. Nicholas sat in a rocker and waited for them to walk his way. He contemplated how long it would take Marlon to bury Rico six feet deep in the ground.

"From this perspective, I'm assuming Rico has no desire to visit family in South America?" Nicholas asked.

"Correct. Diego gave him the option of working for Marlon or going to jail. When we explained he would be blamed for the destruction of Gatos, the murder of three border patrol officers, and all the thirteen innocent people hanging in the basement of Gatos, Rico went ballistic. By the time I arrived to help, Diego was sitting on Rico while Billy added iron shackles to the bastard's ankles. Marlon sent a text a little while ago to let us know his men were on their way," Robert explained.

"Rosa's working on breakfast. I'm going to go see how long and will let you know," Diego said as he turned and walked away.

Robert sat in the rocker next to Nicholas. "Rita and I are leaving after breakfast. We have to drop Sheila off at the river crossing."

"I know."

"You do?"

"Yes. After I showered last night, I grabbed a beer and came out on the porch. Sheila came out shortly after and we talked for a few minutes. You and Rita make up for lost time?"

"Are you serious? It was all we could do to shower and cuddle. I think I was asleep before my head hit the pillow. My phone vibrating on the nightstand woke me up. By the time I walked outside, I heard Rico yelling every cuss word imaginable. George and Ellen will be working for a couple more days, so we're going to stop in San Antonio for a night or two. You rode with us, so I assume you need a ride."

"No. I would like to use your truck. I want to make a stop in McAllen then I'll drive it back to Grapevine."

"Good. I've been trying to figure out a way to get it there, but something more important kept pushing it to the back burner. My truck is newer, but Dad's is customized. An extra layer of protection if we need it. Rita let me read the text Sebastian sent you and her about Hasan's little convoy of trucks," Robert said as Rita appeared in the doorway.

"Unfortunately, the female teens are being transported back to Tijuana to find their families. We're working on getting their names moved up on the list for refugees approved for asylum in the US. Marlon never ceases to amaze me. He has contacts high up the chain of command in Monterrey. Somehow his shipment of cocaine disappeared off the truck before it reached evidence lockup. The driver of the tanker truck lit a fire in the cab, jumped out into bumper-to-bumper traffic on one of the exit ramps officers were supposed to have blocked. The driver found a way to escape before the truck exploded. No one else died, but the two cars behind it were destroyed. Not sure what will happen to the six men the officer's arrested. Bandit can't find where they were taken for processing," Rita ranted as she leaned against the rail.

"Are you pissed off about it?" Robert asked.

"Well...no...maybe. Why?"

"Because you repeated Sebastian's text almost word for word. All three of us have read it," Robert said.

"Okay, yes, I'm furious. We worked hard on this case, gave up pursuit, and turned it over to the locals in Monterrey. They fucked it up." Rita took a deep breath and exhaled.

Robert shook his head. "No. Not all the cops in Mexico are corrupt. It just takes one to give them all a bad name. Anyway, I called Bandit while you were in the shower last night. The problem is, the one pulling the strings has most likely been bought and paid for by Marlon. Losing Chief Tito Rojas last year was detrimental to Marlon's chain of contacts. This new person would be way above the Federal Police with more power than he deserves. The six men left in Hasan's little army were all witnesses. Chances are,

245

all of them were buried in the desert somewhere before we went to bed last night. Those bodies will never be found."

"Does Bandit have a name for who he believes is on Marlon's payroll?" Nicholas asked.

"Yes, but I told him I preferred not to know. I told him to send Sebastian a text with his thoughts on the subject," Robert replied.

"Maybe not, but it may be of use somewhere down the line," Nicholas replied.

"What did you do with Hasan's backpack?" Rita asked.

"Gave it to Billy. I told him to give the refugees enough to buy new clothes and the rest to Diego. It's going to take a small fortune to repair what Hasan so easily destroyed here. Chances are all the money came from Marlon anyway."

They all three turned their heads when Diego stepped out on the porch. Breakfast was ready.

Chapter Sixty-Three -- McAllen, Texas

By the time Nicholas reached Saint Vincent's, it was late afternoon. He stopped on the steps in front of the chapel then glanced across the street. The parking lot was almost full of vehicles. Children were playing on the playground, parents were strolling around with their children visiting the animals, and the petting zoo was alive with activity. He was happy to see smiles on the children's faces from the orphanage next door.

He pondered a moment about checking the grape and muscadine vines behind the administrative building, but decided it was too soon for that. The sanctuary was empty except for Father Simon kneeling at the Alter. Nicholas walked halfway up the aisle. He took a deep breath and exhaled as he sat at the end of a long pew. *What do I say? How do I apologize? This man knows me better than I know myself.* He wished he had taken Robert and Rita up on their offer to tag along.

As Father Simon stood and turned, Nicholas made his way up the aisle.

"So good to see you. The children have really missed you."

Nicholas hugged the old man. "I've missed them too."

"Come. Have a seat." Father Simon sat on the front bench.

Nicholas sighed. "I'm sorry for running off. I have no excuses for my behavior."

"You have no reason to apologize. I understand the shock. Now that you've had time to ponder your past, if you stop and consider all persons involved, you may find comfort in knowing you were loved by many. Micha could not have loved you more. You were truly his son and always will be. The blood that runs through our veins has nothing to do with the ones who love us. If Mr. Sebastian knows you are his son, then he let that fact go when he lost the woman he loved to Micha." Father Simon smiled then stood. "How long are you going to stay?"

"Overnight. I would like to spend a little time tomorrow visiting the animals across the street. I know it has changed."

"Yes. Due to the pandemic, this is the last day the playground will be opened to the public. We will be working through a Facebook page for adoptions and making appointments for visitation. You know, since Michael returned from New Orleans, he's taking on extra responsibilities. With the loss of Miss Jillian, he's created schedules for feeding and maintaining each animal. He starts vet school at Texas A&M in the fall. George and Ellen keep the administrative office in shape. They're attending church here." Father Simon stood, turned, and started down the aisle. "You now Jillian loved you."

"Yes," Nicholas replied. He had realized Jillian wanted more than just friendship when he began the sanctuary project. He thought he would eventually feel the same, but those feelings never came.

"Some things don't have to be spoken when they are felt. Let's go up on the roof to watch the sun set."

Nicholas followed him up the stairs through the bell tower. He admired the man for his compassion and dedication. A daily routine that rarely varied. A trip every morning and every evening up the stairs to watch the sun rise and set no matter if the clouds created an overcast sky or rain fell. An umbrella hung on a nail at the top of the stairs if he needed one.

Father Simon leaned against the block wall as he placed his hands on the stucco façade. "I spoke with your Mr. Sebastian today. He told me you were headed this way."

"He seems to know my schedule better than I do."

"Did you bring your two fur companions?"

Nicholas glanced down at Robert's truck. The windows were rolled down about three inches to allow the cool breeze to circulate. "They were asleep in the passenger seat, but it appears they've awakened." Shadow and Coal were hanging from the driver's side window with their noses poking out.

"So, you rescued eighteen refugees and recovered over a million dollars in cocaine."

"I had help. Hasan survived, but somehow, I don't believe he will make it to prison. I'm sure Marlon Garcia will manage to get his drugs to his distributors. Rumor has it, the cocaine never made it to the evidence lock-up in Monterrey. So, wasted weekend."

"You sound as if you believe you failed."

"I used to receive all the information I needed for my contract assignment. I completed the job and received payment. Success. Why does doing the right thing for the right people make me feel like I'm on a losing team?"

"Because the war on evil is so much bigger on the right side than it is on the wrong side. The occasional assassination of one drug dealer, murderer, or sex trafficker only solves problems in the small picture. No matter who you are, God can use you. He doesn't wait for us to be perfect. If He did, we would all fall short of his Grace."

"Not you."

"Yes, me. It took me years to come to grips with the fact I would never see the world outside McAllen. Except for a few trips for Mr. Sebastian, church related meetings in the San Antonio area, and to visit a sick friend in New York. I don't count New Orleans."

"I can understand that."

"Sometimes I've been very angry with God for the burden he has laid on my heart, but then He showed me the results of my work. Be patient. You will eventually see the bigger picture."

"The visits to New York?" Nicholas paused to swallow the lump in his throat. "To see my mom?"

"Yes."

Nicholas sucked in a deep breath of air as he pushed back tears. They stood in silence as the sun drifted below the horizon. Nicholas watched Mother Mary line up the children. It was nearing dinner time. "You are missing two?"

"Yes. Rosalee, and the youngest, Annabelle. Soon we will be losing little Joshua. A young couple unable to have children of their own are going through the long process to adopt him. You ever see the movie *'Field of Dreams'*?"

"Yes."

"The famous line, *'Build it and he will come.'*" Father Simon removed his glasses, wiped the lens with a handkerchief from his pocket, then put them back on. "Memory slipping with age. I don't remember the whole movie, but the main character heard a voice in his dreams. You oversaw and paid for the construction of the animal sanctuary. People come to see the animals and find out about the orphanage."

"I beg to differ. Your memory is as sharp as a man half your age. Remembering a movie from beginning to end would be impossible for most people unless they're a movie critic or fanatic." Nicholas dabbed the corner of his eye with the back of his hand. "Let's go see the children."

"Tonight, is pizza night. Will you have dinner with us?

"Love to, but I'll need to capture the furballs trying to escape out the window first."

Father Simon led the way down the bell tower. "You know, God is our dream weaver. He weaves faith into reality even if it's not quite what we expected. Your expectations of what you accomplished may seem to be a failure to you, but your small success will impact the lives of many down the road."

Chapter Sixty-Four -- Grapevine, Texas

Nicholas ended up staying two days in McAllen. He took time to visit all the animals, from the horses and donkeys to the piglets in the petting zoo. He spent time behind the administrative building talking to Jillian as if she could hear his voice. He wondered if he looked like a crazy man talking to grape and muscadine vines, but realized it was no different than talking to God. After all, they were both in Heaven.

It was early afternoon before he made it back to his shop in McAllen. No cars in the parking lot except his car and Robert's F-150. Nicholas had driven Carlos's truck. He parked in the back and entered through the warehouse entrance. In the mud room right inside the door, a framed, floor to ceiling mirror hung on the wall. Behind the mirror was his secret entrance to his apartment upstairs.

He let Shadow and Coal out of their carrier, fixed their food and water then headed downstairs to find Robert. The pandemic had affected the number of people allowed in the shop and the wine bar would currently be shut down until the week of Memorial Day. On the other hand, on-line orders had tripled. Robert was thumbing through one of the latest vendor catalogs as he walked up the center aisle.

"What are you doing?"

Robert jumped and grabbed his .45 from under the register. "Shit! You scared me."

"I see that. Now, can you put that away? I was going to open a bottle of wine and thought I would see if you wanted a glass."

Robert checked the time as he glanced out the window. "I doubt we'll have any more customers today. This damn six-feet apart thing needs to go before summer arrives." He locked the front door and followed Nicholas.

Nicholas pulled up a barstool behind the bar as Robert sat across from him. "I haven't answered my phone in a couple of days. You want to catch me up?"

"Anita and little Rafael spent the morning here. They just left. It was good to see her before she headed back to Nuevo Laredo. Catching you up on shop business would be a waste of time. I can always sense when you're watching the shop."

"I'm not checking up on you. I do it because I miss being here."

"I know or I would've mentioned it a long time ago. Rita's back in New York, but only for a few months. An agent is retiring in the Dallas office and Sebastian told her the slot was hers if she still wanted it."

"That's good news."

"How did your visit go with Father Simon?"

"I don't know why I waited so long. It went very well. I didn't need to call Sebastian as Father Simon seems to talk to him every day. I heard Diego is allowing all the refugees to stay in the bunkhouses."

"Yes. We decided to rebuild Los Rancho. The teens have agreed to help around the property for their room and board costs. When we start construction, Diego wants to let them take turns being apprentices to the different trades."

"What about the smoker? Is Rafael still buried there?"

"Yes. Anita agreed to let us clean up the immediate area around it, fence it in, and put up a headstone. She also wants to construct an enclosure to preserve the site."

"Great idea." Nicholas refilled their glasses. "I also heard that Billy's back in Tampa. Sebastian has assigned him to the Tampa special task force for sex trafficking."

"Father Simon knows more than we do," Robert laughed. "You know, I've known Father Simon most of my life. My family has supported the orphanage because one of my cousins lived there most of her life."

"Maria, right?"

"Yes. Now that my dad is out of the picture, she can finally live without looking over her shoulder every day."

Nicholas took a deep breath and exhaled. "Your dad…my uncle…two of a kind. What about Gatos?"

"Chief Vito's pissed. The explosion destroyed the street corner. Basement was still intact, but Diego found out two of Vito's men were upstairs when the bomb went off. He seized the property for illegal activities. From what I gather, Vito's fighting with the city records office on who to contact. He has no idea the SVR director owns it. You want to call Barobnakov and let him know about his little whore house?" Robert asked.

"Hell no. It's probably under a shell corporation, but I'd be willing to bet he already knows."

"Oh! I bet I know something Father Simon doesn't know yet. I don't even think you know about the spiral notebook Sheila found in one of the trucks they drove back to the property. Anyway, written in a basic code Sebastian had deciphered. A long list of Hasan's contacts, where drug shipments were delivered, and names of the dealers he worked with. It was filled with dates, times, and quantities. Also, since you decided to ignore your phone messages for two days, Hasan mysteriously died of a drug overdose last night. One other thing, you were right. Marlon does have contacts in Monterrey. His drug shipment is on its way south."

"I guess Sebastian has already dispatched teams to follow up on Hasan's contacts?"

"Yes. He called this morning. Plans to be in Grapevine next week and wants to meet with both of us."

"Who? You and that mouse in your pocket?" Nicholas smiled.

"Real funny. I'm hungry. How about dinner and you can tell me about your future dinner date with Sheila. Rita told me she asked you out on a date."

"Yeah, but I figure she'll back out."

"Nope. Rita invited her up next week. We're all going to Juarez for dinner."

Nicholas stood. "Okay, let's go. Time for a real drink to ease back into the real world."

"Yep. Just as long as we stay six feet apart, wear masks, and wash our hands." Robert smiled and followed Nicholas out the front door.

"Is that an admission you still need to be reminded to wash your hands?"

"Ha ha…not funny. Now, I'm questioning the fact that maybe I really didn't miss you."

"Sure, you did. Because I damn sure missed being here."

NOTE FROM THE AUTHOR: Hope you enjoyed *Broken Road to a Ghost*. Even though the story line and characters are fictional, many of the places are real. All Bible references are from the NIV Bible. My next project, *Fine Line* is a sequel to *Broken Road to a Ghost*. I hope to have it completed sometime next year.

Made in the USA
Columbia, SC
17 August 2022

64803275R10143